WHERE OUR TURN BEGINS

USA TODAY BESTSELLING AUTHOR
A.M. WILSON

Copyright © 2022 by A. M. Wilson

All rights reserved.

No part of this book may be reproduced in any form or by any electronic or mechanical means, including information storage and retrieval systems, without written permission from the author, except for the use of brief quotations in a book review.

This is a work of fiction and any resemblance to persons, names, characters, places, brands, media, and incidents are either the product of the author's imagination or purely coincidental.

Editing: Jenny Sims Editing4Indies

Cover Design: T. E. Black Designs

(https://www.teblackdesigns.com)

ISBN: 9798831304794

CONTENTS

Books By A. M. Wilson   v
About This Book   vii

Prologue	1
Chapter 1	9
Chapter 2	18
Chapter 3	27
Chapter 4	36
Chapter 5	43
Chapter 6	52
Chapter 7	60
Chapter 8	69
Chapter 9	75
Chapter 10	85
Chapter 11	93
Chapter 12	100
Chapter 13	111
Chapter 14	121
Chapter 15	131
Chapter 16	144
Chapter 17	151
Chapter 18	160
Chapter 19	174
Chapter 20	187
Chapter 21	193
Chapter 22	203
Chapter 23	210
Chapter 24	219
Chapter 25	225
Chapter 26	235
Chapter 27	240
Chapter 28	245
Epilogue	252

Also by A. M. Wilson   261
About the Author   271

BOOKS BY A. M. WILSON

Arrow Creek Series
Where We Meet Again
When Morning Comes
What Tears Us Down
Where Our Turn Begins

The Revive Series
Unleashing Sin
Redesigning Fate
Resurrecting Her
His Deliverance (A Novella)
Revive: The Series

Westbridge Series
Pitch Dark
Broad Daylight

Standalone
Indisputable

ABOUT THIS BOOK

Caiti Harris thought her story ended the night her husband died.

She packed their history away like trinkets in an old box and held steadfast to the ache. Life granted her one love, and after he was cruelly ripped away, she knew there wouldn't be anyone else.

When a tempting bartender invites her to stay for a drink after closing, she agrees to one night, not a lifetime commitment. His sinful smile promises to chase away the pain of the past while his chiseled body guarantees to ward off the unrelenting chill.

Her love life ended, but that doesn't mean she's sentenced to an existence of total solitude.

Dane's world is exactly the way he wants. Tidy. He keeps a watchful eye over his bar, and remains a pillar for the people he cares for most. So when the woman he's dreamt about for three years shows up at his door with a toddler in tow, he's ready for the challenge. The two come as a package deal.

Caiti only wants to establish a connection with him in the event something happens to her. A backup plan to keep their daughter safe. She didn't expect to be whisked away in an ambulance before she could explain her sudden return to Arrow Creek.

Dane's vision soars beyond an eighteen year commitment. He sees a lifetime of settling down. And he's not ready to give up his turn without a fight for their daughter.

Or her.

PROLOGUE

Caiti

GRIEF IS a knife severing my life into two parts—*The Before and The After*. While looking at *The Before* hurts like nothing I've felt before, existing in *The After* is a void.

Hollow. Aching. Alone.

I've cried all the tears my body could produce. The anger bled free from my fingertips as I packed up the remaining pieces of a life now gone, occasionally pausing the jerky efforts to throw something I couldn't bear to keep. Fear swept me into its grip day after day, week after week, month by month, tossing me against the rocky shore every so often to remind me that I couldn't escape this.

The love of my life—gone. Like *that*. The universe was cruel enough to keep from me the painful memories of the lasts, so my final recollections of Eric are tainted with regret.

A chaste kiss. A mumbled good night. A flurry of shifting limbs and shaken blankets as I crawled in beside my beloved for the last time.

Time drifts in a lonely, chaotic blur. The stimulation of grief keeps my body stressed to the max, to the point I exist daily with these sensations. The random pounding heart, as if it's calling out to him in rapid bursts. A trembling in my arms, as if they're mourning the loss of his body pressed deeply to mine.

I miss it.

Watching Eric's sister, Evie, leave this bar with her new love slices my inside to ribbons. I want that. I *had* that.

I miss him.

The condensation on my glass of water cools my hot palms. The welcome sip quenches my cotton mouth. Only a minute after being left alone does the quiet bartender set down his own drink beside mine and join me on a stool.

"Hey." The word produces a graveled tone. Low and soothing, somehow heard above the bar chatter and music.

I twirl my ice with my straw. "How many shots did you water down?" I expect a wince for being called out, but he holds his features steady.

"How'd you know?"

"I haven't drunk enough not to notice, and I'm not getting any drunker."

"A couple."

I tilt my head back to suck an ice cube from my glass between my lips. "I'm not paying for them."

"I already comped your tab."

"Why'd you do that?" I lean toward him and plant my elbow on the wooden bar top. His silence draws me nearer.

"You're a friend."

"You don't know me," I argue hotly.

"Friend of a friend, then." The side of his lips twitches as if he's holding back a smirk.

"I don't even know your name."

He holds out a large hand. The nails are clean and

trimmed, and callouses surround his palm. "I'm Dane Blackwood."

Touching him casts light on the shadows in my chest. "Caiti Harris."

"Now we're friends."

A *hmm* sneaks out under my breath, but I have no retort. I can afford my bar tab. The energy to argue is what remains in deficit. Right now, I have more money than I know what to do with, but the thing nobody tells you about life insurance money is how tainted it feels. I'd return the check in a heartbeat if only to have Eric back.

The sound of his bottle hitting the wood drags me away from the thoughts of my dead husband.

"Where'd you go just now?"

"That's a scary question to ask a stranger you meet in a bar."

He leans closer, wafting the scent of bourbon and smoke. He's drinking a beer, though. The enticing aroma must be a soap or cologne. "Luckily for you, I'm not afraid of anything."

I slurp the remnants of water stuck beneath the ice in my glass. "Sounds like a challenge."

"I'm game." He turns fully, feet on the rungs of his stool. His knees open in a relaxed way that seems like an invitation to crawl between them.

Fine. He wants to play and won't ply me with any more alcohol. I guess it's time to scare him into bringing me back to Evie. I shouldn't have stayed.

"If you know Evie, then you must have heard about her brother. He was my husband."

I don't know what I expected. A tick of an eyebrow or the downturn of lips. His face reveals nothing. The lack of reaction means he's not surprised by this information.

"I did, yeah. I'm sorry for your loss." The genuine sentiment strikes my heart where all the others reside. "It never gets easier. The distance just gets longer."

The hand holding my glass freezes halfway to my mouth. I slowly lower it back down without taking a sip. "That's right. God, I'm so tired of hearing that time makes it easier. The only thing time does is keep moving when I want nothing more than for it to just stop."

Dane reaches over the bar for the soda gun and refills my glass with water. "You can't stop time, and you can't move around it. The only way to beat grief is to go through it. Face it head-on."

"You sound like you have experience." I appraise him from the corner of my eye and jab the straw between my dry lips.

"I've grieved both of my parents. They aren't dead, but… they aren't coming back."

"I'm sorry." The warmth of his forearm leaches into the palm I lay on him. Realizing my mistake, I quickly draw it back.

Dane's eyes lock on my appendage as if he either wants to drag it closer or throw it off. His wary gaze reveals nothing once more.

"I suppose I should be grateful it's just me. Eric and I didn't have kids, and at first, that hurt, knowing I'd never have a piece of him to live on, but now…I couldn't imagine having to care for someone else for the past six months. I barely took care of myself. I don't see myself ever having them." The notion is severely understated. Somedays, I still feel on the brink of death. Grief is a horrible process.

"Agreed." Dane tips his bottle in the air in a mock salute. A smile tugs free from my lips at the first sign of playfulness.

"Oh, really?" I use the levity to chase away the perpetual fog inside me.

"I won't have them. Don't want them," he says with a lip

of distaste. "This bar and other responsibilities are more than enough to keep me fulfilled and occupied. I don't have the time. Not to mention that raising kids is fucking hard. My childhood…" He trails off with a wince and a hearty laugh. "My poor mother."

His amused rumble infects me with mirth. "But you seem so polite and respectful."

He laughs harder, swiping his beer from the bar to down another pull. "Time and maturity can fix a lot of things. I think the world would be an even bigger mess if nobody grew out of their childhood antics."

My faux shudder could deliver me an award. "I don't even want to think about what I thought was cool and acceptable as a teenager."

The way his gaze roams my face feels physical. "You? I don't believe for a second you were anything other than as beautiful and collected as you are now."

"I was the nerd with big, thick glasses and frizzy hair who thought wearing patterned pajama pants to school made me cool." I deflect from his beautiful comment.

"You did not." Dane leans forward on his stool again, his face near mine.

"I swear."

"I can't picture it."

I dig my fingertips into my roots and mess up my sleek, glossy locks. A big grin slides across my face when I meet his disbelieving gawk. "Can you now?"

Heat suffuses his gaze. "You look more like you just finished in the bedroom than a high school nerd." He bites his lower lip.

"You…you…" I sputter, leaning forward to smack him on the arm. My foot slips from the bottom rung, sending me headlong straight into Dane's lap.

"Whoa." His hands catch my shoulders, one in each strong

grip, and haul me upright directly between his spread thighs. Mere inches span the distance between our faces. His ardent gaze roams over my face. "You okay?"

"I think so." Just centimeters below his fingertips, my heart gallops. I swallow past the knot blocking my throat. His left hand drops from my shoulder to settle at the curve of my waist, and the saliva leaves my mouth parched, begging for a sip of water.

"You should be careful," he susurrates, close enough his breath wafts warmly against my parted lips. His attention fixates there.

I lower my eyelids, my heart racing, and my thoughts call out to him to just do it.

Kiss me. Please.

For a moment in time, I don't want to be the young, sad widow everyone regards with pity. I just want to be a young woman kissed in a bar.

Make me forget I'm supposed to be sad. I'm tired of the heartbreak.

Dane edges closer, and I pause my breath.

"Caiti."

My lashes flutter before opening fully to meet his heated gaze, and my brows pinch together.

"I'm going to kiss you now." His index finger brushes a wayward strand from my cheek.

A gasp, and then he's there. Warm lips connect with mine, gentle and soft and slow. He inhales sharply through his nose before increasing the pressure. His top lip fits flawlessly between mine. Heat crawls up my torso, spreading the length of me. When he hauls me against his sturdy chest, I throw my hands to his shoulders for balance, not caring how we might appear to onlookers as I stand between his spread thighs. He snakes an arm around my upper back to hold me steady as his lips devour mine. Tentatively, I open my mouth to let him in, wanting to take this further.

A grated groan scrapes up his throat.

"Yo, boss!"

The deep gravelly voice thunders between us like a cymbal crash. The spell is broken, yet I can't seem to move from my position between his legs. I'm dizzy from the intrusion of his lips.

"What?" Dane barks back. I may not be the only one ruffled by the interruption.

"Closing time, you dingbat."

A giggle bursts free in total disregard for the situation. Dane glances over at me with a smirk.

"Does that entertain you?"

"I found the insult amusing."

"Duke has no respect for my position."

"I'm old enough to be your father, young man!" Duke hollers back.

Dane's palm cups my cheek, his touch tender as if he knows exactly what this means to me. "Do you mind hanging around while I close up?"

I shake my head. An older man pops out from the kitchen area. The gray hair pulled into a sleek ponytail and shaggy beard are not what I expected to belong to the deep voice.

"I have it covered," Dane announces to the man who, indeed, could be his father's age.

Upon seeing me, Duke shares a look with Dane. "You sure?"

"Yep." Even I hear the period at the end of Dane's clipped sentence. And I hope my interpretation—that he wants to spend more time kissing me—is correct because I'm more than open for a round two. Maybe this is exactly what I need if time won't make this easier. To jump the first hurdle. To kiss another man like a check mark off the list of things I need to do in order to move past my husband's death.

With a two-finger salute, Duke tucks a key in the exterior lock and moves out the door, leaving us completely alone.

"I didn't realize we were the only ones left." A short laugh conceals my heaving breaths. Even their few minutes of conversation weren't enough to ease the breathlessness in my lungs.

"Caiti."

"Hmm?"

His eyes are serious. The muscle at the joint of his jaw pulses. "I want to kiss you again, but I'd rather not do it in this bar."

My heart sinks for half a second before resuming double time as his meaning resonates. "What are you saying?"

"My apartment is upstairs." Before I can decide, he holds up his hands, palms out. "I'm not going to make a move any further than you're comfortable with. I promised your sister I'd get you home safe, and I intend to do just that."

"Well, in that case..." I toss my black hair over my shoulder and lift my purse from the bar. "I guess you should pour another drink and show me the way."

"Preference?" Dane's fingertips skate along my lower back as he passes by to access the bottles.

The monumental weight of what I'm doing sits squarely on my chest, but I don't care. I brush the rampant thoughts aside with a mental flick. For one night, I don't want to lie alone with my head on my pillow, begging God to ease my pain. I don't want to feel so lonely. I don't want the images to fill my head with regret. For one night...

I look at the man currently waiting for my answer to his question and shove aside the welling pain and guilt and shame. "A vodka soda is fine."

1

Caiti

A SQUEAL OF laughter drags my attention from the bright laptop screen to the little girl in the corner. She claps her hands along with the melody of her favorite television show. Noticing her audience of one, she points at the television mounted in the corner.

"We go to park today?"

The brittle smile on my face goes undetected by the almost three-year-old.

"Why don't we go in the backyard instead?" I gesture out the patio to the quarter acre behind the house enclosed with an eight-foot privacy fence. Often on warm days such as today, I leave the sliding door open so Ophelia can run in and out, and I can supervise while doing my remote work as a data analyst. My job is to pull data from older systems and edit and format it for migration. Tedious work, but the job pays the bills and keeps me busy, and the remote option means I never have to leave my house. Something I've done as little as possible for a while now.

My daughter throws on a scowl made for the big screen. "We no have swings, Momma."

Her words drive a stake in my already fragile heart. She's been asking for swings since she started watching this preschool show three months ago. The guilt I feel at my inadequacy reaches a tipping point. I fight back the tears welling—crying doesn't fix shit—and lift my chin.

"We'll swing another time. Are you ready for a snack?"

I'm going to give her a food complex if I can't find a more suitable replacement. But how can I explain to a toddler why her mother's too afraid to leave the house when *I* don't even know why I'm too afraid to leave the house? I should be stronger than letting a random man scare me into hiding.

"No!"

"No?"

"I want swings! I want park!"

"Baby girl, we can't today. Mommy has work to do." The lie feels like sand in my mouth. This isn't the foundation I want to build my relationship with my daughter on. Not for the first time, I wish I had someone to help.

Oh, but I do.

There is someone who could help, except he doesn't know his daughter exists.

"No work, Momma play!"

"Ophelia Louise." I sigh.

An incoming text interrupts her meltdown. The unknown number clues me into the sender before I even click to open.

UNKNOWN: *Hello, beautiful. You and your daughter have a nice day today. The weather is great. I hope we can meet soon.*

. . .

The innocuous-sounding message sends shivers straight down my spine. And not the good kind. For several months, I've been on the receiving end of unwanted attention. Added to the loss of my husband, raising my daughter on my own, and the unease of not knowing what this guy truly wants has raised my stress level to catastrophic limits. Each day becomes harder. The unpredictability holds me on a precipice of fear.

I screenshot and save the text to a folder with the others for evidence. The police won't help. One officer even had the audacity to suggest I accept the strange man's proposition for a date, and maybe he'd move on. As if I'd ever put myself in that vulnerable position.

Supposedly, his name is Trevor. He works for a client who hired my firm. I don't know how he found my contact information, but through a series of texts, he's detailed how he saw me through a video call and needed to get to know me, so he tracked down my information.

Blegh. Why are some men so damn creepy? This isn't the sexy advance he believes it is.

My daughter's wails break through the static in my ears. Her hand closes around my pant leg and tugs as tears stream down her chubby cheeks.

I never wanted this for her. Hell, at thirty-four, I never wanted this for me, either.

Hoisting her into my lap settles the strongest cries. I rock her gently and pick up my cell phone. A thought I've contemplated a hundred times settles back in the forefront. One glance at my precious toddler steals my choices. I have to do this for her. To keep her safe.

I press my contact button and tap on my boss's name.

"Hello, Caiti." His welcoming voice greets me and settles some of the rioting in my stomach.

"Jason. Hey. I just wanted to let you know I'm going to be

off until Tuesday. I need to head out of town for a little while."

"Can you bring your laptop and work while you're away?"

"That should be fine."

Something bangs on the other end of the line. "It's that motherfucker again, isn't it?" Jason is the only person, other than the police, who knows about my situation. Mainly because I don't have any friends, and I needed to know if he'd heard of anyone asking about me. Otherwise, I would have kept it to myself.

"I just need a vacation." I sigh. He might be my boss, but I don't divulge anything further than necessary these days.

"Can I do anything?"

"Just pray he finds another way to entertain himself."

"Caiti..." He pauses, and I know what's coming before he says it.

"No, Jason. Just no. Getting him fired will piss him off, and he might escalate things."

"He might escalate anyway."

I pray that's not the case. "He has to get bored eventually, right?"

"Some creepy asshole is harassing you, and you've got jokes. Nice," he deadpans.

"What would you prefer I do?"

"You're always welcome to stay with Kathleen and me."

The breath I take releases a substantial weight. "Thank you, but I'll be okay."

"Just stay safe."

"Will do." I hang up, feeling lighter than I have in a while. I've had this job since I found out I was pregnant, but Jason's only been my boss for about six months. Between the remote work and his understanding nature, I'm grateful for the ability to temporarily escape.

Now a new problem lies ahead.

Showing up on the porch of the only man I've slept with since my husband died and explaining why I kept his child a secret.

I didn't want to drop the bomb over the phone, and I live on the other side of the United States.

The first few weeks after her birth, I'd lie awake between late-night feeds and dream about getting in my car to make the two-day drive from Denver, Colorado, to Arrow Creek, West Virginia. I'd show up with a small bundle wrapped in my arms, her full head of dark hair peeking out of her favorite pink fleece blanket. Night after night, I'd script out a full apology for not disclosing the pregnancy. But as time moved on, the less likely it seemed I'd ever get out of this house and across the country. The flimsier my excuses seemed until it felt like I simply waited too long.

What would I say to him now?

He never wanted kids. He stated that with such finality, I knew it wouldn't be fair to burden him. We both fell into bed that night, and even though I fled with tears of guilt by morning, his lack of contact felt like a sign.

A little hand fists a lock of my hair. "We go to park now?"

"How would you like to go on a trip instead?"

Two days of travel later, I click the blinker and turn down a street I've seen once before. The dense fog in my head slightly recedes. A memory from years ago jogs free from the heavy veil separating me from the brunt of my reality. One filled with laughter and love and friends.

As if conjured by the thought, my cell phone rings. I don't have to check the time to know it's Saturday at noon. Evie's calling to leave me my weekly voicemail, knowing I won't pick up. Hearing his sister's voice after I left her without so much as a goodbye cuts me to pieces and reminds me how badly I fucked up.

I automatically flick my gaze into the rearview and scan the back seat.

Facing Evie is only a matter of time.

Especially now as I cruise painfully slow down a quiet street. My eyes slit against the midday sun in order to scan the buildings. My fingers wrap tighter around the leather steering wheel as the sign to the bar comes into view.

Calypso's.

Pain immediately assaults me. Sweat coats my palms, slickening my grip. The light memories from a few moments ago assail me at full force upon seeing the building in person for the first time in years, pummeling me until I might actually be sick all over my plain white long-sleeved tee and black leggings. Despite my feelings, the nearly empty street allows me to easily navigate the alley behind the building without incident. The cease of the engine as I turn the key is deafening.

We made it. The lack of relief is telling.

I shove down the guilt rising with the other emotions plaguing me and swing my door open.

"Momma?"

I slam my eyes shut and suck in a sharp breath through my nose at the sound of her sweet little voice. Thankfully, she can't see my face from her seat when I stand.

If she could, she'd witness her mother breaking. The slip of hot tears wetting my cheeks. A steady tremble of the same lips I use to kiss her before bed each night and upon waking each morning. How can something feel so selfish and selfless at the exact same time?

I use the moment outside the car to compose myself. My sleeve works as a coarse tissue to dry my eyes. The crisp breeze shocks my overheated system into calming down.

Only a few minutes of composure are needed. A few minutes, and I can be free to break down completely alone with Ophelia safe until I'm wrung out.

With a steely breath, I tug open the rear passenger door and tack a plastic smile on my face.

"You did great, baby." I press a kiss on the top of her head, not missing the opportunity to inhale her unique scent. The second the buckle releases, she launches into my arms. I'm unprepared for the ball of weight crashing into my chest, and I can't tell if it hurts from the force or from all I'm holding back.

"Where we going?"

My throat seizes and threatens to reveal all the cracks in my plan.

"We're going to meet your daddy." I manage to whisper.

Her little eyes, so dark like mine, squint adorably in confusion. In response, I pull her tighter against my chest. No words will be able to adequately explain to an almost three-year-old what's going on, so I don't bother to try.

With the reminder of why I'm doing this attached firmly to my hip, I sling the overnight bag I hastily packed over my other shoulder. I dip my gaze down to the head of curly black hair and the chubby thumb wedged between a pair of soft pink lips, and crack a brittle smile just as a sharp pain grips the left side of my chest.

"Ouch," I mumble beneath my breath and force myself to forget it. We make the short walk to the door that I know firsthand leads to an apartment above the bar.

I swiftly shove down the mounting memories and raise a hand to knock. Maybe I should have called first. Or checked with Evie to verify he still lives here. The sudden intrusion of second thoughts jars me into surveying my surroundings. Before I can decide to turn back or forge ahead, another chest pain, followed by a squeeze, sends fear hurtling through me.

Somewhere through the roar in my ears, I register my fist connecting with the wooden door, the intensity increasing until I'm outright banging. Sweat coats my palms, another one of the many strange sensations running through me at once. A current races down my middle, my legs, my feet, turning the limbs weak and numb. My keys fall from my grip onto the concrete step, forgotten.

I'm going to collapse.

The thought courses on a continuous loop to the soundtrack of my fist.

The minor trembles that have remained somewhat of a companion the past few years become an earthquake of shaking limbs. Fearing I'm going to drop my daughter, I set her on her feet in order to grip the doorway with my now-free hand. The other clutches at my chest as a painful squeeze rockets through me.

I can't breathe.

The tightness in my chest grows into a fist around my throat. My breaths become sharper and shallow until I feel like I'm gasping for precious air. A buzzing hums in my ears, drowning out the sounds of my daughter. I notice the tears on her cheeks but can't make out her fearful cries. It's as if a veil has separated us. I'm forced to watch her from the outside as I lose control.

What feels like an eternity later, the door finally swings open. Shirtless, in a pair of gray sweats, the only man I've been with since losing my husband answers with a puzzled expression. Dane's face morphs from confused to angry to concerned in half a second.

"Are you hurt?" He leans halfway out of the door and tensely scans the street.

"I think I'm having a heart attack!" I gasp, convinced my

broken heart has finally given out.

I'm in the best place if I suddenly die. To stop fighting and let go.

Our daughter won't be alone.

2

Dane

I've never wished to be an inanimate object as much as I wish to be that fucking bead of sweat.

I can't take my eyes off the shimmering dew clinging to her bronzed skin. A lucky liquid drop cascades across the sharp bone of her clavicle, increasing speed as gravity draws the moisture into the valley between her small tits. Her breathy sigh lingers in the air between us.

She pleads and breaks the spell.

I curse and piston my hips against her center. Each of us only covered by thin cotton and silk.

"More," she whines.

A rumble catches in my throat. I dive to take her lips and do exactly as she begs me to do. My hand makes contact first with the intention of moving the material out of the way. The slickness between her thighs chases away the insecurity that I might be doing something wrong. She's fucking begging.

Still...

"Tell me again you want this before I go any further."

"Dane," she pants and shifts against my hand. Her head falls back.

I withdraw my hand from the warmth between her legs and use the other to palm the back of her head, bringing her gaze back to mine.

"We've both had a few drinks, beautiful. I know it's been hours, but consent is sexy." I dip my mouth to the hollow of her throat, stealing a salty taste before pulling back. "I won't go further without your answer, but I also won't ask again. I promise," I say with a half-grin.

Her delicate finger brushes the hair across my forehead.

"I want you." Her gaze is steady on mine. She moves her finger to run across my parted lips. "Please make me feel good."

I catch the rogue finger with my hand before she can pull it away and suck it between my lips. She moans and shifts her thighs.

"I promise," she swears on her words, staring me dead in the eye.

"No regrets?" I ask one last time.

"No regrets," she answers soberly.

Not needing anything else, I take Caiti to her back in my bed, feeling like the luckiest man alive.

Knock! Knock! Knock!

THE POUNDING at my door shakes me from my dream. A dream I've unfortunately had on repeat over the last three fucking years. A groan slips free as I rub the sleep from my eyes, wishing I could also rub something else away. Waking up with a boner most mornings isn't exactly the best way to start the day, especially when it comes to something completely unattainable.

If I hadn't sobered up before taking her that night, I might have questioned whether she existed at all.

What fucking time is it? I closed the bar last night, so even if it's not early for most, anything before noon is early when I didn't fall asleep until four in the damn morning.

The knocking increases in desperation and volume, forcing me to abandon my search for a clock. Nerves leech away my usual calm. I race through the numerous people who could need my help without a phone call. Being the owner of a popular bar in a small town has a lot of people depending on me. Acquaintances, regulars, and friends all know I'm only a phone call away when I'm not working and the central location means anyone could stop by without notice. I sprint down the steps of my apartment two at a time, reaching the bottom and yanking the door open without stopping to catch my breath.

I must still be sleeping.

The woman of my literal dreams stands hunched over on my doorstep.

And she's not alone.

A little girl with curly dark hair and tearstained cheeks cries loudly for her mom. A flash of anger strikes me before it's washed out by concern for the woman I haven't successfully evicted from my memories.

"Caiti?" My throat is parched with disbelief.

"I think I'm having a heart attack!" she gasps through a strangled-sounding breath.

"Hang on," I command and run back into my apartment for my phone.

Before I return, I'm already connected to dispatch and requesting an ambulance for the medical emergency. I drop to a knee beside the terrified girls as the dispatcher informs me help is on the way. I open my free arm to the little girl and drag her close. Anything to dispel the frightened wails. Her sobs transform into wet hiccups that wrack her tiny body.

"Thank you," I tell the woman on the line before hanging up. "Talk to me, Caiti. The ambulance is on the way." I shove my phone into my pocket before reaching over to touch her hunched shoulder. Her shallow, quick breaths reveal she's still with me, but I need to hear her say something.

Wide dark eyes lift to mine. The terror there is stark. "I'm scared."

"I know."

"It hurts," she pants. Manicured fingertips curl and clutch at her chest.

Desperate to relieve any discomfort, no matter how small, I scoot over and pull her head against my chest. Her breathing loses its sharpness at the small contact. I ignore that she's basically a stranger and tamp down the part that wants to know what she's doing here. Though I have a pretty good idea already.

"Hang on. They'll be here any minute."

Her petite hand clutches at my uncovered pec, making me acutely aware of my lack of shirt.

"It's coming again." The tremors invade her once more.

"I've got you both," I mumble into the crown of her hair, at a loss for comforting words to say. The woman shows up on my doorstep in sheer distress three years after a one-night stand that she ran out on in the middle of the night with a kid I'd be blind not to notice the resemblance. I have a thousand questions, but none of them matter at this moment. The least I can do is see her through her medical emergency. The time for answers will come.

The whoop of the ambulance precedes the red and blue

flashing lights into the alley. Relief coats my insides at the sight of professional help.

"You're going to be okay." I hold our positions as the crew unloads their bag and stretcher. Something in my chest loosens at the sight of a familiar petite brunette and her partner climbing from the rig. Caiti is in good hands with my friends Cami and Nathan.

"Are them doctors?"

I almost forgot about the little one pressed into my shoulder. The flashing lights captured her attention enough for her hiccups to subside.

"They're paramedics. They're here to help your mom," I answer without looking over. Is it just me, or are they taking a damn eternity to get over here?

A small palm caresses my stubbled cheek and turns my face. I swallow hard as her eyes lock onto mine, unable to deny the likeness staring me in the face. Not in her eyes. Those are purely her mother's. Round, and dark, and like the last time I saw them prior to today, filled with life.

"Does Momma need fixing?"

"We're going to take her to the hospital and find out."

"I don't…need…a hospital," Caiti interjects.

"Stubborn woman," I mutter. She's not the first to fight medical treatment, and she sure as shit won't be the last.

My friends reach us. Cami schools her questioning glance on her approach.

"Hi. I'm Cami. Tell me what's going on today?" She crouches beside Caiti. Nathan follows with a bag of supplies. He gives me a nod but remains engaged in the task at hand, removing items for checking vitals.

I help Caiti shift into a more upright position beside me.

"I just arrived from a long drive and started getting this weird pain in my chest over my heart," Caiti says.

"Has this happened before today?" Cami jots something down on a tablet.

"Sometimes my heart races, but I usually ignore it. It doesn't normally hurt," Caiti answers.

I reject the desire to cut her a sharp glance. She should know better than most never to ignore heart symptoms if the rumor of how her husband died is true.

"Have you been under a lot of stress lately? Anything more than usual?" Cami asks in a gentle tone.

Caiti shifts to allow Nathan to apply a blood pressure cuff. "A little. I probably haven't been taking care of myself as much as I should."

A sense of pride washes over me at watching my friends work. Even I can feel their calming presence as they take vitals and history, and I'm not the one with the emergency. Though as much as I try to ignore, I do care something for the woman in pain, even if she isn't mine to care for.

Lord knows enough exists on my plate as it is. The last thing I need is another person under my watch. The little girl chooses that moment to wiggle in a sudden reminder that I don't have a choice about making room on my plate. And I'm guessing the two come as a pair.

"Her heart rate's come down from one-seventy-five to one-twenty," Nathan remarks. "Blood pressure is 140/95."

"It's best to get checked out. Make sure everything is okay. We can take you and get an EKG on the way," Cami relays to Caiti.

"I don't...I think I shouldn't..." Caiti stumbles over her thoughts through choppy breaths. "I'm probably fine."

She whips her gaze between the three adult faces. The fear etched into her features is distressing. If she's searching for someone to agree with her, I doubt she'll find it here.

"Caiti, let them take you. Your heart isn't anything to mess with," I add.

"But I wasn't planning on staying," she pleads, the notes of fear infiltrating her tone. "Who's going to watch Ophelia?"

I assume that's the name of the little girl. Of my *daughter*. *Ophelia*.

"Do you have family in town?" Cami's question wrenches me back to the present and out of my thoughts. Nathan busies himself with packing up their supplies.

Caiti runs her palms flat over her thighs. "Just my sister, Evie. But she doesn't know I'm here."

I'm shocked at her admission. What is she doing here if not planning to see her sister-in-law? It wasn't a coincidence she ended up at my doorstep? I thought she had an emergency and stopped at the first place she recognized. Now it sounds more like she drove here to see me. The pressure in my temples tempts me to squeeze my eyes shut. I feel like I'm still dreaming.

"Rhett's Evie?" Nathan pauses his tasks with a cock of his head.

"Do you know her?" Caiti asks.

I nudge Caiti with my elbow to ease the tension. "Arrow Creek is a small town. Everyone knows everyone around here."

"She's a friend of mine. I can call her to meet us there if you'd like," Cami offers.

"No!" Caiti's mounting fear is palpable. "I don't want her to know I'm here."

What is she hiding? The number of questions I have rises the longer we sit here.

"Are you sure? I'm sure she'd love to help with Ophelia." Cami places a light hand on the crook of Caiti's arm and tries again.

"I've got her," I interject brusquely.

Something rubs me wrong about calling in Evie to keep an eye on presumably *my* daughter. Forget the fact I found out about her existence ten minutes ago, and Caiti hasn't officially introduced her as such. I'd be either blind or feigning ignorance to fail to notice the resemblance, and I'd be downright stupid to shirk any fatherhood responsibilities. I'm nothing like my biological father.

Caiti attacks her lower lip with indecision, frozen like a nervous fawn. I've seen firsthand what grief can do to a person, but this... this is something else entirely.

"I've got her." I dip my gaze to lock on hers. "Let them take you, and we'll follow right behind."

"I don't know..." Her furrowed brow exposes her mounting tension.

"I'm not giving you a choice. You aren't getting back in your car and leaving until you get checked out. Simple as that." I swipe her forgotten keys from beside us, emphasizing the motion.

My theft doesn't go unnoticed.

"You can't keep me here." Caiti breaks my heart with the undercurrent of fear. I take Ophelia with me as I stand.

"If only for your daughter, you're going."

Caiti moves to counter, whether intending to chase me or satisfy my demand doesn't matter. Her movement scores a win for me. Cami eases Caiti to her feet and tosses me a concerned glance. Nathan's matching expression is unmistakable as I move passed to give them room.

"Where we going?" Ophelia asks, her voice lilting with sunshine now that her personal storm has cleared. The sweet melody soothes fragments of the tension in my chest.

"Your mom is going to take a ride to the doctor." A furrowed brow clouds my scrutinizing gaze as I try to interpret how much she understands. She can't even be three years old. I don't want to scare her with too much detail, but I have no idea how she's going to react to being with a stranger when her mom is wheeled away on a goddamn stretcher. She pats my chest.

"You go naked?"

I crack a smile. "You're right. I need a shirt. Are you hungry?"

Ophelia nods solemnly with a pout of her lower lip.

"Let's grab you a snack, and I can finish getting dressed."

"Are you sure you've got her?" Caiti asks me as Nathan moves the gurney closer.

"We'll be right behind you in a few minutes. But it's probably better she doesn't see any more of this. You can trust me."

I let out a tight breath when she nods her agreement. The first easy surrender.

"See you soon, Ophelia. Be good for Dad—Dane."

The slipup may go over the three-year-old's head, but it sticks right in the middle of mine. Fuck. She practically admitted to it right here with my friends present.

Ophelia doesn't verbally answer. She lays her head on my shoulder and waves.

I don't linger any longer. Caiti is in the best hands with my friends. I push her into a box in my mind and focus on the hours ahead.

A clean shirt and morning hygiene for me.

A snack for Ophelia.

Call Duke to cover opening the bar at two.

Drive to the hospital, and on the way, phone The Legendary to let them know I won't be in today. Mom never does well when I go off schedule, but what other choice do I have? This is my new reality, or at least I'll fight like hell until it is. But how do I balance my responsibility to the person who raised me with the person I'm supposed to help raise?

3

Caiti

My heart whips up in a frenzy the moment Ophelia is out of my sight. Cami instructs me to sit on the stretcher, but I can't help looking back to the apartment door.

"She's safe with Dane." The paramedic rests a reassuring hand on my arm, forcing my gaze back to her face. "He's a good friend of ours."

"I know she is." I swallow hard. "He's her father after all."

If the admission surprises Cami, she schools her features quickly.

"But if I die, I should have hugged and kissed her one last time." The regret in my tone is crafted through experience.

The pretty brunette lowers herself to my level. "I think it's likely you're experiencing some intense anxiety. You're going to see your daughter again when we get to the hospital, okay?"

Anxiety?

"I don't have a problem with anxiety." I mean, sure, I don't like using the phone to order a pizza or schedule a doctor's appointment, but that proves true for ninety percent of millennials. I don't think the intense dislike constitutes anxiety, though.

With a nod to her partner, Cami unlocks the wheels and steers me toward the ambulance.

"Whoa." I squeeze my eyes shut. A rush of dizziness washes over me.

She slides me in before climbing up after me. Once the doors shut, Cami works on placing sticky pads on my chest and ankles and attaches the wires to the pads. They lead to a machine I assume is the EKG.

"This will give us a quick look at your heart before we get there."

Moving backward while driving sends a wave of nausea to accompany the other sensations I've felt today. My mind races until I can't even focus on Cami. She takes another blood pressure and disconnects the wires but leaves the sticky pads attached to my skin. Cars drive behind us, and I wonder if they're thinking about who's in this ambulance. If anyone out there can understand the experience I've gone through today.

That's absurd. I'm not the first person to have an emergency, but I've never felt more alone in my entire life. Eric isn't here. He hasn't been for years, and I have nobody to call for support.

Neither did he. The thought flashes before I can stop it, followed swiftly by the images of him dying alone beside me.

I squeeze my eyes shut. Intrusive thoughts, a therapist called them. He said they're normal and harmless, and the best course of action is not to dwell on them. A skill I'm far from mastering at this point.

"How are you doing?" Cami's kind voice retrieves me from my thoughts.

"As good as I can be."

"Try to calm yourself down. Breathe deeply into your stomach, almost like you're trying to push it out," she coaches. "We're almost there."

As I try what she says, I feel some of the tension ease and the palpitations slow.

"You're good at this."

She casts me a proud smile. "Are you staying in town?" Her attempt at conversation reminds me of my plans—or lack of. I mentally mapped out my steps for this impromptu trip, but this detour cramps my strategy.

"I might need a hotel room. Depending on how long this takes at the hospital."

"Dane can give you directions once you're all fixed up. I'm sure you have enough on your mind right now and don't need to add remembering where to go."

"Thanks."

"Your EKG looks normal, so that's reassuring."

I manage a weak smile but internally brush off her statement. One normal EKG doesn't mean I'm in the all clear. There could be another defect somewhere that she doesn't know about. It happened to Eric.

The thought sends my heart racing again.

"Remember to take slow, deep breaths." When I glance her way, she waves her hand at a monitor.

"Oh," I say in response to the 150 beats-per-minute heart rate flashing on the screen.

The duo unloads me a few minutes later with practiced ease and pushes me inside. The torpid emergency room seems chaotic in my mind. My focus is shot as I try to assess everything around me while taking stock of each internal twitch and pinch and pull.

The click of the wheels locking rings as loud as a prison

door locking me inside. The last thing I want right now is to be trapped and alone.

"Don't leave." I capture Cami's forearm.

"I wasn't going to. We're just transferring you to the hospital bed."

The breath expelling from my lungs shakes on its exit.

"I'm sorry. I'm not usually like this." I swipe a loose lock of hair from my forehead. I can only imagine my frazzled appearance after the morning I've had. "I've lived alone for the past three years and managed." *Just barely.* The words spill forth as a means to fill the silence. Or explain why I seem like a crazy person.

The thought of actually losing my mind sends a lightning jolt through me. Is this the beginning of true insanity? I toss the pulse oximeter off my finger and throw my legs over the side of the bed. A feeling of doom surfaces, and something inside begs me to flee.

"Wait, where are you going?" Cami blocks my path.

"I need to go. I need to get Ophelia and leave. I can't stay here."

The thoughts continue pummeling me. Images of doctors in white coats locking me away and social workers taking my daughter. Thoughts of lying sedated in my bedroom, unable to get up and function. With each powerful image, the hot sensation spasms in my stomach, encouraging the fear to grow.

I squeeze my eyes shut.

This isn't me. I fight against the riotous sensations.

"Caiti, listen to me. You're panicking. Today has been scary, but you aren't alone. You're going to get through this."

"How do you know?"

"Because we were built for hard things. There's no other way around but to push through."

My chest tightens in response to her words, and I rub my

fist against the spot to alleviate the burning ache. A noise from behind the sweet paramedic snags my attention. I'd never admit it out loud, but the perfidious heart in my chest ticks a few beats slower at the stoic, dark-haired man leaning against the doorframe with my daughter tight to his hip.

And my next breath in stutters with a mix of relief and unshed tears.

"Hanging in there, Mama?" Dane asks in a low, unreadable tone.

"Yeah," I force through a dry throat and pair it with a super-cool thumbs-up. I am the picture of composed today. This is nothing like how I imagined his induction to fatherhood would go. By the looks of the two of them, I'd say Dane's figured out why I'm here, and he's staking his claim. On his daughter. Not me. I'm ninety-seven percent certain if I hadn't had a mysterious episode outside his door, I'd already have received an ass chewing and an order to turn my car around and leave town.

Or something along those lines.

Someone finally arrives, a nurse or a tech, nudging Dane out of the way to triage me with more vitals. My heart rate has decreased to around one hundred, which surprises me because it still feels like the organ is trying to flee my chest, but my blood pressure remains high.

"We're going to take you for some blood work, an X-ray, and another EKG."

I slap on a brave face for my audience, not wanting to show my fear of what the tests may reveal.

"We'll be waiting here when you get back," Dane says while I transfer to a wheelchair for my tests.

"I'm sorry."

The tech pushes me toward the door.

"Nothing you did wrong, Mama."

My heart flip flops. I choose to believe the sensation

stems from whatever inflicts me at the moment and not his calling me Mama or the gentle graze from the single finger he blazes across my shoulder.

ONCE ASSURED I've returned to my room after all my tests, Dane takes Ophelia to the cafeteria for a snack. I rest in the unyielding hospital bed, closing my eyes to block out my racing thoughts. Regret lies heavy at the forefront, leading the emotional pack. I made a mistake by coming here. Fear persuaded me to believe Dane would take one look at our beautiful daughter, step in, and allow me to step back, all while keeping my reasons close to my chest. He's a good guy and not just in the looks department.

His unruly dark hair that falls over his forehead, perpetual five o'clock shadow, and tall, broad stature project the image of a man at home in a wilderness cabin. Not a local bar owner who'd give the shirt off his back. But within minutes of meeting him the first time, his stable presence became known. His quiet calm and wisdom stem from a life of difficult experiences.

Hours spent quietly together in an empty bar drew me in and allowed me a night of freedom. The only one since Eric died, and for that, I refuse to feel regret. Not only because it gave me our daughter, but Dane offered me a few hours of oblivious hope for a future I could never have. In one night, he was a Band-Aid for the fear I had carried since Eric died, and the moment I fled Arrow Creek three years ago, I haven't been able to rid myself of it since.

The swish of the curtain sliding back startles me with another zing in the center of my abdomen, and my heart takes off again. Disappointment chases away the feeling when a man wearing a white coat and stethoscope walks in rather than Dane and Ophelia. Every muscle in my body locks in a brace against the news regarding my health.

"I'm Dr. Patel." He ambles over, unwinds the stethoscope, and starts listening to my chest. I follow his instructions to take a deep breath, and within a minute, he steps back.

"Everything appears fine." His kind face matches his soft tone. "Your EKG and X-ray were normal. Your bloodwork was unremarkable, including troponin level, which helps rule out a heart attack."

"So I'm not having a heart attack?"

"No." Dr. Patel sits on a stool and opens my electronic chart.

"But why does my heart keep beating so fast?"

"I'm going to put in a referral for you to meet with a cardiologist. They might want to look into some more tests like an echocardiogram. I think you might be experiencing some anxiety. Have you ever had a panic attack?"

"I've had some increased stressed since my husband passed away." I attack the cuticle on my thumb with my index finger. Though I've experienced high bouts of nervousness, what with having to pack our home overseas, move back to the States, and live alone without the love of my life, getting pregnant by a one-night stand and abandoned by my family, I wouldn't classify any previous experience as a panic attack.

"Are you seeing someone to help with that? Taking any medication?"

My reticent answer apparently doesn't pass undetected, and Dr. Patel's counter question gives me a defensive sting.

"No." Not without trying. A doctor back home gave me medication to try shortly after Ophelia's birth, but it only worsened the sensations. I couldn't handle raising a newborn alone and dealing with them at the same time, so I tapered off at my doctor's direction.

"I see. I'll add a referral to a therapist. In the meantime, I recommend you take two weeks to rest and bring your stress level down. It'll help with the sensations and your palpitations."

"Thank you." I don't bother telling him I no longer plan to stay in town. My body is clearly signaling my mistake. Any follow-up is none of his business. His job is to make sure I'm not about to drop dead right this minute, and it appears that's not likely, so I'm free to be on my way.

"A nurse will come back with your discharge paperwork. I wish you well, Ms. Harris." Dr. Patel exits the room, drawing my attention back to the door.

"How long have you been standing there?" I ask Dane, following it immediately with another question that sparks my heart. Dr. Patel has to be kidding himself with his order to rest. "Where's Ophelia?"

"She's with Evie."

"You're *kidding*," I practically growl and throw my legs over the edge of the bed for the second time. "Shouldn't I be protected by HIPAA or something? I told you not to have the doctor call her."

Before I regain my feet, Dane's across the room, blocking my path.

"I'm not your healthcare provider, so HIPAA doesn't apply to me, and I made a judgment call and called her myself. Like it or not, you need her help."

"*Not*," I seethe. I'm being unreasonable, but so is he, stepping out of line as if he knows what's best for me. I'm not ready to face her. Hell, I wasn't sure I was ready to face *him*. Coming here was a huge mistake. "I shared about myself with you for one night years ago, and you think you can make decisions for me?"

"I'm really glad you brought that up." He crosses his arms over his broad, muscled chest, making it totally hard not to notice the way the short sleeves of his black tee hug his rounded biceps.

"Forget about it."

The way he swipes his palm over his mouth gives the impression he's hiding his amusement. When he draws his hand away, seriousness steals across his face. The softness around his eyes draws me in and acts as a balm to my frayed nerves.

"You need a moment to worry about yourself. You can take the afternoon off to rest, and Ophelia will be back after dinner."

"I don't know." My teeth pinch my lower lip.

"I'll take you back to my place while I check on the bar. You can take a nap, and I'll bring up food for all of us when Evie arrives. Doctor's orders."

"I hope you know I'm not staying. I'll rest, but only because I'm beat, and I need to get back on the road sooner than later."

My discharge paperwork arrives, cutting off any long-winded retort.

"We'll see," Dane mutters.

Damn right, we will.

The loose plan I outlined before arriving might be altered, but spending the afternoon in the hospital only proves there are decisions to be made for everyone involved.

I'm too unreliable to be the only person Ophelia needs, but I'm too selfish to let her go.

So where does that leave us now?

4

Dane

The dull throb in my temples demands I take an extra-strength dose of ibuprofen once Caiti is settled, and I can disappear for a few hours to check in with my staff.

"You can bring me to the nearest hotel. I'll text Evie to meet us there, and I can pay for a cab to return you home."

Make that two ibuprofen and a shot of something strong. She's repeated the same thinly veiled demand several times since we left the triage room. I shift my eyes to the side before returning them to the road. Damn, she's pretty. Having her beauty seated beside me hits me straight in the solar plexus. Even when she sat at a table in my bar with her husband three years ago, I had a hard time keeping my gaze to myself. Allowing myself to enjoy looking, but nothing more. When she returned to my bar six months later a widow, all bets were off. I thought she was on the same page, or I would have never taken her to my bed. The way she fled by morning speaks to her regret.

Though more important matters persist at hand.

"How are you feeling?" I evade her request and ask the question nagging at me for the last eight hours. Even in a small town, emergency room visits are not swift.

Caiti lifts her head from resting on the window and stares blankly ahead. The silence stretches. At the next stop sign, I chance a glance to find her chewing her bottom lip.

"Caiti?"

She shrugs. "I'm really tired."

"To be expected after the day you've had." I ease on the gas. "We're only a few minutes away. Do you want something to eat now or after you've had a chance to rest?"

"I'll wait, thanks." The softness in her tone convinces me she's battling her emotions.

She remains silent when I park her car at the curb and lead her up the walkway to my apartment. I wonder if she remembers the last time she was here in as much detail as I do.

"It's not much," I mutter. I don't need to take stock of my bachelor-style abode. Maybe she won't look too closely either.

"It's just what I need." Caiti yawns and toes out of her black flats near the door.

"If you weren't taking a nap, I'd tell you to leave those on."

"I'm not going to make more work for you by tracking dirt in. You've done enough for me today." Her lingering sigh quells any further argument from me.

"Come on. There's a bed this way."

This morning, I had a few minutes while Ophelia demolished a snack to straighten up my room, which mostly consisted of picking up a week's worth of laundry from the floor and shoving it in the hamper. I'm a pretty clean guy. I can proudly admit my bathroom is free from piss streaks and beard clippings, and I know many dudes who can't say the same. Or whose wives would declare otherwise.

Entering the dim space, I'm thankful I had the foresight to straighten the black comforter from the crumpled mess I flung off me during the loud awakening this morning. I chance a glimpse over my shoulder. Caiti travels at a sluggish pace into my room. Without pause, she meanders straight passed and climbs onto my king-sized bed.

Does she know how fucking sexy she makes the simple act look?

"I'll, uh..." I clear my throat and rub the back of my neck. "I'll be down at the bar if you need anything."

Silence stretches. My body burns to walk over and check if she's already fallen asleep. To cover her with my blanket and trap in her flowery scent. The only time she spent in my bed left my sheets smelling of her for over a week until I was ready to wash them.

I walk to the door and wrap my hand around the bronze handle, pulling it closed behind me. Before the latch clicks, I swear I hear her voice calling out a faint, "Thank you."

My chest tightens. I've kept a lock on my emotions all day, but I think it's time for that shot or two.

I'm down the stairs, through the bar's back door, passing the kitchens, and into my office without a single distraction. For once, I'm thankful for a slow afternoon. My mother's old clock on my desk says it's nearly four-thirty. The aides will be helping her get ready for dinner any minute, then it's television time, a bath, and bed by seven-thirty. I scratch out a note on a scrap paper to my left to bring her a box of her favorite cookies when I visit tomorrow. It doesn't make up for the distress I probably caused her today, but it's a start.

A knock sounds when my door swings open, and my best friend, Rhett, pokes his head inside.

"You must have heard from Evie." I slide out my bottom

drawer to grab the bottle of vodka I keep stashed. I own the place, but I don't like to take from my inventory, and it doesn't set a good example for my staff if I'm on the floor serving myself drinks.

Rhett steps fully inside and closes the door behind him.

"She was goddamned over the moon to show up at our place with that adorable little girl in tow. Evie and Tommy have been busy all afternoon keeping her occupied with toys and snacks."

My stony face gives no indication of the burn as I toss the first shot back. "Want one?"

"Nah." My friend waves his hand. "Evie and I have a pact while we're trying to conceive. No alcohol for either of us."

"How noble of you to decline in her honor."

"If you're going to spit sarcasm, mind sharing with the class what's up your ass?" Rhett sits on the arm of the green-velvet armchair I keep in the corner and rests his ankle on his opposite knee.

I swallow shot number two and flick the cap back onto the bottle. If I don't stow it away now, my entire evening might be shot, and I have important shit to do. Like find out what Caiti is doing here after all these years and why she didn't try to find me sooner. I'm trying to reserve judgment on calling her out for keeping my kid from me until I hear her reasons. I firmly believe people deserve the chance to explain themselves. But waiting is fucking hard.

I stop peering at the mess of papers on my desk and fix my gaze to Rhett's. "You remember the last time Caiti was here about three years ago?"

"You mean the time you banged on my door half naked at seven in the morning searching for her, and all you could say was you fucked up? Yeah, man, hard to forget. Evie was pissed for months and blamed you for running Caiti out of town."

I release some irritation with a sigh.

"Ophelia's mine."

"You're shitting me."

"Caiti hasn't made an official declaration, but c'mon. The resemblance is undeniable."

Rhett rubs his chin. "I don't know, man. She's pretty cute. Either she got it all from her mother, or you're off the mark because you're dead ugly." He grins to soften the mock blow.

He would say that with his cover-model good looks. He takes the trophy for a pretty boy, where I fall somewhere on a spectrum between clean and rugged depending on how much scruff is on my face.

"Save the wisecracks for another time, if you wouldn't mind. Maybe when I don't have so much on my plate."

"What are you going to do besides calling your urologist to demand a refund?"

I ignore the jab. "I want to know why she's here after all this time. Is it guilt? Or is it something more serious?"

"Serious how?"

"She collapsed on my steps this morning." I run a hand over my tired face. "Maybe she's here because she needs my help in some way."

"That's a lot to take in. It might be best to see how this plays out and keep your distance."

I level Rhett with my gaze. "I want to know how to convince her to stay."

"Are you breaking your rule for her?" Rhett leans back in the chair and lowers his foot to the ground as if he's stabilizing himself for my response.

Yes.

No.

Fuck.

"I don't know," I spit in answer. The very thought turns my stomach. Only those closest to me know about the rule I set to keep me from ending up in this exact situation, and look how that fucking turned out. The rule was supposed to keep us all safe. The sentiment from that morning three years ago swirls again in my head. *I fucked up.* "Does it matter? The deed is done, and clearly, my vasectomy failed. She doesn't have to stay with me. She just needs to stick around town. I'll be damned if I let her run off with my kid now."

"Evie might be able to help you with that."

"How?" I lean back in my chair and drag my fingers through the hair atop my head. The vodka dulled my frayed nerves, but I'm still restless.

"She's refused to set a date to marry me until she could get Caiti to agree to come. Since Caiti's been avoiding Evie's phone calls for the past three years, I'm thinking she has a pretty convincing reason to guilt her into sticking around."

Having good friends is absolutely fucking priceless. It hasn't even been one day, and they're already lending solutions.

"She's a known runner." The memory of waking up to disheveled, empty sheets flashes through my thoughts.

"Evie rolled into town after running from her family and her ex. She ran from me once too. If I can get her to settle, I think this plan has a decent chance of working out."

"If Evie can crank the guilt up to one hundred, I'd be grateful."

Rhett slaps his hands against his knees and stands. "You got it. It'll all work out." He fishes his phone out of his pocket. "I have three missed texts wondering when I'll be home so Evie can get Ophelia back here, so I better go."

I rise from my office chair. "That's my cue to put in an order with Duke. I promised to feed all the girls tonight."

"Give us an hour. I want to fill Evie in and give Tommy a little more time to play with his new cousin."

Thinking Ophelia might already have a friend in Rhett's six-year-old son puts a rare smile on my face.

"You got it."

"If we weren't already like family, this would have sealed it."

"Yeah." The word draws out on a sigh.

Rhett exits left out the back, and I head right to the kitchen. I give Duke, my assistant manager and cook, an order to have six bacon cheeseburgers with fries, condiments on the side, and an order of mozzarella sticks ready in an hour.

"Feeding a small crowd tonight, Boss?"

"Something like that. Are you good to cover for the rest of the night?"

Duke's head bobs while he cleans the sizzling grill. "Not a problem. My old ball and chain is at book club until nine, in which case he'll catch a ride home with one of the gals' husbands and be conked out by nine fifteen."

"Is book club a code word for something I'm unaware of?" Duke's partner Ronnie is naturally the life of the party. Even in their sixties, the couple knows how to have a good time, but I can't imagine how a book club could be enough to knock the man out.

A snort from across the room pulls me from my thoughts. "Let's just say the stuff he reads keeps us young. I'd think the books were an excuse to get rip-roaring drunk with his friends if it weren't for the way he puts out while reading 'em."

"That's a visual I didn't need." I shake my head.

His cackling laughter follows me out the swinging door into the restaurant.

5

Caiti

THE DOOR OPENING sounds like a gunshot in the quiet darkness startling me from sleep. I don't remember much about the dream, but it must have been a nightmare judging by the sensations rushing through my body. Electric bolts sizzle beneath the surface of my skin, and my heart races again. I sit up, noting the cold sweat covering my chest and dampening the shirt clinging to my back, while my eyes take in the room.

The simple space hasn't changed since I was last here. The memory dredges up a guilty pang even though it shouldn't.

Quiet voices break through the static ringing in my ears, and I breathe a sigh of relief, recognizing Ophelia.

"I see Momma now?"

"If you keep your voice down, I will check and see if she's ready. Why don't you take the coloring crayons Tommy gave you and make her a picture while you wait?"

My stomach pitches. The other voice belongs to Evie. I rub my sweaty palms together and shake my arms out, knowing she's moments away from coming into the room. There's no use in pretending to be asleep now. Evie would wake me up without hesitation anyway, and I'd rather not get busted faking it.

The dim light from the other room grows fractionally as the door opens silently and Evie slips inside. I'm grateful she closes the door behind her, blocking out the potential for Ophelia to hear something she shouldn't. She's not even three years old yet, but she is smart as a freaking whip, and I don't need her repeating anything she might hear in the next five minutes.

My sister-in-law's scrutinizing eyes meet mine in the dark room. I can tell without the light on she's not surprised to see me awake.

"Nice to see you're still alive." Evie crosses her arms across her chest, the disdain in her tone intended for me to hear.

"Look, I'm not going to make any excuses. You've met my daughter. I'm sure you can conclude for yourself why I haven't been answering the phone."

"Don't even think you can use her as an excuse for not picking up the damn phone, Caiti. That wouldn't have worked for Eric, and it damn sure won't work for me."

The guilt and shame burn deep, mingling with the other sensations coursing through me. "I know," I mutter meekly.

Evie rushes toward me, knocking me to the side. Her arms wrap me in a tight embrace that until this moment I didn't know I needed. Tears burst forth. After three long years, the dam holding them at bay has finally broken free. I choke on the sobs, my throat tightening as every breath becomes nearly painful to take.

"I'm so sorry," I cry into her thick curly red hair, soaking her neck and the collar of her T-shirt with my torrent of tears.

"Shush." She strokes my back with a motherly hand. Spending time with Rhett's son has unleashed her maternal instincts.

Sitting up straight, I throw my arms on her shoulders and hold her at arm's length. "I didn't know what to do. I still don't know what to do."

Evie's thumbs catch the tears streaming from my eyes and running down my cheeks. "It's okay. We'll figure it out. And now that you're here, you're not alone." Her stern tone reveals her unhappiness with me keeping my distance for all this time as if she didn't once do the same.

"I'm not ready to talk about him," I say quickly to head off further conversation.

Evie's eyes slit as she regards me, and her head cocks to the side. "Which him?" she asks, not cruelly based on the curiosity in her tone.

"Eric." Saying his name out loud for the first time since I saw her last hurts more than I could've ever imagined. The loss of him still lances me from time to time, sure. But I think the fact I've dishonored him by not saying his name is what hurts the most at this moment.

"Did something happen?"

"What do you mean?"

Her gaze scrutinizes my face. "It's just… You're different."

"I lost my husband." I can't quite keep the perplexity out of my tone. What did she expect after all this time? That I'd be the same old carefree girl she knew and loved? That I was somehow strong enough to endure the loss of my husband and becoming a widow at the ripe old age of thirty-one? Don't forget to throw in a meaningless one-night stand and a baby, oh and the fact I kept said child a secret.

"You were so strong when I flew out to Colorado after he

died. You comforted me," she says, choking on the words of the memories.

"I think I was in shock. It was both incredibly real and unreal at the same time. And I had you, and I had Tate, and I had my parents. That was the last time that I didn't feel alone." The truth is, people only linger for so long after tragedy as their lives begin to resume again. Evie's held out the longest. Eric's best friend, Tate, drifted shortly after the ceremony we held to honor him. I suspect his grief pulled him down, and I was too lost to ask. As for my parents, the minute they realized I wouldn't put my bastard child up for adoption, they ceased speaking to me.

Evie nods. "When you flew out here six months after that, I knew something was wrong. But you didn't give me a chance to help you. You showed up sad, demanded we go to the bar, and spent the rest of the night drinking and refusing to talk. I thought I'd let you sort out your emotions, and we could talk the next day, but then you left."

This is the part I've been dreading. The part I've been hiding. "I think you can now understand my reason for leaving."

"I believe you thought you were doing what was best for you. That doesn't mean I'm not pissed you left without talking to me."

I brush a loose strand of hair out of my face. "I deserve that. I hope you can forgive me."

"I'll forgive you because I love you, but I have a stipulation."

"I'm scared to even ask."

"You should be." Evie shoves my shoulder. "But I'm afraid you don't have a choice."

"What is it?" I groan. I lean back against the pillow behind me, sending a waft of bourbon-scented soap into the air. The scent of Dane renews old memories. The mixture of alcohol and smoke has been branded into my brain. For a moment, I allow myself to breathe in the fragrance I associate with comfort in this strange place.

"You have to stay."

I straighten from the pillows. "I can't."

"You've always been close enough to me to be considered my sister, so while I love you, I'm not going to mince my words when I tell you if you leave again, I'm done."

A spasm around my middle makes me grateful for my empty stomach. "You don't mean that." My attempt at calling her bluff sounds weak to my own ears.

"I have to mean it, sweetie. Because while you've been trying to figure out what you need to take care of you, I've put my life on hold waiting. And I can't wait any longer. Not even for you."

"What are you talking about? Waiting for what?"

"To marry Rhett. I won't put it off any longer."

"You shouldn't have waited."

"Well, I did. And now that you're here, I'll never forgive you if you leave before my wedding."

The pillow behind my back ends up clutched against my chest. "When's the date?"

"In one month."

"And after I can…I can leave again? You won't hate me for it?" I slowly inhale through my nose with the new wave of rising panic. Evie's hand lands on my bouncing knee.

"I won't hate you for it, no. But I hope by then you might have a reason to reconsider."

"I won't," I state with finality. Nothing's changed even after a few hours of rest.

She shrugs. "We'll see. One more thing."

With a huff, I throw my curtain of hair over my shoulder. "What else?" I'm starving for food after not eating for most of the day, but at this juncture, I'd be happy with falling back into another ignorant sleep.

Evie sinks her teeth into her lower lip in a clear warning I won't like what she's about to say. "You're both needed for the wedding party. At first, I just needed you as my maid of honor, of course, but seeing Ophelia playing with Tommy, ugh, you should have seen them, Cait. They're going to make the cutest flower people."

I wrinkle my nose. "Flower *people*? Isn't he supposed to be the ring bearer?"

"I've already given that job to Ghost." Her smile brightens at the mention of her sweet deaf, blind pit bull. "I figure Tommy would be a good example to Ophelia on what to do."

I lose the pillow in my lap in order to cross my arms over my chest. "How long exactly have you had this planned?"

"Three years," she deadpans.

Of course. While I've been stuck in a Groundhog Day scenario, lives went on, even if I wasn't actively partaking in one. I'm grateful she can't see the tears pricking the corners of my eyes.

"I'm sorry you've been on hold for me. I'll be there. We'll stay until after the wedding."

Evie sniffles quietly in the dark. "That's all I've wanted. I've missed you."

"I've missed you too. So much." If only I could tell her how much, but she wouldn't understand. With the corner of my sleeve, I dab my eyes. "What happens now?"

"We get you settled somewhere."

I run my hand over the duvet to ground myself. A lot of big decisions happened in the last five minutes. "I'm not hard on money, but I don't think I can put us up in a hotel for an entire month. Eric would've had a conniption if I wasted money like that." The joke feels like a pinch more than a jagged dagger.

Evie giggles. "You're not wrong." She waves her hand between us. "Doesn't matter. Rhett and I moved back into the main house ages ago, so you can have your pick of the tiny houses on our property."

The sudden intrusion of light from the door flinging open temporarily blinds us both.

"They're staying with me." Dane's deep voice accompanies the burst of light.

"Holy crap, Dane." Evie recovers first to chastise the man responsible for the rude interruption. "I thought you were an intruder."

His stormy gray eyes are steady on mine. "You'll be safest here."

All my words stick behind a swollen tongue.

"What are you talking about? They're definitely safe with us," Evie chimes back in, ready to defend her and Rhett's abilities.

"I want them close."

Evie opens her mouth to argue again, more than likely on my behalf, but Dane cuts her a glance that has her jaw shutting again.

The irony is they aren't far off. I should stay where I'm safest. Not that I think the man texting me could actually find me here.

"Not my circus," she mutters and stalks out of the room. She pauses at the door to peer up at Dane with an expression I'm not privy to. Their silent communication snaps me out of my temporary muteness to fight on my own behalf.

"I'm not staying." I dig my heels into the mattress to scoot myself toward the edge of the bed.

Dane steps into the belly of the room. "You are. You both are."

Ignoring the wave of dizziness that washes over me takes

effort. It's like my brain wants me to be afraid of every sensation. "We aren't," I bite out.

He tilts his head. "I don't remember you being so intolerable."

"I don't remember you being so demanding."

Dane strides the two steps separating us until we're mere inches apart. His eyes sparkle in the light seeping in from the hall, and his smirk turns downright sinful. "Well, I do."

I bite my cheek to stifle the gasp his words provoke. Not touching that with a hundred-foot pole, I change the subject. "I'm hungry."

"I'll feed you."

"I'll stay at Evie's tonight, and we can meet to discuss this tomorrow." With my chin held high, I stomp past him. I misjudge the space between his rock-solid body and the bed, and our shoulders brush. One simple touch, but now that I'm not bogged down in panic, I feel that touch everywhere. Even more so when five fingers wrap tightly around my bicep and bring me to a halt.

"I have a better idea. Evie brings Ophelia to her place for a sleepover, and you and I can talk tonight."

"You won't stop me from leaving first thing in the morning and staying at Evie's for the rest of the time I'm here?"

Dane gives nothing away as he holds my stare.

I mull the option over. He can't physically force me to stay here, and I don't get the impression that he would. I can't blame him for wanting answers as soon as possible, and he's already been patient for most of the day. He probably wants to know what his new reality looks like as much as I do.

I nod. "Compromise. After I've had some food, I'll talk to you, then I'll settle in at Evie's when we're done."

"I have a feeling you won't want to."

"I'm not here to play house with you."

"You sure about that?"

My mouth dries. I twist the vial I wear around my neck on a gold chain. "It's not you that I want."

"Tell me she's not mine." His eyes darken. I struggle to maintain the connection.

"You know that I can't."

The muscles surrounding his mandible bulge.

"I'm sorry." I squeak the first of many apologies to come.

His hold slips from my arm. "Save it. Food is ready."

Without waiting for my response, if I could even come up with one after that exchange, he stalks from the room.

6

Dane

THE GIRLS PERCH in a row on my sofa. With three fries in one hand and a quarter of her burger in the other, even little Ophelia does her best to mimic the adults. I stand off near the kitchen in a struggle not to hover. My ability to steer small talk away from the questions raging around my skull is next to none. This is my attempt to give Caiti breathing room. At least until the others leave.

I finish my burger and fries in record time, silencing the hours-long gurgle in my stomach as the girls chitchat away. I can't deny that something warms inside me seeing Caiti and Evie bonding again after so long apart. When I called Evie earlier to inform her of the situation, she was as surprised as I was to hear that Caiti was back in town and shared with no small amount of attitude that she hadn't spoken to Caiti in three years.

I busy my idle hands with loading up last night's dishes into the dishwasher, only half listening. The girls decide to put on a movie to keep Ophelia occupied. The show gives me an excuse to dip out and make some much-needed phone calls. With two new guests about to take up much of my time and space, my normally quiet routine will experience a shift, and I need to see to that shift before it becomes a problem.

I shrug into my black jacket hanging by the door and slip out of the apartment, seemingly unnoticed. Nobody summons me back, not that I expect them to. With my phone in hand, I jog down the steps to my apartment and out into the chilly air. The sun has gone down, the first stars of the night peeking out of the charcoal sky. With a hand in my pocket for warmth, I dial the number to connect with one of the nurses taking care of my mom.

"Thank you for calling The Legendary. This is nurse Erika."

"Hey, Erika. It's Dane again. How is she tonight?"

The sigh leaving Erika's lips is telling. "She's okay. You know her confusion worsens when you don't come to visit."

I clench the fist in my pocket. "How bad was it?"

"She was fine, Dane."

"How bad?" I question again. She knows as well as I do that I won't stop until I get an answer.

"She waited by the door. She told everyone who walked in that she was waiting for her son. We were able to get her to relax by telling her we were going to curl her hair for your arrival, hoping she would forget when you didn't show, but as soon as we were done, she just kept asking where you were."

My head falls heavily between my shoulder blades, and my face tips up to the sky. A guilty sigh fractures the quiet air.

"Dane," Erika starts.

"No," I say, low. "It's okay. Thanks for letting me know, and I promise I'll be there tomorrow."

"It's okay, you know, to do what's best for you. We've got her here. We've got her."

I don't bother responding to her attempted reassurance. Her words do nothing to soothe the yoke of responsibility sitting on my shoulders. "I'll see you tomorrow."

Without waiting for a goodbye, I hang up.

The weight of my duties adds to the gravity keeping me tethered until each step feels like trying to pass through quicksand. I don't want to return upstairs until I can sort some of this shit out. I don't want to be liable right now for softening the words coming from my mouth. Not until I've had some time to fortify myself.

My screen brightens when I tap the phone again and punch out a text to Evie.

Let me know when you're leaving, and I'll come back.

Not that I have anything to do to occupy my time until then. My work is done for the night, and I trust Duke to close the place up. I'd call over a friend, except I'd rather not divulge much without having details myself. Even the short chat with Rhett this afternoon set me on edge and heightened my need for answers I'm yet to receive.

Without much thought to the decision, I walk into the back patio of my bar and find an empty seat along the perimeter. The place isn't too busy tonight, and the cool air means only a few straggling smokers remain outside. A part of me wishes I had a few drinks to ward off the chill, but I know cool, sober heads are necessary.

I have a little girl.

Leaning back in the iron patio chair, I let that phrase sink deep into my brain. I have a daughter. A husky chuckle sneaks out with no small amount of disbelief. This was never supposed to happen. I even went so far as to ensure with surgery and limited one-night stands. Caiti was an exception to a carefully constructed rule. I have a couple of women in town, who I've known for years and trust implicitly to take their birth control, that I've let into my bed on occasion. And the one time I make an exception…

Fuck.

The problem is, it's already happened. The deed is done. Caiti doesn't know what my family, and these genes, are capable of, and now it's too late. That little girl is tainted with my blood, which makes it my responsibility to raise her through whatever comes her way because of me.

Her cherub face pops into my mind. Her dark curly hair and round eyes. The innocence only a baby can carry for a few years until the reality of the world chases it away.

Thoughts of my own childhood taint her image, and I brush them all aside.

I'll be damned if I let them walk away now.

Caiti's reasons for showing up in town after three years remain a mystery, and I don't care. She might feel she made a mistake coming here, but I hope I can show her another side of regret. Because there's no way I'm about to let them go. They don't know it yet, but they need me to care for them. I refuse to let them down.

I can handle it just as I've handled everything else life has dished my way.

"Hey, we're ready to head out." Evie's voice beside me yanks me from the abhorrent walk down memory lane.

"Shi-oot. You scared me." Seeing the tired toddler in her arms triggers me to censor myself.

"Sorry. I was about to text, but then I spotted you."

I crane my neck to view beyond her shoulder. "Where's Caiti?"

Evie looks down at the little girl resting her head on her shoulder. "She said she was coming."

"She's probably poisoning my milk."

"Maybe," Evie sing-songs.

"You know, between you and your boyfriend, this isn't that amusing."

"Fiancé. And I think it's pretty dang fitting."

The legs of my chair scrape against the concrete patio as I stand. "How so?"

She adjusts the little girl on her hip. I can't help my drifting gaze roaming Ophelia's face. It's as if my brain is trying to find all the similarities in order to claim them as mine.

"You ran my sister out of town, and I haven't seen her for three years. Karma is dishing it out, and I am here for it."

"I didn't run her out of town. She chose to leave."

"Yeah, well…" Evie trails off and shrugs. "You have a month this time to get it right."

My head rears back in affront. "Get what right?"

She twirls a finger between us. "This. You and her and Ophelia."

"Get that out of your head right now," I hiss and lean closer. "There is no *us* where she and I are concerned."

"You are acting mighty territorial for that statement to be true."

"Keep your opinions to yourself," I grouse and send a rock skittering across the patio with the toe of my shoe. I'd never admit her assessment nears the mark.

"Whatever. I'm just saying, I've convinced her to stay until the wedding, so do with that information as you will."

I grasp her arm with gentle pressure and direct her back to my door. "I really hope you're not filling her head with dreams that won't come true because I can tell you, this isn't a fairy tale."

Evie yanks her arm away, her red hair spinning behind her on a whirl. "Yeah, I'd say more than most, she gets that this isn't a freaking fairy tale, Dane." Her mocking tone hits its mark.

"Just keep it to yourself."

"Will do. We'll get out of your hair."

We reach my apartment with still no sign of Caiti. I look at the tired girl in Evie's arms. "You don't need to carry her back up the stairs. I'll go check and text you if she's good."

"Thanks." Her tone loses some of its heat. "She already said her goodnights to this one, so maybe she's waiting upstairs for you."

My eyes travel to Ophelia. "Good night, princess. You sleep good for your Auntie Evie, okay?" The endearment feels foreign but oh-so right for my little girl.

She lifts her arms straight out in my direction. A warmth spreads through my chest as I take her into my secure hold. Her little body snuggles right into my chest, and her arms wrap around my neck. My voice is hoarse when I tell her, "I'll see you tomorrow."

She nods against my shoulder. I soak her in for a moment longer, not wanting to make Evie linger when she's already doing so much to help, and relinquish her back to her aunt.

Silence greets me when I reach the top of the stairs. I swear if she found a way to sneak out of here, the ensuing fight won't be pretty. I'm not interested in an ugly custody battle, but she can't show up here after three years and expect me not to be involved. Otherwise, what was the point?

That's exactly what I'm hoping to find out.

Both my bedroom and spare room are empty, and the door to the bathroom is wide open. I pass through the living room on my way to check for her car when a rustle ensnares my attention.

A smile twitches my lips and chases away the burden for a moment. The visual of her dark hair tousled over the side of her face, her parted pink lips, and her arm thrown across her eyes inks itself in my mind.

Caiti fell asleep on my damn couch.

A piece of me wants to be mad. What in the stall tactic dictionary is this? If she hadn't had such a trying day, I'd accuse her of faking. But knowing she spent over twenty hours in the car the past two days and eight more in the emergency room today testifies to her exhaustion.

Even with her nap this afternoon, she deserves to catch up on her rest.

The only problem is I didn't intend for her to sleep on my couch. The old furniture is as uncomfortable as it is ugly.

I stalk to the kitchen for a glass of water while I ponder what to do and send Evie a quick text that she's able to take off. I could risk moving her and court her wrath if I wake her in my arms, or I could leave her there and feel like a jackass for sleeping in my king-sized bed.

A sharp cry cuts the contemplation short.

"Nooooo." A gut-wrenching sob tears from her throat. "Please don't go."

The wail is so loud, I swear she's awake. "Caiti?"

"Don't leave me. Promise you won't go!"

Reaching the back of the couch, I look down. Tears stream down her cheeks from behind closed eyes. "Caiti, you're having a bad dream." I move around the side and crouch down at the front. She doesn't seem to register my voice.

"I don't want to be alone." She hiccups through a sob. Without any other ideas in my inventory, I reach out a hand to gently shake her. My fingertips barely graze her shoulder. She sucks in a sharp breath and rolls over, cradling my hand against her chest.

"You're here," she breaths through a choppy exhale. The sobs calm to gentle waves, and her breathing begins to even out. She's still asleep.

"I'm not going anywhere."

"Don't leave me." Her plea splits me into two.

"I won't." I swallow against the knot in my throat. "I won't leave you." Not sure what else to do, I hoist her into my arms. She doesn't stir more than to snuggle into my chest much like our daughter had not long ago.

I walk us carefully into my bedroom and close the door partway with my foot. With gentle movements, I lower her to the bed and pull my duvet up to her chin. I notice the tracks from her tears left imprints on my shirt, sending another twinge to my chest. I really got myself into an unfamiliar position here. I'm not cruel enough to rip a child away from her mother, but where does that leave me when she ultimately decides she can't stay?

I deposit my boots next to my closet door, and without removing a stitch of clothing, I lay on the other edge of my king-sized bed.

A million thoughts race around my head. Some encourage me to go. Others urge me to stay. Some want to pull her into my arms and not let go like she begged even though I'm certain it wasn't me filling her dreams.

I settle for a compromise.

Close enough in case she needs me, but not too close to invade her space. Once I know she's fast asleep, I'll return to the couch.

But for now?

I'll wait.

For as long as she needs.

7

Caiti

I WAKE with a flutter in my chest after a restless sleep. My stomach shifts like a lava pool as my consciousness kicks in, sending my heart into overdrive. *Not again.* I squeeze my already closed eyes tighter. Another morning waking with fear in my veins.

Why didn't I know anxiety could be like this? These all consuming feelings happening at random without identifiable triggers. I always assumed an anxious person would be afraid of attending a party alone or speaking to a crowded room or driving over a bridge. Why is it that I'm merely afraid of waking up in the morning?

I take slow, deep breaths through my nose, something the therapist I saw after Eric died tried to get me to practice with regularity. I found it to be a bunch of garbage, but as time went on, the simple way of calming myself eased some of the sensations. Now that my fear has returned with a vengeance, I find the action annoying.

Fluttering my eyes open, I'm met with a strange room and dim lighting. The memories from the day before rush back in. What am I doing in Dane's room again? The bed beside me is messed but empty. I grip the vial around my neck and listen. Except for my breathing, the rest of the apartment appears silent.

I locate my phone in the side pocket of my leggings. It's a miracle it stayed put all night. The battery is down to fifteen percent, and all my belongings remain in my car. I'm not sure where my keys ended up, but they have to be nearby. Unless Dane's holding them hostage to force a conversation.

A message from the home screen waits from Evie, and guilt sinks into my stomach. I'm so used to ignoring her attempts at reaching out that I almost missed it. With a hurried swipe, I open the text and read.

EVIE: *Ophelia slept great! She's having some toast and a banana for breakfast. Call me when you're up. Love you.*

I TYPE BACK: *Thanks for the update. I miss her so much! Let me figure out where Dane is, and I'll call you in a bit. Kisses!*

I CLICK the screen off and head to the bathroom. The rest of the apartment is vacant. I definitely need to find my keys so I can change my clothes. I've been in these pants for so long that they're going to start to adhere to my skin, and a shower sound heavenly right about now.

A white sheet of paper on the kitchen counter beckons me forward. The apartment is small but tidy, with an air of coziness I can't quite place. A smoky pine smell reminds me of Christmas without a tree in sight. The kitchen and living room are open, separated by a bar counter with two stools. I imagine as a bachelor, Dane eats most of his meals here or on the couch in front of some sports game.

The vision of his concerned face chases some of the gray clouds from my head this morning. I don't know how he'll take to this entire situation, but his actions yesterday give the impression I can count on him.

Beside the paper are my keys. A phone number is transcribed in a barely legible scribble above a message.

C-

I'll be back at eleven. Help yourself to the fridge. Put this number in your phone and call if you need anything.

D.

A GLANCE at the microwave clock shows I have thirty minutes alone before he returns. I check the note again and add the number to my contact list. My stomach sours further at the thought of food. I'm too anxious to eat. I scratch that off my mental to-do list and grab my keys to the car. I'll shower instead.

Fifteen minutes later, I'm lathered, rinsed, shaved, and clean. With a towel wrapped around my body, I stand on the blue rug in front of Dane's sink, worrying my thumbnail between my teeth. What-if thoughts circle my brain like vultures surveying roadkill. Apprehension at our impending conversation seizes all rational thought. I should have tried harder to stay awake last night instead of putting this off until morning. The fretfulness is nothing new—I've had three years of practice—it's the thought of losing control again like I did yesterday that sends new terror through me.

My phone rings on the sink, jolting me from the

ruminating.

"Hey, Evie," I answer, coughing to disguise the perpetual tightness.

"Morning! How'd it go last night?" She's never one to hold back, except when concealing her own secrets. I crack a small smile, thinking of how hard she tried to keep this town a secret from Eric and me, and ultimately failed. I'm grateful I got to see Arrow Creek before. The slight sense of familiarity made the return bearable.

I clutch the knot of the towel between my breasts. "It didn't. I fell asleep."

"No! You're kidding."

"Sleep got the better of me, I guess."

"Caiti." Her tone is one of a disapproving mother. "Well, what happened this morning then?"

I dance from foot to foot. "It didn't. He was gone when I woke up."

"Do I have to lock the two of you in a room to figure this out? Because I will."

"You're supposed to be on my side," I whine, glancing back at my reflection in the mirror.

"Oh, I am. You have no idea," she mutters. "How about I bring the kids and pick you up? We can do some shopping until Dane's back from his errands."

The thought does nothing to settle my nerves. If anything, it sends my new-friend anxiety back to the forefront. "I don't think that's a good idea. He should be back soon. Actually, I'm standing naked in his bathroom right now, so I should take care of that."

"Why? It's not anything he hasn't already seen."

"One-time thing."

"That's no fun. Who else is servicing your needs?"

"My toys are none of your business."

Evie snorts. "No men in three years?"

"I learned my lesson." Though I'd never regret having Ophelia. The survival mode and nonexistent babysitters weren't conducive to my dating profile.

"Oh, honey," she says in a sober tone.

"Save the pity and go play with your niece. I'm hanging up now. I'll be by later."

"Good luck!" she sing-songs before we disconnect.

The smile remains etched into my face. I can't believe how long I denied having her in my corner. Gaining back one person makes everything that happened yesterday worth the turmoil. This spontaneous decision continues to conjure inklings of good things to come. I can feel it.

I lay my phone on the sink beside the pile of clothes I deposited there before my shower and locate my underwear. A frown chases away the smile. The pile now looks incredibly thin. Where the heck is my shirt? I swear I pulled the powder blue Henley from my bag and brought it in here. With a grunt of frustration, I yank open the bathroom door.

There.

The dumb shirt lies halfway between the bedroom and the bathroom.

I scoop it off the floor with an automatic huff just as the apartment door flies open. Dane looks to the kitchen, whipping his head back when he notices me standing frozen in a towel. Our eyes lock for a brief second before he skims down my unclothed body. We barely know one other, only in the most intimate ways but nothing about who we are as people, but I swear his face fills with no small amount of heat. An identical flame flickers within me.

"I'm sorry!" I call over my shoulder while I scamper back to the bathroom.

"Do you mind putting some fucking clothes on?"

The towel pools at my feet, and I jam the shirt over my head. "I was trying to," I grumble beneath my breath. Once all my body parts are contained in their proper clothing, I yank open the door, only to find myself alone once again. "Dane?"

"In here."

Apprehension fills me on my way to his bedroom, not knowing what'll come once I get there. Dane sits on the edge of his bed, a frame clutched in his hand.

"How'd you sleep?"

I shrug. "Fine," I answer, keeping this morning's sensations to myself.

"Here." He thrusts it in my general direction without raising his head.

"Oh." The frame holds a picture of Dane around Ophelia's age with a woman I presume to be his mother. His resemblance to our daughter is irrefutable. If we cut her hair, they'd look like twins.

"As you can see, I knew she was mine the second you showed up on my doorstep. All I need to know is why you're here."

"Is this your mom?"

He nods. "Why are you here, Caiti? Is someone sick, or are the two of you in danger? Because I can't think of why, after all this time, you'd show up with my kid without even figuring out a way to call."

My fingers remain curled around the frame. "I should have tracked you down. I'm sorry I didn't know how."

"Tell me now." His soft voice triggers the words to flow.

"I remember everything about our night together." Heat creeps into my cheeks. That simple statement sends images flooding through the barrier. Gasps and moans. Skin set ablaze with touches and exploration. "You don't want kids. I thought I lived far enough away that you wouldn't have to find out." I don't know why, but I skip the catalyst for sending me across the country and keep the weird text messages to myself.

"So you went at it alone?"

Sticky saliva slows my response. "I made the decision to keep her, and I already knew your position. I figured I could handle being a single mom. But the grief...I didn't have enough time to heal. She was a good distraction, but as you saw yesterday, I'm not one-hundred percent."

Dane shifts forward on the bed as if he's trying to hold himself back from standing. He wipes his palms on his jeans. A heated admiration shifts his features. "Did you have any help?"

A humorless laugh escapes before I can smother it. I move my gaze to the far corner of the room and numbly search for the vial around my neck. "My parents couldn't stand the thought of a bastard child tarnishing their reputation. They wanted me to put her up for adoption or to beg you to marry me. When I refused both, they cut all ties."

"You're shitting me." I glance back in time to see a stormy cloud move over his face.

"I don't want to be here, Dane, standing in front of you and admitting I'm a failure in multiple ways. I never wanted to drag you into this. I also didn't want to keep her from you to hurt you. If you can even try to believe, I did it for you."

Three lines appear between his brows. "For me?" The gravelly tone stokes a fire in my belly. Unable to hold himself back any longer, he stands. A foot of distance separates us, but with the intensity he's looking at me, I feel mere centimeters away.

"I'm sorry." The inadequate apology is all I have to offer.

His hands clench into fists at his side. "I can't remember the last time someone's done something for me."

The admission shocks me into silence.

"Even as fucked up as this is..." He chuckles without humor. Dane captures my gaze. "I want to kiss you so damn bad."

"I'm not here to be with you." I've had my one love of my life. This is about a co-parenting partnership and keeping our daughter out of harm's way. Nothing more.

"Are you sure about that?" His tone lowers to a decibel that provokes an electric sizzle.

"I'm sure. She deserves her dad."

"And what about you?"

"What?" I take a half-step back.

"What do you deserve?"

"I have my daughter. She's all I could ever ask for."

Dane matches my half-step with a full step of his own. "You made sacrifices. For me. You might have gone about them in the wrong way, but I don't miss your intention."

My breath hitches. "I kept memories from you. Precious firsts you'll never get back."

"Or maybe you've given me firsts I never, ever thought I'd want."

A change of course is in order. "What happened yesterday was the culminating point. I've had escalating symptoms for a while now, and I kept thinking, what happens to Ophelia if I can't take care of her?"

"You're going to be okay."

"What if he's wrong?"

"Who's wrong?"

"The doctor." I lock my fearful eyes with his, spilling secrets kept locked tight. Tears well on my waterline. "What if there really is something wrong with my heart, and he just missed it?"

His hand locks around my elbow, a comforting point of contact. "He's not wrong. You have to believe that."

"I need you to promise me you'll take care of her. No matter what."

"Nothing will happen to you," he growls deeply, his tone conveying a dizzying distaste for the notion.

"Please promise," I maintain. He needs to say it. He needs to promise. I'm yanked off balance and into his arms.

"Jesus, Caiti," he sighs into my hair.

Gun to my head, I'd never admit how good it feels being held to his warm, broad chest. "Promise me," I mumble against his tee shirt.

"Fuck, I promise. You have nothing to worry about."

I push out from his embrace a little harder than necessary. The space clears my head. "Not anymore. Thank you."

The corner of his lips lowers in a frown. "What happens now?"

"I can bring her over later so the two of you can get to know each other." Indecision slithers through me. It feels wrong to hand over my daughter to a complete stranger. Yesterday was the exception. But that's the result of a one-night stand, isn't it? Why should he be denied any further because I don't know him? He's her father. If I hadn't kept her a secret, he would have had the right to see her from birth.

And if something does happen to me, I want him to be familiar to her.

"If you're nervous, I can have Rhett come over with Tommy," he states as if he can read my thoughts.

"You'd do that?"

"We'll start slow. Give you a few days to adjust. If you don't fight me, I won't fight you."

This is the moment when I'd audibly gulp if I were a cartoon character. Because I haven't figured out how to tell him this might remain temporary. Now that I've made contact and he's agreed to be there for her, maybe a long-distance custody agreement would suffice.

The only certainty is I have roughly a month to figure it out.

8

Dane

I TUCK the realistic-looking baby doll into the crook of my mother's arm while she watches television from a wheelchair. We sit in the sparsely decorated common room at her facility. The same way we do every day. Though I couldn't recall what's currently on the mounted flatscreen. The show occupying my mind is an endless loop of Caiti waving goodbye from her idling red car at the curb as I drove off an hour ago and trying to decipher her unreadable mask. The vulnerability she's shown thus far is either a rare occurrence she can't control or a glimpse to an emotional side. Either option, I find a rare treat. I'd rather her be open than attempt to deceive me behind a stone wall of artificial strength. She came to me for help. I'm willing to give her whatever she needs.

The evidence of a strong woman too stubborn to ask for help sits beside me, and I'd do anything to turn back the clocks and give her the aid when she most needed it.

"What're you doing in my house?"

"I'm here to visit you, Ma." I gently reach for her hand that's holding the wheelchair in a death grip.

My mother crying out isn't a rare occurrence, but what she says in her native Southern twang drives a stake through my heart.

"Get out of my house, Barry!"

Fuck. Hearing her refer to me as my father is a special sort of torture. I thought seeing his features reflected back at me in the mirror was bad enough. The only solace I get is knowing he's rotting in a prison and can't hurt anybody ever again. Unfortunately, the lack of proximity doesn't stop him from occupying my mother's fragile brain from time to time. The chunks of her life she does remember tend to be from the distant past.

I should have known missing a day would set her off. Her confusion worsens whenever I delay a trip, and this time seems especially bad.

"It's me, Ma. I'm your son, Dane."

She yanks her hand from my grasp surprisingly quick. "Someone help me, please!" Her frightened stare moves beyond my shoulder to search out the faces around us. I feel the bruises on my heart with each rapid thump.

"I'll get someone. Hold on." I know from experience she won't settle down until I leave, and she won't remember this ever happened. This isn't a common occurrence, but that doesn't make it any easier to have my mother in such distress over my appearance.

A CNA works her way over at the commotion. "Want me to take her to her room?"

"Please. I'll just make it worse."

Sabrina smiles at me. "We've got her. I'll give her one of those treats you brought, and she'll be good as new."

Or as good as a seventy-year-old with early onset

Alzheimer's can be at this stage. We've had nearly twenty years of practice during her incredibly slow decline.

"Thank you."

I stand to the side, not wanting to leave until her distress dies down. Sabrina speaks to Ma with a soft smile and quiet tone. She touches her arm and hugs her. Knowing my mother is surrounded by people who care so much makes leaving her each day a little easier. Even these hard ones. I know she's well taken care of and even loved.

They wheel past, Ma not even twitching her gaze a little bit in my direction. That's my cue to head home. Tomorrow will be a better day for her.

My heart feels leaden during my walk to my truck. A quick glance in the rearview sends a familiar loathing through me. The day I cease being compared to my father will be one for celebration. The thought sickens me, knowing that day comes when my mom is entirely nonverbal or passes. I clutch the key harder than necessary and jam it into the ignition. A forceful exhale persuades the thoughts away. My cell dings from my pocket, denying their return. For now.

EVIE: *I don't know what the two of you are doing over there, but can you send Caiti soon? She's not answering her phone.*

THE ORGAN in my chest increases its beats. A glance at the time tells me she should have arrived over an hour ago. I punch the truck in reverse and speed off in the direction of home. I'll make the five-minute drive, and if she's not there—why the hell would she be—then I'll sound the alarm. The only thing keeping me semi-calm is the fact she wouldn't leave without her kid. Not a chance.

Except I don't really know her. Not like that. I could describe in detail how she sounds when she comes and the location of a little brown mole on the inside of her right thigh. How she's quiet overall but incredibly responsive in bed.

I also know she's funny and kind. She's not afraid to let loose a few tears rather than holding them inside when something strikes her emotionally. And she can verbally spar with the best in a way that turns me way the hell on.

But do I know her well enough to know this isn't a ploy to leave her kid somewhere safe so she can start fresh?

No. No, I fucking do not.

Heated anger twines itself through my veins until my hands sweat. Coming around the block on my street, I spot her red car. Concern douses the fire inside me. The whiplash from this situation threatens to knock me down. Keeping up with my own life while navigating hers is tricky and unpredictable. Space might do us some good until we figure out our respective roles.

Relief at seeing her in the driver's seat tames the beast within me. I kill the truck engine behind the red sports car.

"Caiti." I follow her name with a sharp knock on her window. The flinch of her shoulders sends my stomach pitching, and before I even think, I'm yanking the handle. The door flies open without resistance. "Are you hurt?"

Her hands shake violently where they grip the steering wheel. "No. Not hurt." The hollow tone is unconvincing. "I-I can't drive."

Not understanding, I order, "Look at me." Her wide, fearful eyes nearly do me in. "Spell it out for me, Mama. What happened?"

"I sat down. I waved as you left, but the panic came back when I turned the key."

"You had another panic attack?"

Tears spill down her cheeks with her nod. "I can't do this, Dane. Why is this happening to me all of a sudden?"

"It's not your fault, pretty girl." I tuck a loose strand of hair back behind her ear. "You've been through a lot, and your body is telling you it needs a rest."

"I've never been afraid of driving before. I just drove across the country to get here, but suddenly, I keep thinking what if I drive off the road, or what if I drive into oncoming traffic, or what if I have a panic attack *while* driving? What if it's with Ophelia in the car?" Her voice vibrates with a repressed sob.

I slide a finger beneath her chin and tilt her gaze to mine. "If it happens, you can handle it. The only way to know is to face it head-on."

"I don't know if I can do that."

"I'll help you." The vow rolls off my tongue with sincerity.

"How?"

"I'll follow you to Evie's right now. That way, if anything happens, you can pull over, and I'll be right there."

Frustration intensifies her grunt. "I can't have you babysitting me. Dammit, I brought you one child, not two!"

The eruption provokes a small chuckle from me. "I don't see it that way."

"I don't want to be a burden."

"You're easy to care for, and this is temporary. But the sooner you start driving again, the easier it'll be. If you wait too long, you'll take twice the time to recover."

Caiti dashes the tears from her cheeks with the back of her hand. "You'll stay right behind me the whole way?"

"I promise."

She moves her gaze to the windshield. "And when they ask what you're doing there?"

"Leave that to me." The most assuring thing I can think of is grounded in trust, and I can tell she's having a hard time believing me. I never said I was good at this, but I'm more than willing.

"Okay. Okay, fine." She twists the key in her ignition and squeezes her eyes shut as the engine roars to life.

"You'll need those open to see the road," I joke to lighten the air. At the provocation she turns a devastatingly sexy glare on me. But then she blinks and turns up the corners of her lips.

"Thank you," she murmurs.

"I'll be right behind you," I answer.

Petite fingers snatch my wrist as I turn to go. "Give me a five-second head start."

I bite down the praise I want to give her and instead reply with, "Got it."

I punch out a concise text to Evie as I walk back to my truck, simply saying we're on the way. She can ask or assume whatever she wants, but I've stepped into Caiti's privacy enough. Telling her sister-in-law the truth is her decision, not mine.

Once my engine roars to life, I catch her eyes in the rearview of her car. My fingers dance from the top of my steering wheel in a gesture to go ahead.

Loose gravel at the curb crunches as she pulls away, and I give the necessary five-second countdown in my head before mimicking the motion.

9

Caiti

DODGING questions from a nosy sister-in-law after three years apart is a game of chess. Staying three moves ahead is impossible when I'm rusty from disuse. I use her upcoming nuptials to my advantage and steer us far away from the topic of my baby daddy. At least for the time being until we can all settle in.

Dane seems to relent on keeping us near and agrees to meet me at the end of the block each day to help me drive back to his place for some father-daughter time. The intention is twofold. He spends time with his daughter and assists me with driving through panic. As terrified as I was to make the drive back to Evie's, knowing he was behind me somewhere eased my irrational fears.

This sudden turn of events is unwelcome at best.

Escaping Colorado was supposed to provide some clarity. Should I make the move permanent or simply establish a contingency plan should something happen to me? Factoring panic into this situation throws a rusty wrench into my plan. Decision-making is on the backburner.

But I refuse to lie down and accept it.

Each morning while Ophelia sleeps, I take my car around the block by myself. I drive in circles until the fear is replaced by boredom. Then I allow myself to return home, only to practice when Dane shows up in the afternoon. I don't know how much it helps, but I'm not giving up until I feel safe driving again.

I turn into the second driveway that leads to the two small houses Rhett had built for Evie deep on their property. The two now live in the main home, and I'm grateful for the quiet space. A part of me considers paying them rent and moving into the tiny house full time. There's space for Ophelia and me, and once she starts having sleepovers with her dad, I'll have more than enough. The seclusion suits me just fine.

Rhett's Jeep idles near the house. Evie stands beside the door with Ophelia on her hip, a black umbrella overhead blocking the drizzle. My baby girl shows off her teeth in a wide grin at something Rhett says. What's going on here? I couldn't have been gone for more than half an hour.

A text stalls me from exiting when I park beside Rhett.

UNKNOWN: *Good morning, beautiful. I hope a rainbow brightens your day.*

I FLASH my gaze to the gray sky. That's a coincidence, right? It rains all the time in Colorado where he should be. And snows. And hails. And sleets. Maybe he's speaking in metaphors or fucking poetry. There's not a chance in hell he could have followed me here.

Shaking off his reoccurring intrusion, I exit the car. "Everything okay?" I ask and pluck my girl from her auntie.

"You've been avoiding me." Evie's fierce glare nearly incinerates me. "So I've recruited Rhett to watch the kids while we go dress shopping."

"I'm sorry. Dress shopping for what?"

Her shoulders straighten. "For my wedding."

"Oh. Of course. I'm sorry I'm spaced out. The client files I'm currently working on are a bunch of medical jargon that steals my brain function." Which isn't a lie. The files do give me a headache. Except I haven't started any work yet today. The truth is, as glad as I am to be here, with so much going on, the wedding is pretty far from my mind.

Evie loops her arm with mine. "No matter. I don't need your input. I just need your measurements."

"Is this the part where I have no say in what sort of dress you stuff me into for your wedding?"

"Yep." Evie grins. "Give the baby to Uncle Rhett so we can be on our way."

Uncle Rhett climbs out of the car and opens the back seat to release his son Tommy. The sweet boy is very much a kid and not the toddler I used to hear stories about. "Hand her over." Rhett scoops her beneath her armpits and into the air over his head, releasing from her a fit of squeals.

"Uncul Wet play?"

"Of course, beautiful." He turns to me. "Do you mind if we take her to the p-a-r-k? Dane will meet us there."

Remembering her desire to go on the swings cinches my heart, and I trust Evie's fiancé implicitly after the way he took care of her when she was homeless. "Oh, not at all. You guys have fun."

Evie loops her arm in mine and starts leading me away. "He already installed Tommy's old car seat in the Jeep. He'll never admit it, but he's excited to take the two kids out on an adventure by himself."

I shove my keys into her hand at the crook of my elbow. "You drive," I call and scurry to the passenger side before she can protest.

Surface small talk fills the car on the short trip back into town. I still haven't gotten my flow back with the woman I once considered a sister, and conversation from my end remains stilted.

"Thank you for dragging me out. It's nice to see something other than Ophelia and my laptop screen."

"Don't thank me. I'm just glad you're here." Evie maneuvers the car to a curb in front of a brick store. Three women loitering around the exterior flail wildly in our direction.

"Do you know them?" The confusion in my tone gives away my solitary disposition. I've never been on the receiving end of such a greeting.

"You've already met Cami. She was the paramedic. Her partner Nathan's wife Kiersten is the blonde."

"So they're what... a thruple?"

Evie snorts. "Oh, God no. Law would lose his ever-loving shit if Nathan put his hands on Cami. Nathan was the other paramedic from the day you arrived."

"And who's Law?" All the names swirl in my head.

"Law is Cami's husband. The other brunette is Cami's daughter, Evelyn."

I study the two brunettes with matching grins. "They look more like sisters."

Evie unlatches her seat belt and hands my keys over.

"Thanks."

"Cami had her young. She was only sixteen or so."

"No wonder they look more like sisters."

"You're going to love them. I know they made me feel

instantly welcome here, and I hope they can do the same for you."

Evie holds too much hope in her eyes for me to quash during such a momentous occasion. Most people only choose their wedding dress once in their life. Myself included. I'll do whatever is necessary not to storm on her happy day.

"I'm excited!" Faking an emotion is a practiced skill at this point. I'm happy for my sister. Summoning up the appropriate amount of external enthusiasm is a challenge I refuse to back down from.

"Me too. I'm so glad you're here." I catch the shine in her eyes before she blinks, and it's gone.

The group on the sidewalk is no less fervent on our approach. Hugs are dished out, and I'm also swept into three different pairs of arms. Cami's hold lingers the longest.

"You look so much better," she says beneath her breath.

"No small thanks to you. You really helped keep me calm," I admit while admonishing myself for any lingering embarrassment.

"I'm glad you could join us so I can meet you in a non-professional capacity. I've heard so much about you." Her exuberance is infectious. "This is my daughter, Evelyn."

The youngest of the group waves from beside her mom. "Nice to meet you."

"It's nice to meet you too."

The remaining woman on the sidewalk rests a hand on her rounded stomach. "Hey, I'm Kiersten, and because my husband can't seem to keep his hands to himself, this is buns number three and four."

Gasps mingle with the chirping birds.

"What?" Cami's remark lands first, followed by her daughter. "You're having twins?"

"No wonder why you're so bitchy lately. Twice the

hormones." Evie's joke sends the other women into fits of laughter. I'm trying to wrap my head around the supportive girl gang while remaining an outsider.

"Congratulations," I add with a soft smile.

"I came straight from my appointment and just found out this morning." She swoops a rigid finger through the air. "Which means none of you better tell my husband before I get the chance to."

A chorus of rejections sounds from the group.

"Can you secretly record him?" Evie asks innocently.

"I bet fifty dollars he faints," Cami adds.

"You two are ridiculous," Kiersten pouts. "He's tougher than that. He'll handle it like a champ."

"You tried to die during your first delivery. I don't think he took his eyes off you for the second, and now you're about to have two at once? Lord help the man." Cami whips open the glass door to the shop.

"Um, Aunt K, I can babysit Cedric and Dean, but I'm not sure I can handle four at once," Evelyn announces.

"Don't worry, babe. You can bring a friend and split the work."

"But not the cash." Evelyn follows her mom inside without waiting for a response.

"I used to change your diapers, kid!" Kiersten calls through the open door.

I nudge Evie with my shoulder. "I like your friends."

Her answering smile radiates her happiness. "They like you too."

"Come on. Let's find you a dress so you can finally get married to your man." I swallow any lingering sadness.

"I'm ready."

A saleswoman greets us with bubbly flutes of champagne. We sip and chitchat while she prepares a room with some initial picks for Evie, then hauls her back to try on dress number one. The excitement in the air is palpable. I can tell these women all truly love one another.

"So, Caiti, the gossip is mighty hot and heavy around here since you showed up." Kiersten waggles her eyebrows.

The champagne has loosened my muscles. And my tongue. "You scratch my itch, and I scratch yours."

"Well..." We lean together conspiratorially, even Evelyn, who's barely a stitch over eighteen. "Obviously, Dane's your baby daddy, but the rumor mill is dying to know when and how that happened."

"What do you mean?" The bubbles sizzle on my tongue.

"Let's just say he's not the type of guy to use his business as a hunting ground. Rather the opposite, actually." Cami furrows her brow. "Calypso's is probably the safest place in the state for a woman to let loose without fear of being taken advantage of. I don't think I've ever heard of him picking up a woman there."

"Whoa, pump the brakes. He didn't take advantage of me."

Kiersten tips her water glass to her lips. "Even Evie says she left you drinking at the bar that night. Not that she's been gossiping," she reassures. "She was pissed at Dane for months after you left. She didn't go to Calypso's for an entire year."

That sounds exactly like the type of grudge my sister-in-law would carry with her fiery attitude.

"Let me put an end to that train now. Dane was nothing short of a gentleman that night, and I wasn't even drunk."

Kiersten cups her elbow and smirks. "Do tell us more about how much of a *gentleman* he was."

"Don't mind her. She's always horny," Cami grouses with a matching grin.

Heat incinerates me from the inside out. "Those details aren't up for grabs, ladies."

"Bummer," Kiersten pouts. "Good for you, anyway. If

you're going to bag a bachelor from this town, he's one of the last ones standing."

"That's not why I'm here." The champagne in my glass sloshes dangerously close to the rim.

Three pairs of curious eyes stare at me.

"Why are you—?"

Cami's question is cut short by Evie's stunning entrance.

The mermaid-style gown hugs every curve and dip along her figure as if it's been painted on until it flares at her knees. Her plus-sized figure can rock nearly anything, but the white, lace, and tulle dress takes the damn cake. The V between her breasts plunges nearly to her belly button, and white off-the-shoulder sleeves will drive Rhett absolutely insane.

"God, Evie," I croak and quickly slam more champagne. "You're so beautiful."

"Your man will be pissed he can't yank that over your ass for a quickie." Kiersten demonstrates once again she has sex on her brain.

"That's how I build tension." Evie winks. "This is it. This is the one I wanted," she squeals.

"You've only tried on one. Don't you want to see any more?" I glance around in confusion to see if the other ladies agree with me on this.

Evie moves off the small dais with grace and stops before me. She grabs my hand and pulls me from my seat without spilling a drop of my drink.

"I've had this dress on hold for two years on the condition if someone came in ready to buy it, I'd let it go."

"I'm sorry." The waterlogged apology sticks in my throat.

"This just proves it was meant to be," she says brightly. She uses my hand to perform a twirl, sending the mermaid skirt floating above her ankles. "Now it's your turn. The color theme is shades of blue, whatever style suits you best."

She waves her hands in a shooing motion. We take the hint and scatter.

"How much are you putting into searching for the perfect dress?" I ask Cami, who ends up at the same rack as me.

"Comfort over everything else. I'll even wear a pair of flip-flops if she'll let me, which means I should choose a long style."

"We wore Converse at my wedding." The admission slides out naturally. My hands pause on the silky material clenched in my fists, bracing for the pain to come. A small twinge pulses with my heart, but not the usual twisting heartache I've become accustomed to. My breath leaves in a slow stream.

"Law and I got married at the courthouse and never looked back." Cami saves me from further expanding on my own nuptials.

"What are the two of you talking about over here?" Kiersten joins our twosome in a sea of fabric and tulle.

"What style to pick." Cami spares me once again.

Kiersten draws out a dress with thin straps, short length, and a slit to mid-thigh in a vivid cerulean. "Access over everything."

"I like that idea." Cami's devilish grin spreads. She holds up a strapless flowy dress in baby blue. A thin sash hangs from the waist. "Your turn."

"Oh, I don't need access to anything." Might as well lock me in a chastity belt.

Kiersten frowns. "Maybe not, but you deserve to feel sexy."

"What about this?" Evelyn, eavesdropping on our conversation, crosses from a diagonal rack carrying a handful of steel blue fabric. She lifts the hanger overhead and lets the material cascade toward the floor.

The sheath dress has thick straps and a V-neck, ruching

around the stomach that wraps to a side bow, and a thigh-high slit in the front. The dress is sexy, all right. Maybe a little too much for a single mother widow.

"Try it on!" The girls cajole.

Before I can protest, the dress is shoved in my arms, and I'm pushed into a changing room.

Excited chatter floats from the stalls surrounding me. The material feels nice against my skin, slipping perfectly over my curves to sit in place like a glove. My admiration in the mirror lingers well past acceptable. I can't remember the last time I wore a pretty gown or dressed up at all. The reflection before me is nearly unrecognizable.

"Come out, Caiti, and show us." That voice belongs to Evie. The last thing I want to do is disappoint her, so I pull up my figurative big girl panties and unlatch the door.

"Yep, that's the one," Evie declares loudly. "No arguments allowed."

"You won't get one from me." I shrug one shoulder. "I love it."

Evie's phone snags her attention. "I've been ordered to tell you to head to Dane's when you're finished. Also to give him your damn number so he can stop using me as a middle man. I added that last part myself." She drops the device in her purse and grins.

Nerves ratchet at the sudden change of plans. "I suppose I should go."

"I'll go with you. Rhett's waiting for me there."

Once I shuffle into the changing room and shuck the gown, I breathe a sigh of relief in solitude. I should be able to conquer driving a few blocks with Evie in the car. It's what awaits me when I get there that has my heart beating faster.

10

Dane

THE PEN in my hand scratches against the notepad as I jot down the last few items on my list at the kitchen island. Ophelia plays happily with a singing stuffed animal in the spare bedroom. I smile at the sounds of her childish enthusiasm. I know there's learning involved, but how kids don't get bored of the same old songs the way adults do is beyond me. She's had the stuffed dog on repeat for over an hour now. I never thought I'd remain entertained to sit silently and listen to girlish chatter, but here I am. Happy as a goddamned clam.

My ticker tracks the seconds until Caiti arrives, quickening my pulse. The sound of the oven alarm sets me in motion. The early dinner I prepared is ready, and she's yet to appear. The enchilada bake smells like a heavenly marriage of chili powder, cumin, and garlic and entices a gurgle from my stomach.

"Is dat for me?" Ophelia wanders into the kitchen. The inquisitive cock of her eyebrow causes me to laugh.

"Are you hungry?"

She opens her mouth and points at the void. "Please?"

"Soon, honey. Why don't you wash your hands before we eat."

"You help me?" She rubs her hands together to finish the sentence.

"Of course." I turn off the oven and lead her to the lone bathroom.

Her little head of hair spans mere inches above the top of the sink. I mentally add a footstool to my list.

"Up we go." I hook one arm around her middle and hoist her above the basin. Her pleasing squeals sing a melody that soothes my soul. I turn on the tap with my other hand and squirt a bit of soap onto her awaiting palms. "Scrub them together."

Her practiced movements reveal some combination of an involved mother and a smart kid.

"You're good at this," I praise, and it strikes me then this isn't one of my friends' kids who I'm babysitting temporarily. This one's mine, and something as simple as handwashing brings me a massive sense of pride.

"Anybody home?" Caiti's voice resonates through the living space.

"Be out one sec," I call out, then twist off the water. "All done?"

Ophelia holds her hands in front of her and flips her palms up and down. "All clean! Time to eat?"

"Go get your mama." A sturdy hand between her shoulder blades propels her in the right direction.

"Momma, I play swings today!"

"You did?"

With eyes averted, I pass by the reunited duo and into the kitchen to finish dinner prep.

"Uncul Wet push me, and Tommy push me, and even Daddy push me!"

My neck cricks with a rapid turn, and I find Caiti's gaze awaiting mine. Unfamiliar emotion bubbles within the cavern of my chest. Never have I been stunned speechless, but hearing her call me Daddy for the first time constitutes a first.

At this moment, it doesn't matter if I missed her babbling Dadda when she first learned to talk. Hearing her call me Daddy at two-and-a-half eclipses the lost moments of the past.

Caiti recovers first. "I'm so glad you had fun."

"And nest time, you come too, Momma."

"I will." Caiti taps the end of Ophelia's nose, and the little girl scrunches her face with a giggle. "Are you ready to eat?"

Ophelia sprints around her mom's legs in the opposite direction of the kitchen.

"I sit wight here nest to Daddy, and you sit wight here nest to me." The little girl wiggles her way onto the brand new dining room chair.

"Where did that table come from?" Caiti's suspicious tone glances off the mental guard I spent all afternoon assembling.

"I bought it."

"Why?" Her perplexity precedes a frown.

"The stools are too tall and not enough of 'em." I carry the casserole dish to the table. "Sit. Eat. I'm sure the champagne sloshing around could use some substance."

Her shoulders remain stiff as she crosses to my new dining set and takes a rigid seat. "Thank you for this. You didn't have to go through the trouble."

I dish up the girls' plates before turning to my own. "It's no trouble."

"You're taking to this better than I expected you to."

"Am I?" I busy myself with filling glasses from a pitcher of ice water I set out earlier.

"Are you intentionally obtuse? Any other guy would lose his mind if a woman showed up with his child. You're being unnaturally cool about it all."

Condensation drips down the glass I place before her. "When have I given the impression I'm like any other guy?"

Her pink tongue sneaks out to wet her bottom lip. As if realizing the motion, she reaches for her glass. Our fingers softly touch. If I weren't already looking at her, I might have missed the sparks in her dark eyes. I definitely don't miss the hefty gulp or the way her other hand clutches at the chain around her neck.

We eat in a stilted silence, occasionally punctuated by Ophelia's remarks about the park or her food or Tommy. She's absolutely enamored with admiration for her new cousin. When remnants of chopped enchilada litter the table, floor, and her hair, the end of dinner is declared.

"I'll clean this up," Caiti announces on a brisk rise from her chair.

"Leave it." With Duke covering the bar this evening, I could use a mindless task.

"Momma, I show you someting." Our girl decides to move the evening full steam ahead.

My attention remains riveted on Caiti. If the quirk of her brow is any indication, she's instantly wary. Her lack of equilibrium may keep her pliable to my demands. I'm an actionable guy. She's about to find that out for herself.

The two join hands, and Ophelia leads her through the living space to one of the bedrooms. She tosses the ajar door to the spare room wide. "Dis is my room!"

A chuckle from me transforms into a cough at her bold declaration of ownership. Caiti's heavily dipped brows display the dispute surely on the tip of her tongue.

"It is?" she asks in a lilting tone to hide from the young innocence that Mommy and Daddy are about to throw down.

"Come see." Ophelia confiscates Caiti's options and tugs her deeper into the newly decorated room.

After a few minutes of slowly circling the space, Caiti announces, "It's beautiful, baby. Why don't you play in here with your new toys so Daddy and I can talk."

The door closing behind Caiti's exit sounds as a warning.

"Why would you do that?"

"Do what exactly?"

"Give her a room here without talking to me."

I gather the three dirty plates on the table to engage my hands. "She's mine, isn't she?"

"Yes."

"And I presume we'll share some form of custody?"

"We haven't worked that far head, but yes."

The plates rattle when I deposit them beside the sink. The counter at my back serves as an appropriate resting place to maintain our distance. "So what's the problem?"

"What's the… are you serious? The problem is we haven't talked about any of this. What are you doing, Dane?"

I rest a palm on the counter behind me and scratch the bridge of my nose with the side of my thumb. "I'm moving you in."

Her mouth falls open. "I…you…what?" she sputters. If she wasn't so damn beautiful, I might muster an ounce of annoyance, but I'm wrapped up under her spell. All I want to do is stare at her and soak her in.

"Now who's being obtuse?"

"How do you figure?"

"So far, I'm yet to hear a plan, so I created one. This way, we don't have to shuffle Ophelia back and forth between houses. When it's my time with her, I'll work out my bar schedule and be here, and when it's your turn, I'll make myself scarce."

"And sleeping arrangements?"

"I'll take the couch, and you can have the bed."

The violent shake of her head sends her hair flying. "No. Absolutely not. I can't sleep in your bed."

"Too many memories?" I quirk my lips. I may be goading her, but there has to be a small price for leaving me in the middle of the night after the best one-night stand of my life.

"I actually can't recall any."

With a quick shove, I take two paces across the room. "Bullshit," I growl.

The hitch of her breath calls her on her lie. "That's not important."

"I can still remember how you taste."

"We're getting off topic."

Another step. "I think we're precisely on track." I don't stop until I'm a pillar before her. Her head tips back, sending her hair cascading down her back.

"I'm not here to be with you," she says breathily. The verbal sparring is a shield against what she truly wants.

"You sang a different tune then."

"It was one night."

"Neither one of us stated that intention."

"That's all it is now."

"Why? Better question why did you leave that morning?"

She moves a fraction closer. "Because I'm a broken mess. My life back home. My health." She grips the hair at her crown.

I'm thoroughly doused by her words. "Are you okay right now?" Caught up in the heat of the moment, I didn't consider her anxiety.

"I'm okay right now."

"Your heart isn't racing?"

"Not like it was the other day."

I want to touch her so damn bad to soothe the frayed edges. But that isn't what she needs, and I'd be smart to keep my impulses in check. "I'll stay out of your way." I revisit our original argument. "You're here until the wedding, that much is certain. Give this a shot until then."

Her teeth abuse her bottom lip. "I guess this makes sense. For Ophelia," she adds.

"Of course." But it makes sense for us too. Someone needs to keep an eye on her. The strong woman before me has shouldered too much for far too long. She deserves a peaceful place to get her head on straight, and I intend to find one for her. Even if it happens to be in my own damn house. With or without me in it.

"I'm glad that's settled," she remarks after a long pause of staring at one another. There's no way she doesn't feel the heat brewing between us. It's nearly palpable.

"We should write down a schedule. That way, I don't tread on your time."

She finally moves away from the guest bedroom door. "I work most days from nine to five, but I'm fully remote, so I can take my laptop anywhere."

The pad of paper and pen remain where I left them on the counter. "I'm needed at the bar for closing Friday and Saturday nights, and sometimes I have to pick up if we're short staffed. But if you ever want to get away, we can call Evelyn to babysit. She loves kids." I jot down our schedules.

"I don't think that'll be a problem."

"I also open the bar Monday, Tuesday, and Thursday and work until dinner."

She studies the sheet of paper. "You can have Sundays with her after you've recovered from your late-night shift."

I add that to my list, and we continue to fill in the gaps, trying to provide as little overlap as possible. When the paper is full, I scribble my name across the bottom with a dramatic flourish. "Here. Sign."

She adds her petite scrawl above mine.

"I'm glad this is settled," I admit. A weight from the past few days lifts off my chest.

"It'll be good." Her voice catches on the last word as she fights back a sniffle. "Sorry," she mutters.

"Hey. Look at me."

The overhead chandelier shimmers off the water collecting on her lower lids. "This will be good. The doctor said you needed rest, and this way, I can take some of the load off."

Her hand flutters between us. "I know. You're right. *Thank you*," she emphasizes the last part.

"I should really be thanking you. I'm happy to be here for you both in any way I can."

"I have one more ask. If it isn't too much." Her hesitance to reach out punches me square in the chest. I push back from the counter and straighten.

"What is it?"

"Our stuff is at Evie's."

My keys jangle as I snatch them from the island. "I'll follow you there."

11

Caiti

Anticipation rips through me as a tech squirts warm gel on a section of my bare chest in a darkened room. The ultrasound screen casts a dim glow over his apathetic features. After a visit with the cardiologist, Dr. Chaing sent me for an echocardiogram. He wasn't overly concerned with my oral history, but putting a visual on my heart gives me peace of mind I wouldn't have found otherwise.

The tech engages in stilted small talk as he captures images of my heart. The painless test doesn't take even a full thirty minutes before he hands me a towel to clean off the goop.

"I'm not supposed to say this, but I didn't see anything concerning. Your doctor will reach out with the official results."

I clutch the opening in my gown to cover my breasts. The sweet warmth of relief floods me like it was injected straight into my veins. "I really appreciate that. Thank you."

He leaves with a nod, and I immediately dress. My heart might still beat hard and fast randomly throughout the day, but nothing is wrong with me structurally. Knowing Eric died from an undetected anomaly, a blanket of peace settles over me.

"If this is your way of watching over me, thank you," I whisper. The answering ache in my chest brings a tender comfort.

Sunbeams temporarily blind me when I step out onto the concrete sidewalk. I snatch my sunglass from my hair and plop them over my eyes with one hand while the other digs in my bag for my phone. Without much fanfare, I tap Dane's name and hit call.

"Hey, how'd it go?"

A gentle exhale gives me pause. "It went well."

"That's great. I suppose you have to wait for any news?"

"I should, but the technician said he didn't see anything wrong."

"I'm really glad you're okay." His low tenor settles somewhere deep inside me.

"Anyway, I don't want to interrupt you two. I just wanted to confirm when you need to be at the bar."

"Three thirty. If you need more time—"

I cut him off. "No. That's perfect. I'll leave you to it. Have fun."

"We will. See you later."

"Bye."

A twitch of my shoulders shakes off the lingering awkwardness. I'm sure with time, our situation will become natural. We'll rock this co-parenting duo for as long as I'm in town. For however long that happens to be.

After three years of being alone, having people to lean on has been a life saver. When assistance is a phone call and a short drive away. The thought of returning to my home across the country packs a boulder in my gut. Colorado was the first home I shared with Eric before we moved to Germany. Even though he's no longer there, moving permanently feels a bit like leaving him behind.

I settle behind the steering wheel in my car with a sag of exhaustion. Sleep is spotty, and mornings begin around five a.m. with a racing heart and churning stomach. The doctor's order for two weeks of rest remains a humorous joke. I don't think parents are allowed to relax until their kids go to college, and even then, nights are fraught with worry. What do I know? Maybe this is just how it is for moms. I haven't had any friends to compare notes.

Cranking the ignition slickens my palms with sweat. This morning, the daily driving practice allowed me to cross town with relative ease. Now I have another location on my agenda, and the idea ratchets the feelings to life once again. I can do this. Nothing bad will happen to me.

The weakness I feel each day pummels my confidence levels. I should reside on a summit for all I've accomplished in my life, yet most days, I'm standing at base camp. Summoning the energy to be proud of myself for trivial tasks most take for granted is an endeavor.

With nothing more than sheer stubborn determination, I travel the main highway to the other end of town and park my car near the back of the lot at The Legendary.

A slight skip infiltrates my step. The whirring air conditioner in the entry greets me, a respite from the August heat. I grip the handle of my purple cosmetic case with undisguised excitement.

"Hello. You must be Caiti." A woman of my height and appearing my age approaches from behind a reception desk.

"That's me. I spoke with Nikki about volunteering."

"I'm Nikki. It's nice to meet you." Her bright rainbow scrubs match her sunny personality, a compliment to her pomegranate-colored locks. "I'll bring you to our spa. It's really just an empty room with a beauty chair and mirror, but the residents love it."

"I'm excited to spend some time with them."

"Right this way." She gestures for me to take the hallway to the left. "We don't have a schedule or anything. Whenever one of our volunteers is available, we ask the ladies one at a time if they want their nails painted. When our cosmetologist comes in, she'll give haircuts. She does operate on a schedule, so you'll know before if she's coming and needs the room."

"Perfect. Well, I'm just looking for a way to give back some of my time when my daughter is with her dad."

"Ah." Nikki's smile is tight and unsure. "I have a situation like that. I hope yours is working out better than mine."

"I'm lucky, that's for sure." Something I don't take for granted, which is part of the reason I'm not hanging around the loft on his time.

"Here we are."

We reach a glass exterior door surrounded by a faux brick façade. The sign above declares it to be The Legendary Salon. Suctioned to the glass is another sign announcing the salon is open.

"I love this." I run my finger across the brick, the bumps bringing surprise at the rough texture.

"I can give you a tour later of the rest of the building. The resident suites are individually decorated in different housing styles, each with a window, a mailbox, and a chair. They love to sit and gossip with their neighbors. Those who can, that is." Her smile holds reminiscence and a touch of sadness. Memory care isn't an easy place to be, I'm sure.

"I've only been here a few minutes, and I can tell you take very good care of the people here."

"It isn't easy, but I love it. They give so much back without even realizing it."

I clap my hands together. "Well, I'm ready for my first client. Whenever you're ready."

"I'll see who's available."

I set up my kit while she leaves, which mostly contains acetone pads and an assortment of polishes. The plan is to donate the stock this afternoon. When I called yesterday, Nikki told me their supply was nonexistent, so I placed an instant delivery order from the nearby department store for a variety of colors.

A little bell above the door dings, and Nikki returns behind a wheelchair. The woman's mouth is stretched wide and open in a silent laugh. The joy radiating from her heightens my own mood.

"Welcome to the salon," I greet cheerily. Already, my spirits are lifted. The nerves I carry around daily dissipate in this purposeful moment. She turns her head, her big, round eyes finding my face.

"H-H-H-H-Hi."

Nikki parks her chair to the left of the door and locks the wheels. "We'll keep her here to avoid a transfer," she says quietly. Louder, she announces, "This is Corinne. She loves to have her nails done."

"It's very nice to meet you, Corinne."

Corinne's head of thick, wavy black hair bobs. I interpret the motion as a nod.

"I'll be back soon." Nikki departs.

"Can I see your hands?"

She holds a trembling limb up to chest level.

"Looks like you have some old polish here. I'll clean it off and put on a fresh coat."

"Thank you," she says in an exaggerated fashion with a twinge of Southern accent.

I grab three colors of polish similar to the one she's wearing. At my approach, her gaze remains fixed in the corner of the room with a faraway look in her eyes. Careful not to startle her, I move into her sight line.

"Can I paint your nails now? Is that okay?"

Her head bobs again. "That's okay."

"Okay." I smile and set out on the removal process.

The tension of the day melts away. I chitter to mostly silence. Every so often, Corinne says a word or sentence that gives the impression she's listening, but her response isn't required. It hits me then how lonely I've been if I can sit here for half an hour and have words spill forth. Mundane things become conversation highlights. After detailing my trip across the country and how Ophelia wouldn't quit asking to stop for snacks every twenty minutes, Corinne startles me with a complete sentence.

"My son is coming." Her voice is monotone, but her expression brightens like a firework burst overhead at the mention of her family.

"You have a son. That's lovely."

"Is he here?"

"I haven't seen him. I can check while your polish dries."

"C-C-C-can you fix my hair?" Her gaze remains motionless on the wall. It warms my heart that she cares so much about her appearance for her son. They must have had a special bond.

"I'm not a hair stylist, but I can try. What would you like me to do?"

A cabinet beside the mirror supplies a comb in its meager contents. I move behind her chair and gently shift her hair from her neck. The strands remain soft and well cared for despite the fact she relies on someone else to manage them. I hope I can provide the same comforting assistance.

"Brush it, please."

Though the black and gray threaded strands hardly need brushing, I fulfill her request. Halfway through the second pass, Nikki returns.

"Corinne! You look like a total babe."

"Th-Th-Thank you. Is my son here?"

"Not yet. Why don't we get a snack while we wait?" As she leans down to unlock a wheel, she murmurs, "He already visited today."

My heart sinks at her impending disappointment. "Oh, no. Did I do the wrong thing? She was so excited."

"She'll forget soon. He visits nearly every morning, and she still asks if he's coming every afternoon. You did just as you should. Trying to convince them otherwise does more damage. We try to live in their world as much as we can."

"Noted. It was nice to meet you, Corinne. I hope to see you again!"

She waves her hand in a shaky goodbye.

"Do you have time for another?" Nikki asks as she reaches the door.

I dig out my phone for the time and smile. "Looks like I have an hour and a half. Keep them coming."

A new feeling ricochets through me, one I haven't felt in a very long time. A sense of purpose beyond motherhood duties. Don't get me wrong. I love being Ophelia's mother more than anything, but it's safe to say I lost my identity in the process. This feels like a step in the right direction to becoming a better, stronger me.

Not just Ophelia's mom.

Not just a widow.

Not just a sufferer of anxiety.

Me.

Caiti Harris.

12

Dane

"You need them ready by when?"

The vein of distress in Caiti's voice pulls me from the puzzle Ophelia and I work on. She wears a path across the kitchen and back as she listens to whoever called her this early on a Saturday. From her side of the conversation, I'm gathering it to be her boss, which, for some reason, pisses me off. This is one of only two days a week we both have open before I head into the late-night shift, and Caiti takes over Ophelia for dinner and bed. She's been attempting to establish distance while I've been looking forward to today since we wrote down our schedules.

She's trying to stay in her lane while I want to direct her firmly in mine.

The time she gives me alone with Ophelia doesn't go unnoticed or unappreciated. After only a week, the little girl has me wrapped around her tiny finger. The way she calls me Daddy only highlights how fucked I'll be in her teenage years when she wants her way from her mother and me.

The problem is I have to convince them to stick around that long first. I'd like to do that in a way that doesn't involve the legal system and expensive lawyers. My finances were tied up long before my daughter appeared at my door, and I'm not the type to tear a child away from their mother if there's another option.

"Jason, it's the weekend, and I—" Caiti pauses her wild pacing. "No. No, you're right. I won't get behind. Monday morning, I'll be on top of it." Another pause. "Yep. I know. I do remember telling you I'd be off until Tuesday, so that's why this week has been short."

She lifts her hand to glide through her silky black strands. I notice it trembling. Not sure if I'm about to hold her or rip the phone from her, I rise. The sudden movement attracts her glare to me, and she subtly shakes her head as if her boss can see my protective stance.

"I'll get to it today. I'm sorry. Okay, talk to you soon. Bye."

Before I can get a word out, she's on the move to the bedroom.

"I have to work. Just let me know when you need to head downstairs, and I'll open the door."

The irritated demand keeps me rooted when I want nothing more than to chase her down.

"Is Momma sad?"

"Your momma is working hard so she can have more time to play with you."

"You make Momma happy?"

Her little innocence flickers a flame to life in my chest. "I think she's happiest with you."

Those little eyes so like Caiti's light up. "I wike playing with Momma."

I resume my seat on the floor beside her and hand her a

puzzle piece. She tugs it from my fingers and turns a pearly grin on me.

"I wike playing with you, Daddy."

Suspended awe fills me as she fits another piece perfectly. I could watch her draw with a stick in the dirt and still be amazed that something so flawless belonged to me. "I do too, princess."

Not five minutes later, she abandons her nearly completed puzzle in a search for something new. She's constantly moving and discovering, often with her mother or me in tow. As much as I enjoy being her adult shadow, Caiti's sudden exit nags at me with a desire to make sure she's all right. I snag the tablet Caiti brought for their long car trip and offer the bribe to Ophelia. "Want to watch a show?"

"Yeah!" She punches two tiny fists straight into the air. She snatches the proffered tablet and scampers to the couch.

Without bothering to knock, I gently push open my bedroom door. The light is off. Only the dim glow of the laptop screen and a strip of the sun between the curtains illuminate the space. The soft glow is just enough to see the red splotches on her cheeks.

"Are you crying?"

"What?" She feels her face with the back of her hand. "No. My face turns red when I'm upset."

"Did he call you back?" Any further communication this weekend would border on harassment.

"No. I'm just tired." A subtle sigh slips out, punctuating her point. Her smile is crooked. "A lot has happened this week."

She's not wrong about that. "Why don't you take a break?"

"I just started working today. I have to get this done."

"Not today. Take a vacation. Your doctor said you could use two weeks."

"That's pretty short notice to give my boss."

"An emergency came up. It's not that far off."

Her huff is adorable. "I had a panic attack. That's far from an emergency."

The reminder of her distress kicks my heart rate up a notch. "You have documentation. You deserve a break."

She spins back to my desk and her laptop. "I can't have a disturbance right now. Please."

By the time she's done arguing, I've moved behind her. My hands fit perfectly at the juncture of her neck and shoulder. The force of my thumbs rubbing the muscles there elicits a moan from her that travels straight to my eager junk. I lower my mouth to the space beside her ear. Her lashes flutter against her tan, freckled cheeks. "You need to relax," I huskily murmur.

"That feels good," she groans. "You're distracting me."

"I'll work out a few kinks and leave you to it." I keep my voice low. The goose bumps erupting on her skin sends my blood pumping.

"You don't have to hurry." She switches course.

I hit a particularly tight spot, causing her to gasp. The little sounds she makes are reminiscent of our night together. If I closed my eyes, I could picture her spread naked on my bed in this very room.

"I'm not the one trying to rush back to work."

"Mmm," she moans. "I really should get busy." Her body undulates with the movement of my hands.

I didn't plan this when I approached her, but now that I'm working over her soft skin, I realize I don't have an exit strategy either. Her breathy moans and rhythmic movements culminate to make extricating myself nearly impossible.

Threading through her soft strands, I tilt her head to the

side and expose her slender neck. Her breath catches, and I pause, lips close but not touching the smooth skin. I offer her an out. A part of me silently begs her to tell me to stop, while the other half nearly comes undone at the thought of tasting her skin again.

The further incline of her neck speaks to receptivity, and I waste no more time before touching my mouth to her pulse point.

"Dane!" She quietly gasps my name, a staccato on an exhale. My teeth follow the drag of my lips down the column of her throat. With eyes closed, I pepper her with kisses, breathing in the scent of cherry blossoms like a parched man brought to a drink.

The ascent takes longer as my journey nears the end. I'm pushing boundaries she doesn't want to be challenged. Though she seems more than open to the prospect of having me close again if the way she melts in the chair is any indication.

A rumble breaks free from my chest. Reaching her ear, I leave one last kiss and position my mouth at the shell. "Now that you're relaxed, I'll let you work. Then I'm going to call a babysitter, and you're going to join me downstairs for a drink and a night off."

She straightens, forcing me to release her hair. I brush it with affection down the side of her neck. "I…okay. That does sound nice." The breathless quality of her voice requires me to stop in the bathroom to adjust myself before I accomplish anything else.

"See you around seven."

"I'll be the hot mess in sweats. You can't miss me."

"I'll be the one behind the bar, but you already know where to find me." Thoughts of our first steamy encounter drift like tendrils of smoke through my mind.

She turns back to her screen in dismissal, but not before I catch her eager grin.

THE STEADY STREAM of customers requires me to keep post behind the main bar on the first floor. When the pace picks up on weekend nights, I like to weave through the tables to observe the mingling patrons. Cameras assist in keeping my customers safe, but nothing beats the aid of a watchful eye. Tonight, with the door nearly revolving and down a server, I'm stuck mixing drinks. I meant to meet Caiti here at seven, but I won't have much time to chat by the looks of things.

A bachelorette party wanders in with multi-colored flashing favors and penis whistles blowing a rowdy tune. They push their way into the far corner, dispersing the few people waiting for drinks there as if they intend to stay a while. I don't bother with a fake smile intended to woo a tip. My bar is the only one in town hospitable enough for this type of crowd.

"What can I get you ladies?" My usual dour appearance seems to attract more than one appreciative glance.

"Hey, handsome. Do you offer body shots? Preferably off you?" the short brunette with the maid-of-honor sash shamelessly requests.

I offer a brief quirk of my mouth. "Sorry, ladies. Not from me. But if you want to travel downstairs, the bartender might be more than willing to set you up." Damien would work these ladies into a tizzy with his outgoing persona and washboard abs. As long as he's not too busy serving drinks, I'm sure he'll find a way to oblige. The man will use just about any excuse to take off his shirt, seeing as he used to work at a strip club in Logansville before circumstances brought him here. I lean in closer. "I hear he has an eight-pack."

Sighs, squeals, and giggles accompany the large group across the room. I chuckle to myself, thinking of the mess I sent downstairs, immediately followed by the thought of Cami, Kiersten, Evie, and Caiti on their own bachelorette party escapades later this month. Mental reminder to check with the guys on a strategy because we all can't pull babysitting duty that night.

The group of rowdy girls clears the entrance, leaving the direction of my gaze wide open to see her. As if I could miss the raven-haired beauty. I clocked her the first time she sat at a table by the window next to another man. As much as it fucks me to think of it now, I shamelessly couldn't take my eyes off her, even though the husband she lost only a few days later was at her side.

Just like all those years ago, I'm drawn to her as the rest of the bar melts into the background. My focus zeros in on tight black jeans, a direct contradiction to the sweats she promised to wear. Following her long, lean legs, I discover the silky silver cami encasing her torso. A far cry from a hot mess. She's fucking beautiful.

The moment she spots me, the tension melts away. Her shoulders relax away from her ears, and she drops her crossed arms to hang loosely at her sides. I'm shocked silly at the illuminating smile that graces her face. I half expected her to stomp down here with a sexy-as-hell grumpy attitude and her hair in a messy bun. Either version I'd take in a heartbeat. But why all the effort if she vaguely hinted that it wasn't worth one?

I flick two fingers in greeting, then direct them at the stool the bachelorette group vacated. She saunters over with an enigmatic smirk, oblivious to the turn of male heads all across the room.

She plants both palms on the counter and hoists herself up. "Sorry, I'm late. I got to chatting with Evie."

I dry my hands with a white towel. "Not a problem. We've been busy tonight."

"It appears so." She bounces her gaze around the room.

"What are you having tonight?"

She runs her tongue across her bottom lip and tips her eyes to the side in contemplation. "How about a vodka soda?"

My stomach bottoms out. The drink order is the exact same as the night we spent together. Not that it's unusual. I just haven't been able to make the drink since without recalling the vision of her sipping the clear cocktail on my couch. "Coming right up."

"I'm guessing you can't join me while on the job."

I want to kiss the pout from her plump lips. "Unfortunately not tonight, Mama."

I swear I catch her shiver when I set down her finished drink on a napkin.

"Thanks." She picks up the clear glass to sip straight from the rim.

"That bad?"

"What?" Caiti lowers the drink halfway before drawing a little more liquid into her mouth.

"Your job." I tease. "You might want to take it easy."

She digs in her purse without answer, proudly waving a stack of bills she produces. "You can't water down my drinks tonight, sir. I'm a paying customer."

I lean over my elbows on the bar. "Do I need to ask our babysitters to stay overnight so we can go somewhere else?"

The surprise in her dark irises holds a tinge of want. "I... no...I just meant I can handle my alcohol."

A customer approaching forces me away from her. "I'm just teasing, Mama."

"Can I get a whiskey and Coke?" He tosses a few bills on the counter.

"Sure thing."

I give her my shoulder while I fill the newcomer's order, keeping a line of sight in case someone decides to harass her. Not that it's any of my business. If she's looking to flirt with a stranger, who am I to stop her? She's the mother of my kid, not the woman wearing my ring on her finger.

That doesn't mean I won't keep a close watch as the hungry wolves behind her decide the best way to descend. I fill this guy's drink with record speed and send him on his way. When I fixate on her once again, I want to throw her over my shoulder and keep her hidden from the lecherous stares.

She sways a hypnotic beat on the stool in time to the music. With closed eyes, the black straw pokes between red, pillowed lips. The way her tank top clings to her breasts is damn near indecent. She's the picture of a carefree woman living in the moment. Then her eyes open, and catching my attention, she startles. She sets her drink on the bar so hard some liquid sloshes over the side.

"I'm sorry. I haven't had a night out like this in—"

"Three years," I guess with a throaty growl. "And don't apologize."

Her fingers glide through the condensation on the glass. "I didn't trust anyone enough to babysit, and I didn't have any friends back home."

The confession sits like a lead weight in my gut. All this time, she could have had me. She could have had help. My captain obvious hat hangs on a rack for the evening. Pointing out what she already knows won't change the past.

Her hand banishes her regrets like dust motes in the air. "Never mind that. I'm here now, and this drink is delicious."

"Plenty more where that came from. Under one condition."

She leans in conspiratorially. "What's that?"

"You only leave with me." I level my gaze with a seriousness I feel down to the very cells that make me. "Either together after I close, or I walk you upstairs, but you aren't going home with anyone else."

The shock expresses itself through her half-open mouth and a rising blush tinting her cheeks. She snaps her jaw closed and twirls the ice in her glass with the straw. "Let's say I don't agree with your little demand. Then what happens?"

"I dare you to try to make it out that door."

"You're making strong assumptions. I agreed to have a drink with you tonight, not find my way into your bed."

"You seemed quite receptive to my mouth this afternoon."

She scoffs, but the deepening blush reveals she's enjoying the fictitious debate. "Put down your club, caveman. You don't need to knock anyone over the head tonight. I'll behave."

"It's not you I'm worried about," I mutter. Whether she realizes it or not, she could walk out that door with just about any guy in this place tonight.

"What was that?" She leans forward, pushing her tits dangerously close to testing the confines of that top. Fuck she's trying to kill me without even trying.

"I said I'm glad you decided to join me tonight."

She leans back. "Me too. My boss has been increasingly demanding since I left town. I don't know what to do besides what he asks."

I buff out a smudge on the bar. "You could always look for a job here."

"The job isn't the problem. This one pays really well, and I can work anywhere in the US. Usually, Jason isn't this much of an ass."

"Just saying it's an option." I lean back and cross my arms over my chest. The way her eyes move over my biceps feels like a physical caress.

"I have to thank you," she says so softly I just barely catch the words over the music. "You've been incredible with all of this. Taking in Ophelia and me, rearranging your schedule. Honestly, I expected a fight."

"When we get to know each other better, you'll learn I'm not a fighter, Mama. Not unless I have to be."

"Whatever happens, and however this works out, I hope you know I'm grateful."

The part she isn't saying hangs in the air like another chandelier strung above the bar—she still doesn't know if she's staying and where that might leave us with custody. I don't take her gratitude as a form of manipulation, though I hope she heeds my own warning. I only fight for things that mean something to me. That includes our daughter, but her as well.

Her fear blinds her to visions of the future, so she might not see it yet. But I do.

We might be more than a night of incredible sex and shared custody.

And I intend to find that out.

13

Caiti

Dizziness fills my head that has nothing to do with my icy drink. Dane yanks my focus in circles with his wildly good looks, protectiveness, and easygoing attitude. When I first met him, he appeared sullen, almost with an unspoken motivation. What I've discovered since is a natural sweetness he reserves for a select few.

"Tell me about her."

The question catches me off guard as he returns from filling another customer's drink order.

"Who?" The left-field question requires clarification. Before he walked away, we were discussing whether or not it's appropriate to wear a band tee if you're not a true fan of the band.

He resumes his earlier position with his elbows on the bar and plucks a peanut from the bowl. "Ophelia. What's her birthdate? Where was she born? I've already learned her favorite color is pink, and her favorite animal is a unicorn."

He grins with amusement at the absurdity of the mythical creature.

I relax on my stool and study the ice cubes in my glass. "Her birthday is January thirteenth. She was actually born at home. I hired a midwife and a doula to support me since I was alone. Her middle name is Louise. Her favorite food is string cheese, which she bites instead of peels like a little monster, and she also loves dogs. She'd make every puppy her friend if she could."

When I look up from my babble, I find Dane staring at me with a touch of sadness.

"You were alone."

I rewind the conversation in my head until understanding dawns. "It was my choice."

"I would have been there for you. One hundred percent."

Guilt sinks in. "You said you didn't want kids."

"Not for me. I know why you did what you did. For you, Mama. *You* didn't need to go through it alone. I would have been there for you."

A stinging starts in my nose. "I should have let you."

He nods solemnly. "I'm here now. And so are you. You don't need to be afraid anymore."

If only he knew how much I wish that were true. Even making my way downstairs was a fear-filled endeavor I had to work myself up to accomplish. The future is one big question mark. I'm learning to regain some normalcy, but what happens when it's time to return home?

"I have pictures of her as a baby." The distraction steers the topic into safer waters. I open the album on my phone designated to her first year of life and spin the device on the bar toward him. "You can scroll through. This is her birth until her first birthday. I have another folder for her terrible twos."

Obvious joy cracks through the dark shadows in his features. "She was born with all that hair?"

Returning the topic to Ophelia lightens the heaviness in my chest. "It was even visible in the ultrasound pictures."

"I'm impressed."

He continues scrolling with added commentary until a customer approaches. "I'll be right back. I want to see more."

I pocket the device. "I'm just going to slip off to the restroom. Where is it?"

Dane jerks his head to his left. "Just down the hall that way." The way his gaze passes through the people milling near gives the impression he's looking for something.

I slide off the stool onto steady legs and weave through the few bodies blocking my path. The goofy smile fixed on my face feels natural after the evening we've had. The zapping nerves I felt about meeting him here dissipated the moment I had a drink in my hand. The last time I sat in a bar with a drink was the night I met Dane, and I started off the evening in a pit of sadness until he gently coaxed me from it.

The humid atmosphere entices me to sip cocktails long into the night, but I should keep my wits about me. A mountainous undertaking in Dane's presence. The feeling of his hands kneading my tired neck lingers like a phantom pain, and the ghost of his lips still electrifies my skin.

It would be so easy, natural even, to offer a repeat situation. But that wouldn't be fair to any of us until I make my life-altering decision.

Return to Colorado and send my daughter cross-country for visits, or move to Arrow Creek and start fresh near the only man who's made me feel anything other than my dead husband.

I promised myself I'd never let anyone get close enough to devastate me ever again, which initially included kids. Attachments are the recipe for pain when someone inevitably gets hurt or dies. Suffering is the unavoidable nature of life, and I've had enough to last me the remainder of this one.

But God sent me Ophelia. And someday, hopefully when I'm old and gray, I'm going to peacefully pass away, and I vowed the day she was born to not leave her in a position to deal with that pain alone. At the time, that meant having my affairs in order and a substantial life insurance policy to take her wherever her heart desires.

Now, I'm seeing where I've gone awry.

Which makes my decision pretty simple. She needs to be around people who genuinely care, and that place is not Colorado.

Arrow Creek might be the only town not to have a line out the door of the women's bathroom at a bar. I tuck the revelations away to sort later and slip inside. The room is cramped but large enough for three stalls and three sinks. I choose the middle one to take care of business and position myself in the center mirror when I'm done.

The humid air teases a frizz near my hairline, and a smudge of mascara sits below my left eye. I wet my finger and clear off the mark, thankful for the dim lighting in the bar. I might have changed my clothes for this evening, but I still look the hot mess I pledged to be.

The door creaks open at my back, drawing my eyes back to the reflection in the mirror. Three women slink inside as if they're up to no good.

"How do you know Dane?" The middle one, a short brunette with a curly ponytail, confirms my suspicion with her prying question.

"He's a friend." I turn on the spot to face the unwarranted confrontation.

She runs inch-long red nails through the curls at the end

of her hair. "I've been here a long time, and I haven't seen him pay one person so much attention."

Her two cohorts exchange a curious glance with one another behind her head.

"I haven't seen him in a few years, so we're just catching up while I'm in town." I inject a casual confidence into my tone. This woman doesn't ruffle me, and she has no business asking questions. "I'm sorry, but I don't know who you are, so if you'll excuse me."

My phone rings in my purse, halting my need to retreat. I dig the device from my pocket and see Evie flash on the screen. Without hesitating, I hit the answer button. There could be a reason she needs me upstairs, and I can hear her better in here than out with the music and chatter.

"Hey."

"Hi, Momma," my sweet baby greets me. I move the phone from my ear to check the time. It's after nine.

"Shouldn't you be in bed?" I give my audience a shoulder and focus my attention on the little voice in my ear.

"Autie Ebie says I say good night!"

"Good night, sweetheart. I hope you're having fun tonight. Be good for your auntie."

Evie prompts her from the background to say I love you. She's such a good aunt.

"Love you," Ophelia sing-songs, and my heart soars.

"I love you and miss you so much."

One of the women in the room mutters something about leaving, drowning out the sound of my daughter's voice.

"What was that, sweetie?" I try not to scowl as I cover my other ear with my hand to hear better.

"I say night to Daddy too?"

"You want to say good night to Daddy?"

"Yes," she says too emphatically for a toddler.

"I'll bring him the phone so you can say good night to

Daddy." As soon as the words leave my mouth, so many things happen at once.

Someone in the room gasps, followed by a shout of "Bailey!" Three people move toward me. The brunette with the curly hair reaches me, and without warning, her palm connects with my face in a stinging slap. Heat rushes to the cheek I'm certain already glows red.

My phone slips from my hand and skitters across the bathroom floor. I lose track of its location when I right my head. Before I can get a word out to tell this psycho to get the hell away from me, the door to the restroom bursts wide open. Dane's broad shoulders and heaving chest fill the width of the entry. His eyes find mine in a nanosecond, and he stalks directly to me.

His hand cups mine where I hold my sore cheek, and his concerned gaze roams my face. "Did she hit you?"

I nod through the sting of embarrassment. "I need to get my phone. Ophelia might be scared."

The look in his eyes transforms into one of fury. "Get to her." The gentle way he runs his fingers over the back of my hand is at odds with his incensed expression.

"You." He releases me to address the woman who hit me. His hand latches around her bicep, and he tows her to the door without sparing her a glance. "Get the fuck out of my bar, Bailey."

"Wait." She pumps her heels into the concrete floor. "Can we please talk?" Her entourage follows without a word of apology to me.

I move down the row of stalls, locating my phone on the floor of the third. The lit screen reveals the lingering connection. I hit the speaker, not wanting to touch the device to my face after it spent time on the bathroom floor, and Ophelia's singing echoes around the bathroom.

"I'm talking to Daddy-y-y. Talking to Dad-ad-ad-y!" Her

words bounce as it sounds like she's jumping on her bed, and my heart mimics the rhythm.

"Hey, sweetie, Daddy can't come to the phone right now."

"How not?"

I could cry at the sudden disappointment in her tone. "He's—"

"Right here, baby."

"Daddy! Autie Ebie tells me say good night."

Dane clears his throat. "Good night, princess."

"Do you love me?"

I cover my mouth to contain a choked breath. Dane's eyes shine in the dim bathroom light when his gaze meets mine.

"Yeah, baby. I love you."

I could almost delude myself into thinking he's talking about more than just Ophelia.

"Wike Momma loves me?"

"Yes. I love you like Mommy loves you." His hoarse voice coaxes a lump to my throat.

My heart swells three sizes at this sudden turn of events. "Time for bed. We'll see you in the morning."

Noise shuffles across the line, and then a heavy breath. "You guys enjoy your night. I'll get her to bed."

"Thanks, Evie," Dane answers as I fight to remember how to speak. The screen blackens. I mechanically tuck the device back into my jeans. What the hell just happened?

Dane secures my hand in his firm grip. "Come with me." He leads me from the ladies' room, giving a short wave to the man with gray hair behind the bar, and pulls me through a door at the end of the hall.

"Wait here." With a gentle nudge to my shoulder, he encourages me to sit in a dark green, winged chair.

I caress the abrasive fabric while I try to wrap my head around what just happened.

He returns before I locate an answer.

"Here."

Dane drops to his knees at my feet. One hand braces himself on my knee while the other extends to hold an ice pack on my cheek. The point of contact sets off fireworks in my belly.

"It's not that bad," I argue with a wince at the frostiness.

"It's bad enough," he growls, the anger rekindling now that Ophelia's no longer on the phone.

A red cheek never killed anyone, but I accept the gesture with a sigh. "I'm going to hypothesize that you have a very possessive ex?"

He lowers himself to his ankles, but his hands remain in place. Dark brows lower over his stormy eyes. "Not usually."

"Your business is your own, but if she lives around here and might see you with Ophelia, that could pose a problem."

"She won't be a problem."

"Really? Because I told her we were just friends, and she still found reason to hit me."

The sight of him sitting below me, face tilted skyward, and gray eyes regarding me has me wanting to slip off this chair and straight into his lap.

He draws dizzying circles on my knee. "We broke it off years before I even met you."

"I would have thought you ended things last week with that reaction."

"We dated for a couple of years. Casual at first and then more serious. She was adventurous back then. We liked road trips. She was even saving to purchase a van and wanted to document the experience."

The details create an uneasy wave in my stomach. "What happened?"

"My mom's illness progressed, and she needed me more. I no longer felt comfortable being far from home, so the dream was abandoned."

The pieces aren't adding up. "And she couldn't handle that?"

He shakes his head. "She handled it quite well, actually. Too well. Instead of plans to travel the continental US, she daydreamed about us starting a family."

"And you didn't want kids," I supply as fragments begin to fit.

"I was always clear I didn't want kids. I've known that since I was eleven and my…my…" He severs our connection and drops his head. Heaving breaths lift his broad shoulders.

"You can tell me." I cup the hand holding the ice against my cheek. He spreads his fingers, and I slip mine between his.

He wipes his face against his shoulder. "It doesn't matter. What matters is I told her repeatedly I'd never have a family, and when she couldn't accept that, it ended our relationship."

Realization dawns. "And she saw me sitting with you all night and heard me tell Ophelia I'd find Daddy so she could say good night."

"She has no reason to feel betrayed and absolutely no excuse to hit you."

"No, she doesn't." I shake my head, dislodging our hands and the ice pack. "But she does deserve an explanation from you."

His brows lift over furious eyes. "How can you say that when she assaulted you?"

"Because I've made plans to spend the rest of my life with someone before, and if I stumbled upon a similar scenario. I'd be hurt too." My trembling hand instinctively searches out the vial around my neck. "Let her know it wasn't intentional."

"She should be apologizing to you," he argues.

"I hope she does someday. But I'd rather you clear the air now before risking the chance she might actually run into the two of you in public. If Ophelia has to witness a scene, I might be the one not keeping my limbs in check."

He squeezes my knee. "I might not like it, but you make a valid point."

"I'm pretty smart."

Dane runs his free hand through his disheveled hair. "I'm sorry your relaxing night took a turn." He hooks a crooked thumb beneath my chin and tilts my face. "How's your cheek?"

His visual inspection moves like a tender caress. "It's fine."

"Good." He withdraws his hand. "What do you say? One more drink to salvage the evening, or are you ready to call it a night?"

The question requires no consideration from me.

"The bartender better pour me another."

14

Dane

SOMETHING PLUCKS MY EYELID. The pleasurable dream of trailing my fingers down Caiti's naked hip dissipates before I can return to sleep. I tuck my chin into my chest, but escape is hindered by a pillow at my neck. A hand slaps my cheek.

"Wook it, Daddy. I made me bweakfast."

A sleepy smile spreads across my face, and I scratch an itch on my pec. "You did? What'd you make?" I ask without opening my eyes. These closing shifts at the bar are proving difficult with a toddler running around at an ungodly hour each morning. Welcome to parenting.

"I made a cherry sandwich!" Ophelia states proudly.

Curiosity persuades my eyes open. An extensive yawn transforms into a laugh. "You sure did."

Ophelia holds out her invention with two hands. A single lone cherry sits held precariously between two slices of dry bread.

"How does it taste?"

While holding her sandwich, she sinks a knee into the cushion at my hip, signaling she wants up. I hoist her and plant her diapered butt on my stomach. Only then does she sink her teeth into the bread, not even far enough to reach the cherry in the middle. She looks at me with wide eyes. "It's weally good!"

I grin at her enthusiasm over two slices of bread. "Do you know what goes well with cherry sandwiches?"

"What?"

"Pancakes!" I launch a tickle attack on her ribs. "Want me to make some?"

"Yes, please!" She fist pumps both hands into the air, hurling the lone cherry somewhere behind the couch. Our soft laughter rings together in the quiet loft.

"Looks like you'll need a new cherry for your sandwich."

She scoots off and zooms from the room. "I get it!"

My gait is much slower than that of a toddler this morning. While Ophelia raids my fridge, I start a pot of coffee and grab the pancake supplies. I carry over a stool and set it beside me at the workspace beside the stove.

"I help you?"

I tap the seat. "Climb on up. Let's make breakfast together."

After I measure ingredients, Ophelia dumps them into the bowl. We somehow manage to get pancake powder all over the counter. Her red pajama shirt is speckled white with a tiny handprint right in the center.

"Do you like blueberries in your pancakes?"

"Da wed ones."

Red ones? "Do you mean raspberries?" I hold up the second option. When I went shopping this week, I grabbed an unnecessarily large assortment of everything, not sure what they liked to eat. Now I'm glad I did so I can give her choices.

She points at the raspberries. "Dose ones."

"Got it. Come here." I heft her onto my hip with an exaggerated grunt. Her squeals are music to my ears. "You're going to help. I'll pour the batter in the pan, and you put on the berries. But be careful. The pan is very hot."

I do that thing all parents do where they hold the kid's hand over the stove to feel the heat. Her dark eyes grow impossibly round, and she tucks her fingers against her chest. "Hot," she repeats.

"Here we go."

She's the best little chef's helper. Her tongue pokes out the side of her ruby lips as she concentrates on dropping exactly five berries on each mound of batter. While we wait for each batch to flip, I twirl her around the kitchen.

"Faster!" she squeals and slaps my bare chest with berry-stained hands. Her curly hair floats behind her. She wraps her arms around my neck and shouts, "Mommy, we make pancakes!"

I execute another quarter turn in surprise. Caiti leans against the frame of my bedroom door, her long, sleek legs on display beneath her pajama shorts. Delight glitters in her eyes as she watches the two of us.

"You are?" Caiti's tone only feeds her daughter's excitement. "Are there any for me?"

Ophelia twists her lips to the side. "Say please."

Caiti crosses the room. A rumpled mess defines her hair, and pillow lines dent her cheek, but she's gorgeous first thing in the morning. Our eyes meet for half a second before she closes the distance and takes one of Ophelia's small hands in hers. "Please, oh please, can I have some of your delicious pancakes?"

Ophelia pats her mother's cheek with sticky fingers. "Duh, Momma."

Caiti loses the battle on a snort and bypasses us to the coffee pot. "I feel duped. She traded sweetness for sass."

"It happens to the best of us." I steal a glance at her mother while Ophelia and I resume our position at the stove. "One more batch. Get the berries ready."

Once the pancakes are done, Ophelia races to the table, I carry the food, and Caiti follows with plates and utensils at a much slower pace. The caffeine hasn't infused her yet.

I spear a pancake from the stack. The family atmosphere slams into me as we pass plates and dish our food. I don't recall this experience in my past because it's not something I had. The normalcy of Sunday morning breakfast in pajamas always seemed like an imaginative theme from '90s sitcoms. These two girls have shared hundreds of breakfasts together, but this feels like a family unit. One I don't want to exclude myself from any longer.

A clattering fork forces me back to the present moment.

"Sorry," Caiti says and seizes the offending utensil. "I was going to ask if you had plans today before work?"

I gaze at her patiently, noting the faint redness lingering on her cheek. "No. What do you have in mind?"

She stares at her half-eaten plate. "Evie's been telling me about a bridge in town. I thought we could go see it if you wanted to follow us there."

The implication is she seeks another driving lesson. "I'll take you both to the Swinging Bridge."

"Are you sure?"

"I can't pass an opportunity to give you another reason to stay."

An unreadable silence lingers. "We can be ready whenever you are."

"After breakfast works for me." There's nowhere else I'd rather be. We can head out for a few hours, and I'll still have time to visit Mom before work tonight. My schedule's grown tighter but nowhere near over extended since the duo arrived. The adjustment is worth the reward.

An hour later, after Caiti wrangled Ophelia into a pair of jeans and long sleeves and I cleaned our breakfast mess, we headed down to the street. Caiti's car is parked at the curb on the opposite side and half a block from my truck.

"Are you sure you don't want to just ride with me?" I offer. Ophelia swings her hand in mine while we stand on the sidewalk.

"I'm sure. I feel myself getting less afraid. This is the farthest location yet. I'm just not quite ready to go alone."

The effort she's applying into her rebound from the panic attacks inspires me. She might feel weak, but her choices exude her strength. "You can call me if you need to, but I know you're going to do just fine."

"Can Ophelia ride with you?"

The lack of trust she holds for herself punches me in the gut. "Nothing's going to happen to you." I flood my voice with assurance.

"Just on the way there? She can ride with me on the way home after proving to myself that I can do it."

A part of me wants to say no. To force her into the position she's trying to avoid. The thought of causing her discomfort when I can bring her peace is a pill I can't swallow. "Okay."

"Let me grab her car seat."

"Daddy dwive me?"

"You want to ride in my big truck?"

"It go *broom broom broom?*" She scrunches her entire face and mimics a rumbling engine. One single person hasn't made me smile so much in my nearly forty-years of life.

"I think I can make it do that."

Caiti latches the seat in the back and demonstrates how to make sure Ophelia is properly buckled. The slam of the back door echoes around us. The urge to tug her forehead to my lips forces my hands into my jeans pockets instead.

"I'll be right behind you."

Just because I fought one impulse doesn't mean I don't stay rooted and watch her sexy hips sway as she walks away. With a shake of my head to erase my grin, I round the hood and climb into my truck.

"Ready?"

Ophelia punches both hands out in front of her. "Weddy!"

I rev the engine with three long growls to give Caiti a head start, much to Ophelia's squealing delight, and gently pull out onto the empty street. I may have driven with Ophelia to the hospital that first day, but the emergency set my pace. This feels like the first time traveling with precious cargo, and my attention is laser focused. I tap the gas to catch up to the red car slowly becoming a speck on the horizon.

The lone stoplight leading out of the town center allows me to nearly kiss her bumper. Unfortunately, a driver in a beefed-up pickup has the right to turn before me and takes my place behind her. Not even ten seconds after I accelerate, my phone rings through my dash, and Caiti's name flashes on the touch screen.

"Doing all right, Mama?"

"I think so. I just wanted to make sure you're still there. I can't see you behind this clown."

My fingers twist the leather steering wheel. "I'm right here."

"Ugh!" An exasperated grunt infiltrates the cab. I twist the volume down a notch. "What's this guy doing?"

"I don't know," I growl. Helplessness lashes me. I can only watch the truck ahead of me ride her ass. His brake lights tap on repeatedly, forcing me to slow down. He swerves to the left as if he might try to pass before crossing back over to the right and on the shoulder.

"There's a gas station up ahead on your right. Pull in there, and I'll follow you," I order her. Safety for us all hinges on her compliance.

Her exhale shakes through the speakers. "Okay."

"You're doing great."

"Thanks, Dane. It's pissing me off more than anything." The return of a little fire is encouraging.

"Just up ahead now."

"I see it."

Just as she flicks on her blinker, the asshat behind her cuts his wheel to the right and moves fully onto the shoulder. The maneuver blocks her turn, bringing her dangerously close to a full-out crash. "Look out!"

"Shit!" Caiti pumps her breaks, allowing him to pass by. His cloud of dust engulfs us as he accelerates off the shoulder and into the gas station parking lot.

"Shit," a little voice barks behind me.

"Oh shit!" I say automatically in response to her cussing.

"Shit!" Ophelia squawks again.

"Princesses don't say that word." My sentence is choked by the fury engulfing me. Caiti pulls her car into the only available spot directly beside the truck before I can recommend we no longer stop. The opportunity she presents me with is too sweet to give up. I whip in behind his rusty box, blocking him from escaping when he returns from inside the store.

"Come on. You're going to wait with Mommy." The click of the harness releases Ophelia straight into my waiting arms.

Caiti swings her door open on my approach. "What's going on?"

I push our daughter onto her lap. "Take her and wait here."

"Dane, stop."

"Nobody treats the mother of my child that way." I move into her space, forcing her back into her seat. Our rising chests nearly brush. "Wait. Here." I hold her stare to convey the rest of what I can't say with little ears around.

She lets me close them inside with a gentle slam as I back away.

The dude-bro exits the convenience store carrying a lofty arrogance. His steps falter when noticing his new predicament. With a puff of his chest, he resumes a measured pace straight into my path. Before he can slip his shades back on, I notice the tension around his eyes.

"You mind moving outta my way?" The air of indifference surrounds him almost as strongly as the scent of stale cigarettes.

"Not until you apologize."

His chin retreats into his neck. "Dude, I don't even know you."

I jerk my head to the girls in the neighboring spot. "To them."

"What the fuck for?"

There's no way he doesn't recognize her car from not even five minutes ago. I step into his space and pull my shades from my eyes so he can see how serious I am when I say, deadly calm, "You nearly caused an accident with my woman."

He raises his palms. "I was in control."

"Now, you already said you don't know me. So you don't get that I don't take kindly to *any* man threatening *any* woman in any way, but most especially when that woman belongs to me."

"Hey, I didn't mean any harm."

"She didn't know that, as she's driving down the highway at high speeds and trying to take the turn lane to pull off when some jackass drives around her on the shoulder instead of waiting ten fucking seconds for his turn." Composed fury blankets my tone. "So you can tuck your tail between those scrawny little legs and apologize like a man with a little bit of integrity, or we can sit here all damn day."

"Fuck dude, you're crazy." His tone vibrates with nerves.

"Not yet, but I can be." I move a threatening step into his space.

"Fuck! All right." He whirls his hands between us. The attempt to stop me is laughable. I could snap him like a twig.

"Make it pretty," I taunt. Not about to let him within a foot of her without my protection, I lead him to her window. With two knuckles, I rap on the glass. "Open up, Mama."

The whirr of the motor withdraws the pane separating us. I level the scrawny kid with a disapproving look and jerk my head at Caiti in a motion that says *get on with it*.

He has the decency to remove his sunglasses. "I'm sorry, ma'am."

"For?" I prompt.

"F-For scaring you back on the road there," he stutters.

I roll my neck with an audible pop. "And for my shitty driving."

His glare attempts to incinerate me on the spot. "And for my...my driving."

"Oh, um...thank you." Caiti turns her confused eyes to me, her gaze warming my skin.

"Wasn't hard, now was it?" I straighten to my full height when he looks like he wants to smart off again. "Maybe next time you'll remember to give other people an ounce of respect before you really do cause a crash."

Swearing under his breath, the guy sulks away.

I take my time climbing into my truck and reversing out

of his path into the now open space on the other side of Caiti's car. This time when I hop out, I swing open her passenger's side door. Ophelia wiggles on the seat, reaching for every button and knob in sight. I scoop her into my arms.

"Still wanting to go to the bridge?" The tension leaks from my body with every second that passes. A calmness infiltrates the spaces left behind.

"Definitely. But first I have to ask, why did you do that? Don't get me wrong, I appreciate what just happened, but we could have gone on our way."

Still holding Ophelia, I crouch outside the open door, bringing myself to eye level with Caiti. The last thing I want to do is tower over her while I explain. "I find you to be a very capable woman, despite your own insecurities at the moment. Regardless of that fact, the number one thing women need protection from in this world is other men, and I will never allow a man to disrespect a woman in my presence without letting them know they crossed a line."

She bites her lip. "That's a little messed up, but I sort of love it."

"Good, because it's not something I plan to stop. For you or Ophelia."

"You're a good guy, Dane."

"You say that like you're just figuring it out now."

She subtly shakes her head. "No. But I'm just now allowing myself to express it."

There are other things I wish she'd find a way to express. "I'm just me. What you see is exactly what you get." And I hope like fuck she likes what she sees because I'm not sure how I'll move on if she decides this isn't what she wants.

15

Caiti

A TINKLING BELL over the door signals my arrival at the town's little coffee shop. The aroma of freshly brewed coffee and sugary sweet pastries assails me as I step over the threshold, the air-conditioning wafting the tempting scent through the air. A brightly lit glass case beckons me for a peek. It's been years since I've selected a sweet treat to devour all on my own without sticky little fingers seeking a bite, or more realistically, half of the dessert. Not that I mind sharing with my baby. I'd gladly give her the entire thing. Not even halfway to the display, I've already counted out three donuts to surprise her with back home.

In moderation, of course.

A white bag pack with scrumptious goodies and an iced coffee accompany me to a circular table near the window where Evie waits.

"This place is cute." I dump my purse, donuts, and drink on an empty chair beside me and settle in my own space. The café isn't large by any standards, but it easily fits a handful of tables around the perimeter. The walls are painted with pink vertical stripes, and the table tops are baby blue. It's very fresh and airy and bright.

"Isn't it?" She scrunches her nose. "But we aren't here to chitchat about the atmosphere. How are things with Baby Daddy?"

"This is your friend Kiersten's fault, isn't it? The one who constantly talks about sex."

She takes a casual sip and lifts her shoulder. "Maybe. Don't avoid the question."

I chew my lower lip. For three years, I've been missing exactly this. Having someone close to seek advice from and share my life with. Someone in my corner celebrating my wins. And maybe even telling me when it's time to get my head out of my ass.

"Things are really good, actually."

Evie leans forward, her eyes growing wide. "Really? Tell me more."

A rush of adrenaline surges through me. "He's all in with Ophelia. You should see them together. I caught them making pancakes and dancing in the kitchen on Sunday morning, and I about had a cavity from all the sweetness."

"Oh, my God. I wish I could see it. He's not usually like that. I mean, Dane's a nice guy, but he's not overly affectionate or even smiley. At first, I thought it was because I was a bitch to him when you left all those years ago, but Rhett told me that's just how he is."

I slurp my caramel caffeinated treat. "I expected him to be really mad at me, and it's almost like he's the opposite." My smile severs into a frown.

Evie lowers her blended drink back to the table. "What's wrong? It's like you hit the sad switch."

I rearrange my face into a more content one. "Sorry. Nothing's wrong."

"Caiti…" she warns.

"What? It's the wrong word. Nothing's wrong per se… I just used to run through all these fake conversations I'd have once I finally told him, and not a single one included him being the way he's being right now. I'm confused. And it makes this harder."

Evie smooths a bouncy red curl from her forehead. "Makes what harder?"

"The decision whether to stay or go."

A shutter slams down on Evie as her guard goes up. She twirls her blue straw around her cup. "I had thought maybe you were settling in. Figuring out a way to stay," she states hesitantly.

I crinkle my brow. "What gave you that impression?" We're approaching the two-week mark of my impromptu visit, but she knows I only promised to stay until the wedding. "Nothing's changed, Evie."

She grabs her napkin and wipes the ring of condensation from her plastic cup off the table. Her profession as a house cleaner suits her personality well. "Have you evaluated that recently or is that just what you tell yourself to keep your option of running away open?"

"If I've hurt you or something, I'm sorry, but you know this is my decision."

"Yeah, you've hurt me." Her lower lip trembles before she smashes it between her teeth. "I know I'm not one to talk, but at least when I ran away from the people who loved me, I kept in contact. I just can't imagine you disappearing again."

Immediately, I reach over and wrap my fingers around her wrist. "I promise I won't do that again." A vibration of breath rides my exhale. I shoot for direct honesty, something I should have attempted from the beginning. "You're right.

Some things have changed for me. Volunteering at the memory care unit has been so rewarding that I can't imagine actually leaving in two weeks. And I spotted an adorable preschool on the other end of town that I can already envision walking Ophelia to each morning."

"We sent Tommy there before he started kindergarten this year."

I nod, stalling to chase away the lump in my throat. "Having Dane in Ophelia's life—finally—I can't fathom taking that away."

Evie tilts her ear to her shoulder. "Is it only Ophelia who might miss having him around?"

I pin her with a heatless glare. "He's been really great and supportive. For *both* of us."

"Is it really so bad here?" An assertive smirk sneaks across her face.

"No."

"Then I don't see the problem." She traps her straw between her teeth.

"I loved your brother," I blurt.

She leans forward so fast her drink hits the table with a thud. "I've never doubted that."

Pressure in my chest forces the air from my lungs. Unimaginable words dance on the tip of my tongue. "I don't know how to move on," I whisper as shame threatens to engulf me.

"Caiti, darling, there's absolutely nothing wrong with trying to move on."

"No, I know that. I—" Can I really admit it? "Dane makes me feel..." I trail off when the words don't come.

"Oh." Evie's singular answer sends a poison dart to my chest. Afraid to meet her probing eyes, I keep my gaze averted. "You want to move on."

"I want to try," I disclose the painful truth.

Understanding dawns on her face. "But you don't actually know how."

I shake my head. "I'm already living with him, temporary as it is. But what if something goes wrong? What if we don't work? What if it somehow makes things worse between us, and we have to keep co-parenting Ophelia for the next fifteen and a half years, except now he hates me?"

"But what if it's nothing short of beautiful? How will you know unless you try?"

"What if I somehow end up the bad guy, and Ophelia chooses to live with her dad over me?"

"A *what-if* isn't a premonition. It's nothing more than make-believe. Unless you want a career as an author, stop telling yourself stories."

"You're right." I lean back in the chair and slurp my half-melted drink.

"Have you considered getting advice from a therapist?" Evie pops the cap off her cup and tips the drink into her mouth.

"Tried that. It helped initially, but I don't know if it would be worth going back."

She tosses her empty receptacle on the table. "It might. You know you can always stay in town and not make any other major life-changing decisions."

I cover my face with both my hands. "Have you seen him, though?" I squeak. Just the mere mention sends an image of him shirtless to the forefront of my brain. Corded forearms and bulging biceps, solid pecs, and a grooved set of abs I wouldn't mind running my tongue through, and a five o'clock shadow he can't fully get rid of that keeps him just on the edge of rugged.

Evie attempts to drag a hand from my face. "Whatever you're thinking about, you can share with the class. Your face is twelve shades of red."

I swat her arm away.

She's undeterred. "So maybe you need to sleep with him. Get it out of your system."

"Did that, have the stretch marks and the college fund to prove it."

Evie grins. "Yeah. Seal's already broken then."

My mouth drops open. "When did you become such a bad influence?"

"When did you become such a prude with a capital P?" she fires back.

"I don't know," I groan. "Motherhood stole my confidence. I want my sexy back, but I'm convinced she's gone on an indefinite strike."

Evie straightens in her chair and glances around the shop. Appeased by whatever she finds, she leans across the table. "Is Dane home tonight?"

Confusion steals over me. "Not until late. He's closing the bar tonight." It's Thursday. One of his regular closers called in, so he's covering for the late-night shift.

"So you'll be alone once Ophelia's in bed?"

Where is she going with this? "Yeah, Evie."

She flops back with a shrug. "Then have some fun. Go take your sexy back."

I roll my eyes. "I've done that over the past few years. Nothing new there."

"Not in his bed." She waggles her eyebrows. "You might find some…inspiration."

Just the thought sends my heart pumping blood to all parts of my body, even the ones in a state of disuse.

She shoulders her purse. "Just think about it. Anyway, we should get going. I have to pick up Tommy from school."

"Shit. I forgot the time." Thank goodness the loft is only a short walk away.

Out on the sidewalk, the sun shines warm and welcoming

on my face as I wrap my sister in a hug. "I love you. Thank you for all the advice."

"Love you too. I may have selfish motives because I want to keep you around, but I really do want what's best for you."

"I know."

"Have a good night," she sing-songs and struts happily to her car.

She's definitely given me a lot to think about. The entire walk home, I feel like skipping too.

"I can do this."

I sit on the edge of Dane's king-sized bed. My shoulders rise and fall with stuttering breaths. What's the big deal? I can wash the sheets while he's at work. It's not exactly an invasion of his personal space when he's already lent me the room for a month. It shouldn't matter what I do when I'm alone. Besides, he won't even be home for hours, and I can get through this in fifteen minutes if I really want to drag it out and enjoy it.

Though it's been so long, all I need is five.

Ophelia went to sleep about three hours ago. She's adapted well to our current situation and loves the new room Dane furnished for her, and nearly every night we've been here, she's slept straight through. She won't be a problem either.

I pad in bare feet to my suitcase near the door. The tee shirt I wear to sleep billows just above my knees. The cool air reaching the most sensitive parts of me sends a tremor down my spine. Beneath the cotton fabric, I'm completely bare.

The zipper of an interior pocket sounds loud in the quiet room. I retrieve the toy wrapped in a black velvet bag and return to the bed. Planting a knee on the corner, I hoist myself up and climb near the middle. Pitch darkness blankets me in comfort, removing the nervous edge. This will be good.

I dump the contents beside me. The toy is U-shaped with a flat, round side meant to lie against my clit. The other arm of the U is thick and cylindrical, meant to be worn inside. Once I turn it on, the arm inside will vibrate with varying speeds and move in different pulse patterns, depending on which setting I select. A round remote allows handsfree, wireless control.

Lying back on the pillow at the head of the bed, I lift my hips to tug the tee up to my breasts. Cool air blasts my stomach, sending goose bumps skittering across my sensitized skin. I let out a deep breath and slip the device between my legs. Just the thought of getting off in this bed has me incredibly wet, and the toy slips in with ease. The feeling of intrusion revs my engine even though I haven't turned the device on yet.

Fisting the bunched tee at the center of my chest, I close my eyes and grab the remote with my other hand. I set it to level two vibrations and put it on my favorite setting. The toy begins a rhythmic swirling pattern that almost instantly coaxes me to gyrate my hips.

I moan quietly and bite my lip to stifle another. Pleasure floods me at the thought that this isn't the first time I've gotten off in this bed. The memories of our night together rip through my mind like end scene credits to one of my favorite films. My clit dances to life beneath the pulsing internal and external vibrations, and a steady throb drums my core.

It doesn't take long before I'm lost to sensation and the memories in my head. The room surrounding me melts away into the darkness.

Suppressed breaths become quiet moans mingling with

the shadows. My heart picks up speed in response to the pleasure sizzling through my blood. I arch my neck, the faint scent of smoke and bourbon wafting from the padding behind my head.

"I'm so close to coming." I gasp and release the tee at the center of my chest to take charge of the toy. I begin fucking myself, needing more pressure, wishing I was filled.

"Dane," I moan as I climb the peak. Something creaks, the bed, the floor, I don't know, and at this moment, I can't find it in me to give a shit. I'm too busy chasing what promises to be one of the most explosive orgasms of my life. My torso heaves with heavy panting breaths, and I continue to thrust the toy between my legs.

"Tell me to leave."

The deep voice sends a shockwave through me, only serving to heighten the absolute pleasure surging through my pussy. My eyes fly open in shock. I'm lost. Lost to this world. Lost to the sensation, to the pleasure, to him. To Dane. Surrounded by absolute darkness, not knowing how or when he slipped in here, how long he's been watching or if he can even see me, I can't find it in me to care.

Right now, I want to come.

And I want him to help me.

"Stay." The word is breathless and rough. A scrape of pure need from behind my vocal cords. I blindly reach for him in the dark.

For a moment, the steady hum between my legs and the sound of our breathing perform a symphony for us.

"Don't you stop, Mama." The whisper of fabric accompanies us as he removes his shirt. "Don't you dare fucking stop."

His words spur me on, wanting to please him, wanting to please *me*. The minor interruption temporarily slowed the crescendo. Knowing what the future holds sets me on a steady pace back toward the peak. Keeping my eyes closed, I push the toy deeper inside, and my hips jerk in response.

"Ah," I cry out. Tingles erupt from my center, cascading outward.

"What's this?" Dane's voice is louder now that he's closer.

"W-What's what?" I pant. The interruption isn't necessary. I'm so close I could almost cry.

Dane's movement dips the bed. His warmth radiates into my naked skin at my hip. His palm settles on my hip bone, the pressure enough to keep me in place but not so much that he's holding me down.

Without warning, the vibration increases speed, tearing through me at lightning speed. "Oh, God," I moan as my hips fly from the bed. Except I don't make it far with his hand on me.

"Seems I found the remote." His voice is full of a sinful desire. "Are you going to come for me, pretty girl?"

I clutch at his forearm, my nails scoring along the corded flesh. "You're going to make me come."

The device speeds up again. Vivid pleasure rips through me, and I nearly bow completely off the bed. "Dane!" I half beg, half sob.

His mouth seals over mine in an unrestrained kiss. He has one elbow near my head, the other hand cradles the side of my neck, and his torso hovers over mine. I spear my fingers through the hair just above his neck, dragging him into me and hanging on for dear life.

"Shh. You can't wake Ophelia." The vibrations slow to the original speed, bringing me back down a notch.

"I didn't come yet," I grumble against his soft mouth. My body trembles from holding my muscles taut.

His tongue chases away my dispute in a kiss that makes my head spin. "You will."

Warm, calloused fingers chafe down, down, down, and

across my lower abdomen. He palms the device, probably measuring its size in the dark before he's there, easing a thick digit in with the buzzing toy. My wetness provides more than enough lubricant for him to glide easily inside.

"Oh, please," I cry. *This* is what I was missing. To be stretched and full.

A second finger joins the first, moving in a circular rhythm with the tempo. "It'll fit," he says before shifting his body to fully cover mine. I drop my knees wider to provide access as his hips slip between them.

The withdrawal of his fingers instigates a sad mewl from my lips.

"No," I whine.

"Hold onto me, Caiti," he growls. The deep tenor has me scrambling to wrap my arms around his neck. He could order me to do just about anything right now, and I'd say yes, so long as it ends in an orgasm.

"Please." My legs shake from the ongoing pleasure. If I don't come soon, I might actually cry from the exhaustion.

"No more talking."

Dane slants his head. His lips touch mine at the exact moment he notches his cock at my entrance. I shudder from the smooth tip running through my soaked folds. If memory serves correctly, he's no small prize, and his girth is a challenge on a good day. He starts to press in with the device continuing to buzz away, proving me correct with a snug fit.

My fingertips apply pressure to the sides of his head. He stops kissing me to rest his forehead on mine. "It won't fit. You have to take the toy out."

"It'll fit," he grunts, resuming a journey with his lips across my cheek to my neck.

"You're too big."

"You can take me, Mama."

God, that sentence alone nudges me to the brink. As he

continues his torturously slow intrusion, I find his mouth in the dark. My tongue slips inside his. Talking is over. I can barely hold back my cries as he seats himself to the hilt.

He was right—he fit. Oh God, does he fit so fucking good.

The fullness is unlike anything I've felt in my entire life. I'm completely filled. The ceaseless vibrations drive me to the edge of the cliff. Dane begins a steady rhythm, and on the third glide, he thrusts me straight over the edge.

A warbled, unintelligible sentence scrapes up my throat as I come, and I come, and I come. The pulsing waves throw me against the shore and threaten to wash me away.

"That's fucking beautiful, baby. Come all over my cock."

I'm wrung out and shaking as the last wave slowly pulses away.

"You have one more."

"Oh, no. I don't think I—Ah!"

The vibrations crank back up a speed or two. The argument drifts away as pleasure tears through my body, immediately transporting me back up to the peak. Dane's thrusts drive with accuracy into the spot I need him most, chasing his own release.

"Together this time. Wait for me, Caiti."

"I'm there. I'm waiting," I gasp. The vibrations make it harder to hang on. I scrape my nails into the skin on his back as he plunges deep.

"Squeeze me with that beautiful pussy, make me come."

Nothing could hold me back at this point. I'm already there. His words dump fuel on the flame, sending me gasping over the perilous edge. I splinter for a second time. My muscles grip his cock as he ruts without control and shudders above me, signaling his heady release as he pumps me full of his come.

Surrounded by Dane in his room and his bed, I come down from one of the most erotic experiences of my life. My limbs are spent and heavy where they cradle his large body to mine.

"Hang tight, Mama."

My heavy eyelids flutter as he pulls himself out of me. The loss of fullness is startling. Next, he removes the toy with a gentle tug. The cease of vibrations quiets the air around us until only the sound of his movements remains.

"Be right back."

I wait unmoving in his bed, wearing only the tee and naked from below the waist. He returns two minutes later and settles on his knees between my legs.

"Just a warm cloth."

The brush of fabric sends a shockwave to my sensitized clit. I bite my lip to contain the sound. After a gentle swipe through my folds, he leans down and presses a single kiss over my clit. The cloth lands with a wet *fwap* near the clothes hamper before Dane crawls up the length of my body in the bed. He drags the end of the duvet with him to fold us in the blanket.

"Just a few minutes, and I'll let you sleep."

"Stay." I grip his forearm around my waist.

His body melts into my side. "Okay."

I'm glad he doesn't probe further because I wouldn't be able to answer any questions. I don't know why I asked him to stay. All I know is I'm sated, warm, held, and most importantly, safe.

Something I haven't felt in a very, very long time.

16

Dane

Three taps in the middle of my forehead rouse me from a peaceful sleep. My new alarm clock stands at eye level at the side of the bed. Ophelia's mouth puckers to the side, and her eyebrows scrunch together.

"You sick or someting?"

I roll to my side and boop her on the nose. She giggles and grabs the end of my finger. "I'm not sick."

"Den why are you in Mommy's bed?"

"Daddies sleep next to Mommies sometimes." There. That sounds like an age-appropriate answer. I never considered how this conversation might happen since Ophelia's used to finding me on the couch on the mornings I sleep in.

She cocks her head. "Is that where babies come from?"

This conversation is sinking me faster than quicksand. "Um, well—"

"Babies come from Mommy's tummy, Ophelia." Saved by the mother herself.

"Up! Up!" Two little hands reach for my face.

Who could ever deny her what she wants? With a grunt, I hoist her onto the king-sized bed. As soon as she clears the edge, she crawls into the space between her parents.

Not wanting to miss a minute now that we're all awake, I roll to lie on my other side. Caiti faces me, a soft smile on her sleepy face. I'm relieved we've retained the ability to maintain eye contact after last night. As I held her in my arms in the dark, I dreaded the morning, not knowing if I'd wake once again to an empty bed and her obvious regret.

Ophelia climbs recklessly over her mother, eliciting playful grunts until she settles on her knees by her head. She grabs Caiti by the nose and chin, yanking her mouth open and peering inside.

"What are you doing?" I ask around a laugh.

Ophelia looks at me with her serious face back in place. "I'm wooking for a baby."

Caiti coughs so hard that she dislodges Ophelia from her face. "There are no babies in there, honey," she gasps.

"Oh. Okay!" Ophelia scoots backward to the foot of the bed and rolls herself over the edge. "See ya!" She disappears from the room with a rapid tap of little feet.

I scrub my face with a groan, the grin still firmly in place. "How old does she need to be before we can officially lock her out in the morning?"

Caiti's giggle is musical as she rises from the bed. It's her turn to overthrow the tiny person in power and wrangle her for breakfast. "At least six. Then she can find something to watch on the TV by herself and maybe even pour her own cereal." She stops near the door to flip her hair into a messy bun on her head.

The words she says zip right passed my ears. I sit slowly and kick my legs over the edge of the bed, planting my feet on the floor. "Caiti, come here." The command scrapes up a throat rough with early morning gravel and emotion.

"What's wrong?"

Once she's close enough to touch, I snag her wrist and pull her between my spread thighs. Her puzzled expression remains fixed on her face, but she moves easily into my hold, resting her petite hands on my shoulders.

I fist the material of the *very familiar* oversized tee she's currently wearing.

"How often do you wear this to bed?"

She glances down at the material covering her naked body, her face stark with guilt. She tries to back out of my space, but my hold on the material keeps her between my legs.

She shakes her head. "I-I don't know. I don't even know how it got in my bag."

"Caiti." My voice holds a warning tone. "Three years ago, you left me after the most memorable night of my life, and my shirt—*this shirt*—was nowhere to be found. You mean to tell me it just happened to turn up in your bag after all this time?"

Her eyes glisten.

"And that the night you decide to get yourself off in my bed, thinking of me, you slip on my tee?"

"How do you know I was thinking of you?" she spouts stubbornly, already retreating from me. Not physically. She couldn't be closer unless she straddled my lap. It's the emotional guard she slammed down the second I called her out that separates us.

"I heard you moaning *my* name." I shake my fist holding the shirt. "Why else do you think I ended up in the room?"

"I'm sorry."

"Don't be. Just tell me how often you slip into nothing but this shirt and fall asleep?"

She bites her lip and studies the blank canvas of the painted wall behind me. "Whenever I needed to feel safe." Her thick, watery voice is my undoing.

Fuck.

For years, I've known she took the shirt. That was obvious when it wasn't lying on the floor when I woke up alone the next morning. But I always assumed she ditched it at the first opportunity or, more accurately, based on her hurried departure, burned the damn thing. Never in a million years would I have guessed she not only held on to it all this time but also wore it to sleep when she didn't want to feel alone.

I feel as if she reached into my chest and tore out my heart with her bare fucking hands, and she holds the beating organ in her palms. The worst part about it is I can tell this is a conversation too far. She's not ready to give anything more to me than she did last night.

Releasing the shirt, I wrap one hand around the back of her bare thigh and stroke a crooked finger beneath her chin. "I believe you have something that belongs to me."

"You can have it back. I'm sorry."

I tighten my fingers around her leg. "I'm not talking about the shirt, Mama. If I had my way, you'd never take it off."

Her dark eyes move back and forth between mine, her gaze a mixture of confusion, hope, and a hell of a lot of fear. "Then what—"

The door flies open, and Ophelia dances her way into the room. "Hey! I still hungry." She throws her hip out and rests her hand on it with more attitude than I thought her little body could handle.

"I'm going to..." Caiti trails off and removes herself from my proximity in answer.

Watching her ass sway beneath the fabric of my tee affirms my thoughts from earlier. I'd die one happy man if she lived inside my shirts. And I'm willing to wait until she's ready to make that happen.

Because Ophelia may have interrupted what I was about to say, but that doesn't mean I won't find another time.

Just like the shirt that was once mine, my heart belongs to her now too. She just hasn't figured it out yet.

A WARM BREEZE blows Ma's hair across her cheek as I push her chair outside to sit on the patio. Birds chirp in their high perches above the grassy yard. The peacefully warm sun has only a few cottony clouds overhead to offer a brief reprieve. I stop the chair beside mine facing the pond and settle a wide-brimmed hat over her head.

"Perfect." I smile at her from my bent position. Her faraway gaze travels over my face, reminding me of my teen years when she'd attempt to catch me in a lie. I never could keep a straight face when she stared stoically at me, and I feel that same bubbling sensation in my stomach right now.

She cups my cheek affectionately, and I close my eyes. "M-M-My boy."

The warmth from her brief recognition envelops me. "I'm here, Ma."

She smiles and looks out at the pond. The words spill forth rather than allow nature to fill the gaps of silence, just as they would when I was a kid.

"You have a granddaughter."

Ma doesn't acknowledge me, so I keep talking. She won't remember this conversation anyway, but this feels like something I need to share with her.

"Her name is Ophelia. She's two-and-a-half, and she looks a lot like me. She has my dark curly hair, and her smile is one-hundred-percent mine. Her personality is full of bubbles and sunshine. Her favorite color is pink, and she's obsessed with unicorns and dogs. I'd like her to meet you soon."

I reach over and hold Ma's hand. The manicured fingers are frail and withered at this late stage of her life but still bring the same comfort fitted in mine. My throat constricts on a swallow. "I'm falling in love with her mother, Ma. I never thought I'd be that guy, finding love so easily, and I'm terrified."

"Why are you scared?" Ma's soft voice disrupts my study of my knees. I glance at her face and find her regarding me with gentle eyes.

I realize we aren't having a normal conversation with her cognitive decline. I need to tread lightly so as not to upset her with the past, so I choose an easy answer. "I'm scared of losing her." Vague, but not unrealistic. I won't ever lose her in the same horrific way Ma lost my father, but there are many bad ways someone can lose a person.

Caiti's own history speaks of one of the worst ones.

"Fear should never be a reason to avoid something. Take the fear with you, like a backpack." Years of providing therapy to her clients haven't faded from her mind. She ran her own practice until she recognized the signs of illness in herself and decided to shut down.

"I know."

"Love is never wasted, no matter how fleeting it may be."

Maybe not, but that doesn't mean it can't hurt like a son of a bitch. "I love you, Ma."

Her attention returns to the water without a response, but her hand tightens in mine.

Being here with her like this day after day proves her statement to be true. She took care of me for nearly the first twenty years of my life, and I've spent the next twenty trying to repay what I can. It's my honor to try to make up for her life filled with sacrifices. Even if they'll never be enough.

17

Caiti

THE CREAMY CONCOCTION bubbles around the spoon I'm stirring, wafting the smell of garlic into the air. My mind runs absently while Ophelia plays happily in the background. I throw a sincere smile over my shoulder at her babbling lyrics. I can't deny the positive changes in her even if I wanted to. She's flourished in ways I didn't even know possible since we arrived in Arrow Creek, and it's clearer by the day how cruel it'd be to force her away.

I've worked hard to provide for her, to make sure she's always felt whole and loved with a single parent. If circumstances required, I'd continue to do so for the rest of my life, no questions asked.

But that was before she knew Dane and started to love him.

And I know he's fallen in love with her too. Every interaction is laced with the heart and protectiveness of a papa bear. There's no doubt the two will continue to nurture a close relationship well into the coming years.

The questions that linger are mine to solve. My relationship with Dane appears to hinge on my feelings, and I haven't decided how to unravel them yet. I set the spoon on a paper towel and clutch the vial around my neck. If this were a chess game, the next move would be mine to make.

My phone vibrates on the counter beside the stove. I wipe my hands on a towel and unlock the screen. A knot lodges in my throat at the text from a random number.

I should stop opening the messages, but I continue to save each one in my pile of evidence.

Unknown: *Your lights have been off for far too long. When are you coming home, sweetie?*

Okay. Calm yourself. Being hundreds of miles away from home feels like a blessing at this moment. The problem is I can't tell if this is an escalation or if he's simply never told me he's been by my house before. The thought of him watching my house at night while I sleep sends a sinister shiver down my spine. My palms sweat as I add the screenshot to the folder with nearly fifty others, purposeful not to swipe and read the tens of other messages.

The sizzle of water pulls me back from the edge of fear. The pasta water boils over.

"Shit!"

An electrical current races through my nerves, denoting a heightening stress response. I need a second to calm myself. I need—

"Smells good in here," Dane says right beside my ear.

My body reacts without thought. As fear punches my gut, I whirl, cock back, and throw my fist straight at his face.

"Oh, my God!" I shriek when I realize what I've done.

He grips my wrist in a powerful grasp, holding it as if he's not sure I'll strike him again. I watch in horror as a trickle of blood runs down his chin from a split in his lip. His tongue skates over the tear in an automatic flick while his heated stare meets mine.

Still acting on impulse, I throw my other hand around his neck, yanking his mouth to mine. The metallic taste explodes on my tongue, and I lap it up. A rush of adrenaline provokes me. "I'm so sorry," I pull away to mumble against his sinful mouth before diving back in.

Oh, my God, I hurt him, my thoughts scream.

He releases my hand, and both of his cradle the sides of my head. He takes control and walks me back until I bump into the counter behind me. I'm lost to the dizzying taste of him mixed with the tang of the wound I caused.

"I'm sorry," I mutter again. A salty tear finds its way to my tongue. With a final swirl in my mouth, he pulls away and rests his forehead against mine.

"What's got you spooked, Mama?"

Another tear splashes against my cheek. I need to get away and clear my head before I break in front of Ophelia. Or Dane.

I dash the glistening drop with the back of my hand and push away. Spinning, I twist off the burners as a distraction. "Dinner's ready if you two want to eat. I need to leave for a bit."

"Hey." He snags my bicep in a firm grip. "You can talk to me, yeah?"

I shrug, my brittle smile splintering into a frown. "I'm not ready to talk about this." Pocketing my phone, I pull from his grasp. He lets me go, but not before I catch a look of ill-disguised disapproval.

"I'm sorry about your lip." The exterior door creaks shut behind me.

For thirty minutes, I circle the town. Up one street and down another. I drive until the anxiety leaks from my fingertips, and I become bored. Until the thoughts of what just happened still. As soon as the regret for hitting Dane fades, a new trail of thoughts starts an endless loop. Desperate to quiet the unending noise, I point my car on the road out of town.

Three years ago, Evie brought Eric and me on a hike in Arrow Creek. We took a winding, elevated trail through the trees until we reached a high ledge above a raging river. The day was filled with Eric's grumbling as he tried to convince Evie to move in with us rather than stay here so far away. It was the last day the three of us spent together.

I know in my heart it's the right place to go to feel close to him, so even though my palms sweat, my heart pounds, and my ears buzz through the silent car, I push on. The fear surrounds me like a well-worn shawl, and I embrace it for the first time in weeks. I allow it to accompany me on this journey because I know this is what I need to do.

The moment I find the trailhead, a dam breaks. The memories race forward like leaves on a rapid stream. One after another, they flit past, giving only a glimpse of the life I once had before floating away. I tie my hair back, lock my car, and start the trek. It's already evening, and I only have a few hours before dark settles in.

The greenery overhead casts shadows from the setting sun. A log threatens to knock me down, but I find my footing and move ahead. Somewhere beyond my sightline, a bird caws, the sound an accompaniment to my mood.

"How did I end up here?" I speak to the crawling shadows

and waning sun, but I think the rhetorical question is for Eric. He used to give the best advice, though I realize now he was very safe. Our love was beautiful and true and deep, but I'm not sure it was crazy and filled with passion. Eric was my warm blanket I could curl up under during a scary thunderstorm. But is it erroneous to believe in other types of attraction out there?

Gravel rolls beneath my sneakers as I hike, nearing the top. A gush of anguish threatens to yank me under. Am I really considering this? Thoughts of Ophelia's future once again fill my head. The way she responds to us as a family unit is a piece of beauty I never allowed myself to imagine. Dane stepped into his father role without hesitation, and I can picture the potential. The three of us together.

It doesn't hurt that he lights me up with a single touch.

I felt weak for falling into bed with him years ago, not extremely long after my husband passed. But once I found out about Ophelia, I couldn't regret our night together. Wearing his shirt became a ritual that replaced the nights of tears. Still, I never let myself daydream about a possible future together. Coming here was about keeping Ophelia safe and nothing else.

Because picturing a future with someone else means I have to let Eric go.

The brush clears at the top of the trail. I stop near a slanting tree, the bark rough against my exposed skin, and catch my breath. Twilight is breathtaking from these heights. Jutting black cliffs surround an inky river below as the first stars of the night glitter in the periwinkle sky. I stroll to the edge and seat myself close, tucking myself tight. Picking up a pebble, I throw it into the sprawling darkness.

An ache seizes my chest, unlike the one I felt that first day in Arrow Creek. This one isn't devastating. I trap the vial between my hand and body, curling into myself, as the past few years of grief for my husband leech out of me. Reaching behind my neck, I unclasp the chain and wrap it around my hand. The vial dangles in the soft evening breeze.

"I miss you," I speak through a clogged throat into the darkness. "You were once the best thing that ever happened to me."

I rest my chin on bent knees. "Not a day goes by when I don't hear your laughter in my head. You had the best laugh, Eric."

The words spilling out are past tense and once was and wishes. Because that's how it is when someone dies. The future doesn't exist. The *what could be* becomes *what could have been*. There's nothing I can do to change it.

But suffering for the rest of my life because he was taken early doesn't seem like what he'd want for me.

"Don't hate me for staying here because I really want to stay."

The idea of returning to Colorado makes me nauseous the longer I spend in Arrow Creek. "My parents cut ties with me. I'm sure you wouldn't be surprised. You never liked them much anyway." A watery laugh bursts free. "Tate met some girl and moved out West not long after you…you…after you died," I force myself to say. "Some best friend. I'm glad he didn't have time to make promises to care for me on your deathbed," I say with sarcasm he could read so easily.

"I loved you, Eric, with my whole heart. But now that you're gone, I think it's okay for me to share a piece with someone else. Whoever that may be."

I wipe a tear from my cheek. "Look down on me from time to time, and if you don't mind, keep an eye on Ophelia for me. If she's going to be anything like I was as a teen, I'll need all the help I can get."

A rush of emotion overcomes me. "I love you so much, Eric." Bringing the vial to my lips, I kiss the glass holding his remaining ashes. "Thank you for always loving me. It's been an enormous privilege being your wife."

I sit a while, not bothering to touch the soft tears drifting occasionally down my cheeks. My heart still hurts but feels lighter somehow. I allow time to adjust to the feeling. When the ache in my back becomes persistent from sitting still on the rock, I stand and brush my hands over my backside. I situate the chain back around my neck before embarking down the darkening trail.

A text brightens my phone as I near the parking lot, Dane's name a welcome intrusion.

Dane: *It's getting late. Where are you?*

I type back, *I'm coming soon.*

Not even thirty seconds later, his reply follows.

Dane: *I'll wait up for you.*

Tears fall harder from his thoughtfulness. As I drive back to his loft, I forget everything else. I forget about the future. I forget to be afraid of driving and panic. The only thought I cling to is reaching Dane before I fall completely apart.

From the street, I can tell most of the lights in the loft are off. A yellowed, dim glow shines from the living room window. It's after ten, and I pray Ophelia's asleep. Ignoring the incessant rumble in my stomach from a missed meal, I climb the steps with heavy feet.

The door flies open before I hit the landing. Dane greets me with concerned eyes and tilted lips, the cut I created a dark line through his lower one. His broad, muscular chest looks like the perfect landing pad, and I rush for the center. He wraps me in a strong embrace. The warmth from his body seeps into my chilled bones. The thud of the door shutting behind me times perfectly with my buckling knees as the sobs I've held back wrack my body.

Dane secures me as we sink together to the floor. If I could crawl inside him, I would. Pain rips through the jagged pieces of my heart. My fingers scramble for purchase on the back of his shirt. A guttural sob ricochets around the small apartment, and Dane buries my face deeper into his chest.

"Shhh." His hand soothingly strokes the length of my tangled strands. For minutes or hours, he holds me and lets me cry.

When the sobs retreat to hiccups, I sit back on my heels, spent and wrung dry. He loosens his hold but keeps close with comforting touches.

"I feel like I'm losing him all over again, except this time it's my choice to let him go."

"Oh, Mama," Dane breathes. He reaches out and brushes a stream of tears from my cheek with his thumb. "If I've pushed you in any way…"

"You haven't."

"What do you need?"

I try to look away, to hide my shame, but he turns me back with his finger beneath my chin. "Tell me."

"Is it wrong if I just want you to hold me?"

Dane rises to his feet and pulls me with him. "Come on."

I let him thread our fingers together, and he leads me to the couch.

"Sit."

I drop heavily onto the worn cushion.

"Do you like white or red?"

"Is vodka an option?"

The corner of his lips twitch. "Not tonight, Mama. I want you relaxed, not numbing yourself."

"White."

"Be right back."

Dane returns first with a glass of white wine offered to me by the stem. Once I take it, he returns to the kitchen. The oven door slams moments before the smell of garlic wafts across the room. My stomach gurgles in protest. Seconds later, Dane reappears, carrying a plate of the pasta dish I created earlier.

He sets the plate on the coffee table. I move to give him room, but he catches my legs before I can and lowers them onto his lap when he sits. Leaning forward, he retrieves the plate. The warmth seeps into my legs from the dish in his hands.

"Open."

A twirled forkful of pasta awaits, and who am I to resist? I open and wrap my lips around the silverware, locking the food inside. The fork slides out slowly, and he retrieves another bite.

He feeds me in silence, the concern on his face leeching away with each morsel consumed. I probably worried him by running out and staying away after dark, but he's yet to pry. Instead, he sweetly feeds me as if he has all the time in the world and hasn't been working and chasing a toddler around all day.

"Thank you," I say after washing down the last mouthful with a sip of wine. Dane deposits the plate on the table and moves his hands to my calves. With strong fingers, he kneads the tired muscles, eliciting a groan from me.

"Come here, Caiti." He gently coaxes the wineglass from my hand and places it beside the plate. I place my hand in his and climb over the cushions to straddle his lap. His arms settle around my waist, tucking me tight into his chest. "Is this all right?"

"This is perfect," I mumble against the fabric of his shirt and close my eyes, giving in to his strong comfort.

18

Dane

A FEW DAYS after the punching incident, I still can't look at the reflection of my cracked lip without feeling a warm swoop somewhere in my gut. The punch was the catalyst for a storm of passion that I want more of. Her embrace, her lips, the taste of her mingled with my blood are the stuff of dreams. Not that I previously allowed myself to have them. Funny how life has a way of dishing out exactly what it wants. My own desires be damned.

Caiti's hand sits firmly in mine as we walk down the sidewalk on Main Street. I finally convinced her to let me call a babysitter so we could explore some time alone. The two of us deserve to test out this new rapport between us. Or whatever she wants to call it. We don't know each other well, and we've spent most days at my place or the bar. She might not know it yet, but I intend to find out everything there is to know about her and offer her the same. In order to have a true shot, the guards have to come down.

Starting with a proper date without the distraction of wild toddlers or serving drinks in a busy bar.

Dominic's Steakhouse is relatively new to town and beats out any other restaurant in impressiveness for over forty miles. Even with Caiti's anxiety calming to a manageable level, I didn't want to cause a flare by taking her too far out of town.

The black dress she borrowed from Cami sparkles in the late afternoon sun, and the mid-thigh slit showcases her flawlessly tan skin. She's a tad overdressed for this small town, but I wear her on my arm with pride. I even dusted off a pair of slacks and a black button-down for the occasion, paired with my only pair of dress shoes.

As if reading my thoughts, Caiti shakes our hands and says, "How bad do you think people will talk?"

"Who gives a fuck if they do."

She brushes her glossy hair over a shoulder with the hand not holding mine. "Oh, I don't, really. I thought you might since this isn't really like you."

"You think so, big city girl?" I can't help the grin sliding into place.

"Small-town bartender out for a fancy dinner. I'm sure the gossip mill will be turning over all night long."

I give her slender fingers a long squeeze. "Let them."

Her chin falls to her chest a little too slow to hide the tilt of her ruby lips.

With my hand in hers, I pull us to a stop. "What is it?"

"This is too easy."

"Isn't that a good thing?" My forehead creases. Fuck, I hope she isn't one of those women who wants a fight every few days to stay interested. I am not that guy.

Her voice drops into a whisper. "It's a great thing. Unexpected. But great."

"C'mon." I set us in motion again. If she doesn't stop questioning, I might have to provide a thorough demonstration of how great I can be.

Without dropping her hand, I hold the door open for her, letting her enter first. The blast of air-conditioning chases away the late summer heat, nearly provoking a chill. The host barring entry immediately grabs two menus and leads us to a table in a secluded corner of the half-filled restaurant. The early hour was my choice to enjoy some quiet before the dinner rush.

The host sets the menus on the table and walks away. I pull out Caiti's chair and gesture with my hand. "Have a seat."

"Now you're just showing off."

Once she tucks her skirt beneath her and sits, I gently push her chair in. My mouth is perfectly positioned near her ear, and I'm not one to waste an opportunity.

"I've always wanted to try that." With a discreet nibble on her neck, I straighten and find my own seat. The table touches the corner wall with only two chairs, putting us in intimate proximity.

"What? You don't usually take your dates to fancy steakhouses and act like a gentleman?" The teasing lilt in her voice finds its way straight to my dick.

"I don't think my thoughts about you in that skirt would be considered very gentlemanly."

Caiti fiddles with the roll of silverware, a blush staining her cheeks. "Have you lived in Arrow Creek your entire life?"

Her transition from gasping under my mouth to small talk is admirable. "Yeah. I was born and raised not too far from where we live now." The pronoun is intentional, and I hope she lets it slide.

"It's a nice place."

The sentiment could send my hopes soaring, but I'm not ready to let them out of my clutches quite yet. "Tell me something I don't know about you."

A server dropping water glasses interrupts Caiti's answer, but noticing we haven't picked up our menus yet, she quickly disappears.

"Well, I'm an only child. I've never had a pet though I'd love to get Ophelia a dog someday." She taps her chin, eyes averted, and shrugs. "I'm a pretty average human being. So much of my identity has been tied to my circumstances. I was a wife, then a widow, and now I'm a mother."

"Those are some of your roles, but they don't describe who you are."

"I think I'm still figuring out who I am." She studies the flickering candle in the glass centerpiece.

"Do you want to know what I think of you?"

A look of surprise crosses her face as she reverts her attention back to me. She rests her chin on her propped fist. "Only if it comes with flattery." She bats her dark lashes.

I lean into her space, inhaling the sweet scent of cherry blossoms she's so fond of. My mouth nears the shell of her ear, poised to divulge dark secrets. Only one of those remains on my end, and at the start of a fancy dinner isn't the time or place to share.

"I think you're brave for letting me into your lives, and I think you're stronger than you realize. I think you rock a pair of sweatpants and my baggy tees with the same level of sex appeal as the dress you're wearing tonight. And I think Ophelia couldn't have lucked out with a better mom, just as I couldn't have asked for a better woman to accidentally knock up."

"You don't have to pour it on extra thick."

"I'm not. I can also tell by your smile when you're extra excited about a food you're about to eat. Your hands are always cold, which gives me a reason to warm them up. And the way you smile at your daughter when you think nobody's watching lights up an entire room."

Caiti pushes a loose strand of hair behind her ear. "I feel like I've done nothing besides pile responsibilities onto you."

I reach into her lap and secure her chilly hand in mine. "You may have barged into my life, but I'm paying attention because I want you, not because I have to."

She squeezes my hand back. "Okay, big shot. If you're paying so much attention to me, it's my turn. Teach me something I don't know about you."

I could groan at the onslaught of naughty images. She doesn't even know how eager I am to teach her things. Like my favorite position and how I like my dick sucked.

"My favorite color is the shade of red in your cheeks when you're turned on. My favorite song is the sound of my name on your lips. And my favorite movie is the one where you're getting yourself off in my bed."

"Dane!" She squeals at a hushed volume, that enticing pink rising in her cheeks.

Rather than respond, I cast a grin her way and take a refreshing sip of water. I set my glass back on the table, noticing the vigor with which she rubs her arm with her free hand.

"Are you cold?"

She shrugs. "A little. I read once restaurants keep the temperature down because studies have shown people eat less and fill up faster when they're warm."

"Well, that won't do. I didn't bring you here to freeze to death."

The wooden legs of my chair scrape as I stand, already tearing through the buttons of my shirt from the top. "Up."

The server chooses that moment to reappear, her eyes comically wide at my state of half-undress.

"One second." I peel the material off my shoulders. Good thing I chose to wear a black tee beneath my shirt rather than a white tank top. Not that the other option would have hindered my decision to keep Caiti warm, but I'd look even more out of place.

Caiti holds out her arms one at a time, and I thread the large material over her. With intense focus, I rethread the buttons, leaving the top three open, then I move to roll up her sleeves one at a time.

"Better?"

She tucks her nose into the collar, her shoulders rising with an obvious inhale. "Much. Thank you."

Mini dilemma solved, we place our orders for two medium-rare cooked steaks with asparagus and twice-baked potatoes and resume our discussion.

Somewhere through enjoying our meal, I end up pulling Caiti's calves across my lap. She leans back in her chair with a glass of red wine in her hand, head thrown back laughing at something I said, the picturesque view of contentment.

This is exactly what we needed.

She sits abruptly, the smile sliding from her face. "Oh. There's Bailey."

My muscles tighten as I scan the tables surrounding us. "Where?"

"Behind you. She's waiting on that table. Did you happen to talk to her yet?"

"No." I recognize Bailey where Caiti indicated, though her back is to us now.

"You should."

"Not now," I growl. This night has been one for the books, and I'm not about to intentionally ruin it.

Caiti pushes to her feet, relieving me of the warm weight of her legs. Fuck. "Caiti," I warn, though I'm not sure why. I need a few more minutes to determine if she's upset before she does something rash.

"Bailey, wait," she calls out.

Damn, she's going for it head-on. I have to bite my lip to

contain a grin. For all her anxiety, there's still a bold woman just lingering beneath the surface.

My ex pauses near our table. At least she has the capacity to look appropriately ashamed. "Yes?"

"Can you just point me toward the restroom?" Caiti asks.

Smooth. Or a jab. Seeing as the last time they were in a bathroom together, Bailey committed a punishable assault.

"Oh. Sure." Bailey's shoulders relax. "Take a left at the windows, and there's a hall. You can't miss them then."

Caiti smiles. "Thanks. I'll be right back." She pointedly glances at me, then takes off. From the back, she's nearly indecent. My shirt hangs so low that it looks as if she's not wearing anything but my button-down and a pair of heels. My dick hardens at the view.

"I'm sorry," Bailey's sincere apology drags my attention from the corner Caiti disappeared around. The image of her sexy calves dances in my head.

"You need to apologize to her." I don't bother softening my tone. I still think Caiti should have pressed charges.

She nods. "I know. I will when she comes back."

I wrap my hand around my glistening glass. "I'm sorry you had to find out like that."

"So it's true then? You have a kid?"

The smile stretching my lips is automatic but not meant to gloat. "I do. And I'm not going to tell you more than once, if you ever make a scene like that again, in front of my daughter, her mother, or me, you won't be waiting tables the next week. You'll be sitting before Judge Nelson."

Bailey nods again, the shimmer in her eyes producing zero effect on me. "It won't happen again."

I wipe my fingers wet from my glass on a green cloth napkin. "You need to know I never lied to you. I meant what I said way back then. I never intended to have kids, but it's happened."

"What about the rest of it? Does she know about your mom and your dad?"

A storm cloud darkens my mood. "I'll tell her when I'm ready." Soon, if I can get this conversation over with.

She waves her hand between us. "That seemed to be a pretty big deal to you back then and why you broke up with me, so maybe you should let her know before she finds out from someone else."

"It's been six years since your opinion meant anything to me, not to mention that's none of your business."

"You're right. I won't cause trouble for you." She shifts uncomfortably from foot to foot.

If I didn't know her so well, I'd suspect the opposite, but her sincere tone is one I'm familiar with. "I appreciate that."

Caiti reappears at the other end of the restaurant.

"She's coming back," I announce.

Bailey restores space between us now that the private conversation is over and fixes a smile to her face.

Caiti's hesitant approach slows. She appears to study my expression from across the distance. I lift my chin in assurance. Her responding smile settles some of the lingering tension. As she resumes her seat, that smile remains firmly fixed in place.

"I should get back to work, but before I do, I want to apologize," says Bailey.

Caiti turns a quarter in her seat. "Okay."

"I'm sorry for hitting you." Bailey's voice drops to a mumbled whisper.

"I accept your apology. You made an assumption. It wasn't a wrong one, but it could have been." Caiti flicks her attention to Bailey. "You don't need me to tell you that."

"I'll leave you two to the rest of your dinner. Enjoy," Bailey says and slinks off to the kitchens.

Palming Caiti at the back of the neck, I hold her steady

and bring our faces close. "You meddled," I grouse while staring at her sweet lips. My tongue sneaks out to run across mine as if preparing for a feast.

"I moved us past it."

"Are you ready to go, or do you want to stay for dessert?" The heat I feel inside infiltrates my words with low seduction. The type of dessert I want doesn't come on a menu at a steakhouse.

"I'm ready to go." Her response drips with unconcealed desire.

I throw down a stack of bills on the table, including a tip, and thread our fingers together.

"Wait. Don't you want your shirt back?" Caiti plucks the material away from the center of her chest.

"Keep it. Looks better on you."

We weave through densely packed tables until the front door comes into view. I release our grip, guiding her with my palm settled into the low curve of her back.

Fresh evening air greets us with our first step on the pavement. The further we move from lingering classical music and patio chatter, the more nature replaces the noise. Crickets hum in the swishing grass of a nearby field, and birds sing their final songs.

"Where to?" I break the silence and jostle our entwined hands.

"Nowhere particular. This is refreshing, taking a quiet walk."

She's not wrong. I can't recall the last time I held the hand of a pretty girl just to stroll along the sidewalk. "It is different. I don't usually have time in my day to slow down."

"Even more so with a toddler in the mix."

"Ah, I knew something was missing. Next time, we're bringing her with us."

"I'll suggest somewhere a little more toddler proof. She'll

eat a steak, but only after throwing half of it on the floor first."

She paints a vivid picture in my head. "Noted."

We come to a halt at the single stoplight in town. The cross traffic has the right of way, stalling our progress. I turn into her and grip the shirt billowing on each side of her hips. Caiti tilts her head back to regard me. Her hooded eyelids tell a tale of longing she's yet to voice. If only I could add some persuasion.

Lowering my head, I watch her eyelids droop until the moment our lips touch. Under gentle coaxing, she parts for me, allowing my tongue to explore the cavern of her mouth. She tastes intoxicating, of bitter wine and her own unique sweetness. I want nothing more than to pop the buttons on my shirt and strip her bare, but the public environment hinders that craving. Instead, I dig my fingers into her curves to keep from wandering to indecent locations.

A horn honks, followed by a verbal *whoop!* Caiti and I reluctantly separate. A cherry blush stains her cheeks, and she swipes her tongue across her lip. "I don't think I've ever made out on a street corner."

I lace our fingers and tug her across the road. "I'm happy to be your first for anything. You just have to ask."

Safely on the other side, we resume our walk. Only a few paces forward, Caiti stops with a tug on my hand.

"Sorry. My phone's buzzing."

"Take your time." This leisurely stroll has no expiration.

She digs in her purse. "I wouldn't answer it, but with Ophelia not being here, I have to check." Her audible gasp raises my protective instincts. Adrenaline has me ready to throw her over my shoulder and race back to my apartment. "What is it?"

Color leaks from her tan skin, leaving her pale. She stares at her phone before seeming to conclude with a shake of her head. "I haven't been completely honest with you."

"Start now." Imagining the worst provokes my insistent tone.

"I didn't paint the entire picture of why I came to Arrow Creek. I wanted you to know your daughter in case something happened to me, and I think because of my panic attack you only took that to mean medically."

The urge to touch her nearly does me in. "And?"

She exposes her phone screen. "Someone's been harassing me."

"Since when?" I nearly snarl when I see the text on the screen.

UNKNOWN: *You haven't left me, have you, Caiti? How long will you keep me waiting?*

"IT'S BEEN ABOUT FIVE MONTHS." Caiti's hand trembles when she pulls back the phone and swipes the screen. "There are screenshots of every single message."

"Tell me everything." White-hot fury reverberates through my body, coiling my muscles for a physical fight that doesn't yet exist.

"His name is Trevor Wright. He works for a client my company did business with and found my information through a project I worked on. Honestly, I'm not sure how. He sends me messages nearly every day, usually of the *good morning, beautiful* variety, but sometimes, they're more detailed than that."

The more I swipe, the angrier I become. "Has he ever approached you?"

She shakes her head. "No, he's careful not to actually

break any laws. As far as I know, he's never made contact, but if you look at the message from the other day, he mentioned my house being dark. He knows I'm not home. I went to the police, but they said they can't help unless he makes physical contact."

A different number is attached to each message. He must be using a program to clone phone numbers to cover his tracks. I wouldn't be surprised if he's working with an alias.

"I know I should have told you. I don't think he'll hurt me, but just in case he did, I didn't want Ophelia to be alone."

I know the look on my face is downright scary when she retreats a step. "You're not going back there."

"I live there," she fires back.

"Not until he's dealt with."

"You can't—"

"What was the point?" I move a step back into her space. Not to scare her but to make her see reason. Because for the first time since I was a little boy, I feel fucking fear, and it's not an emotion I'm familiar with. "Why come here if you were just going to run back? Do you think I'll be okay to get a call in a year that I can come pick up my daughter because he killed you?"

Her breath catches. "No. I mean, I haven't thought that far ahead."

"What's your plan then?"

"I don't have one!" she explodes. "I didn't plan any of this, and if you can back off and let me breathe, I can come up with one."

"I can't." My voice cracks, the raw sound unfamiliar to me. "I can keep you safe here, but I can't protect you from a thousand miles away, and I can't leave Arrow Creek." Sorrow drips from my tone. "My mother's in a nursing home, Caiti. I can't ever leave."

"Oh, Dane," she breathes and threads her hand through my hair, dragging my forehead to hers.

"My dad's in prison for murder," I abruptly share. Her startled gasp coaxes the truth from me. "I was eleven. Nobody knows why he did it, but he drugged a woman at a bar and killed her. Everything I do is because I don't want to be anything like him."

She clasps the other side of my head, holding me steady. "You are nothing like him."

"My bar is a safe place. My staff is trained to watch for creeps trying to take advantage of unsuspecting women. You have to understand that there's no chance I can let you return across the country with someone stalking you like this." I shake the phone in my hand. "Even if he doesn't escalate beyond harassing messages."

"What are you saying?" Her eyes flit between mine.

I grip her hand against my cheek. "It means I'm willing to do anything, even if it makes you hate me, in order to keep you both safe."

She forces herself back a step as understanding dawns. "You can't take her away from me."

"I don't want to."

"Then don't!" she snaps. "Don't dangle your power to manipulate me. I said I'd come up with a plan."

I spear my fingers through my hair. "If that plan has anything to do with you returning to Colorado before he's dealt with, then you're leaving me no choice."

"You have a choice."

"No, I don't." I turn my face and kiss her palm. "Not when I'm falling in love with you. There's only one choice."

Caiti closes her eyes as if in pain. "You shouldn't fall in love with me, Dane."

Half my mouth quirks in a grin unsuitable for the moment. "I think it's too late for that, Mama."

Her index finger smashes against my sore lip in an attempt to silence me, but I have to finish. "I'm already there."

"What am I going to do?"

"Let me help you. It's that easy."

"How can you help?"

"You stay. Either he gets bored and fucks off or he tries finding you, which seems unlikely. Either way, you'll both be safe here with me."

19

Caiti

"Are we really going to be that group of women?" Cami grumbles, a hue of pink covering her normally pale cheeks. She fiddles with the hem of her short black shift dress. The plunging neckline is sexy for the normally covered paramedic.

"Have we met? Am I not the same person who once called you over to help me retrieve a lost condom from my vagina? Yes, yes, and yes," Kiersten unashamedly adds while passing out a bag of surprises with enthusiasm.

"I didn't know you used condoms," Evie interjects, looking pointedly at Kiersten's rounded stomach encased in a purple dress. The floor-length fabric beautifully accentuates her new curve.

"You are the most one-of-a-kind friend I've ever had." Cami retrieves a black sash from the bag. She wrinkles her nose at the text as she pulls it over her head. "Shot queen? You're going to get me killed."

"Mine isn't much better," I grumble at the gold *designated drunk* lettering.

"Someone had to wear them. I'm pregnant, so I'll be taking shots of water, and she's of course the bride." Kiersten gestures to Evie, who sports her own sash in white. *Soon-To-Be-Wife of the Party* stands out brightly from her white dress.

"Neither of you can complain. I've seen both of you hammered, so don't pretend you intend to drink virgin drinks all night." Evie grins at my eye roll. She's joined me flat on the floor after a night of too many a few times over the years, usually to Eric's disgruntlement.

"What are the boys up to tonight?" I fix a pin in my hair to hold back a curl. I left Dane with Ophelia with a promise to be home much later tonight. Dane's words have echoed in my head the last two days, so this evening couldn't have given me a break at a better time.

The sentiment mingles with my hopes and fears, along with a pinch of guilt. I never thought I'd hear another man tell me he loves me in this lifetime. As the words left his lips and infused me with a solid warmth, it was all I could do to hang on and not tell him the absolute truth. That I might be falling for him too. The steady confidence as he told me he'd help me makes it easy to give in to the temptation.

The hang-up comes from within me. Weakness exposed its hand the moment I showed up at his door, and the last thing I want is for him to see me as another obligation. He's a caretaker for his ailing mother, and he shoulders a sense of responsibility for the town's safety with his bar. It's all too clear now why he stepped so easily into his role for Ophelia. I want him to see me as capable. Not a weak flower needing tending.

Kiersten shrugs. "Wrangling our brood, I suppose. He didn't say."

"Law either," Cami adds. "I assumed he'd be joining one of

your men for a few beers and moral support since Evelyn's too old to need a babysitter."

"Rhett's supposed to be on a dry spell with me, but we agreed to a truce for the wedding week. Baby-making will commence the night of our wedding."

"My fingers and toes are all crossed for you." I wrap my arms around her from the back in a snug embrace. This journey has been incredibly hard on her, but she's yet to give up her dream of becoming a mother. "I can't believe you're getting married on Saturday."

Evie fixes a red ringlet in the mirror in our hotel room. Our eyes meet in the reflection. "Me neither."

The four of us carpooled to a town forty miles away for the festivities and rented a room even though we weren't planning an overnight stay. Kiersten insisted in case anyone was too drunk to transport home and so she didn't have to use a public restroom. Dane's bar is a perfect place to enjoy a rowdy evening, but the atmosphere was too familiar. We could have easily hopped a plane to a beachy destination for a wild weekend if we weren't on short notice. Something I wouldn't mind planning with these ladies in the future.

"All right, don't get sappy. There's a pregame shot in your bags. Hit those, and let's get downstairs," Kiersten commands the room.

"I'm sorry for shirking my maid of honor duties, but I'm really glad we let her take control," I whisper to Evie. We locate the small bottle of liquor in our gift packs. I wrinkle my nose at the amber color.

She knocks her hip to mine. "You might regret that by morning. Cheers!"

"Hold on, girls, it's about to be a bumpy night." Cami taps her mini bottle to mine.

"Payback is such a bitch. I hope she knows that." I tip back my own shot with a grimace.

"Who knows," Evie adds, her mouth twisted in a pucker. "There might be another wedding in the future."

The burn of the whiskey renders me speechless. Or maybe I can't truthfully refute her.

"Someone should have warned me this place turns into a karaoke bar after ten o'clock," Evie argues as a cordless mic makes the rounds of the hotel bar. We stayed on-site for the evening. This place is huge and open to the public. It's properly packed to drown out our raucous shenanigans.

"Where's the fun in that?" Kiersten remarks with a straw poked between her lips. "It's an unwritten rule that the bride has to do whatever we say during their bachelorette party."

"Whatever!" Evie shouts over the thumping pop music. She sucks down her third cocktail of the night and wipes her mouth with her hand.

"It's true." I punch my way into the conversation louder than necessary. "Don't you remember what you forced me to do?"

My sister throws her head back with a laugh. "I can't believe I forgot about that."

"Do share with the rest of us," Cami adds, leaning drunkenly into the table.

"First, they forced me into babydoll lingerie. Thankfully it was solid and not lace, so it wasn't any worse than running around in a bathing suit."

"Don't forget the mask." Evie's laugh is devilish.

"How could I? It was one of those disguise getups with glasses, bushy eyebrows, and a fake nose, except the nose was a giant penis." I rehydrate my dry mouth with a sip.

Cami nearly sprays the table with her drink. "Shit, sorry. Oh, you poor thing."

"That's not even the worst of it," I continue.

"Oh, fuck. What happened?" Kiersten asks, her face a mask of curious horror.

"They put a blindfold on me, basically kidnapped me in the back of a van, drove me around town, and made me trick-or-treat at our friends' and family members' homes."

Various cringe faces stare back at me.

"Instead of candy, they handed out sex paraphernalia," I finish.

"That's so mean!" Cami's eyes are huge. Her grin belies the obligatory statement.

Evie waves down a server for another drink. "It was hilarious. I've never seen Caiti so many shades of red."

I shove her arm. "You try taking a finger condom from your old-ass uncle-in-law with a straight face."

"What's a finger condom?" Cami asks.

Kiersten nearly cackles. "It's for keeping his finger clean while he shoves it up your ass. Or your finger if you like to put one in him during a BJ."

"Oh." Cami's cheeks turn rosy. "Law's never needed to use one."

Apparently, we've consumed enough alcohol to venture into talking about ass play. I down a hefty swig and look away.

"Someone looks mighty uncomfortable talking about a finger in the butt." Kiersten's call out draws my attention back to the table.

"Kiersten," Evie descends with a note of caution.

I wave the tension away. "It's okay. That's a territory unexplored." Even though I was once married. I brace for the swift ache, surprised when it doesn't come.

This is new for me, finding ways to respond when my widow status is brought into the conversation. I can't avoid the truth forever, and I don't want friends walking on eggshells around me. The more I spend around these women, the stronger the desire is to have them as my circle of friends.

Evie slings her arm around my shoulder. "Another round of cocktails it is!"

"Saved from the butt. Thanks, sister." I rest my floaty head on her shoulder.

"Anything for you." She plants a sloppy kiss on my forehead.

"Aw, shit. Have we already reached sappy drunk status?" Kiersten slams her fist down, sending the table into a wobble. "I swear next time there's a wedding, someone stop me from getting knocked up so I can join in the fun." She peers into her water glass with a scowl.

Cami grips her proffered cocktail from the server. "That's impossible when your husband can't keep his hands to himself."

"I think it's time for a little sisterly payback." I extend a hand for the karaoke mic as it passes by and shove it into Evie's chest. "Up on the table, chick."

Cami covers her face with both hands. "If she falls, you're the one who gets to explain to Rhett why his fiancée has a broken neck."

"Good thing you're a paramedic." Kiersten winks and offers her hand to Evie.

"I hate all of you." She looks pointedly through the group as she rises and tugs down her dangerously short skirt.

"Any further and you'll pop out a tit." I can't believe she's going to do it.

Once balanced in the center of the table, Evie hold the mic to her mouth and gives a throaty, "Hey."

To all our surprise, cheers and hollers erupt in the vicinity.

"Oh fuck," Kiersten mutters. Cami bursts into a laughing

fit, doubling over in her seat. I immediately dig out my phone and hit record. There's no way she's getting out of this now that she has the attention of the entire bar.

"I'm getting married on Saturday," Evie continues, inviting another round of cheers. She swishes her white skirt around her thighs. "I have someone very special here with me tonight. Someone I haven't seen in three long years."

My phone stutters in my grip as my jaw drops. "Don't you dare!" My whisper is as hot as the whiskey shot from earlier.

"She should join me, shouldn't she?" Evie draws in the crowd. A few people even mingle near our rowdy table. A sea of faces spread far and wide.

"You're in trouble," Kiersten whispers in my ear.

"Who knew she was so comfortable in front of a microphone?" Cami slurs in amusement.

Me. Neon arrows appear overhead. I should have known. Evie's personality is large, and her confidence is even bigger. I've never known her to shy away from a dare or back down from a confrontation.

"Get up here, Caiti." Evie gestures to me with a wild hand. "I even have the perfect duet in mind." She slides her phone into the handle of the microphone to read the lyrics through the app.

"You're lucky I'm just *this* side of drunk to let you do this to me. Here, take this." I toss my still-recording phone in Cami's lap. "I need evidence for future retribution."

The beginning thumps, rattles, and tings of Marvin Gaye's "Ain't No Mountain High Enough" blare through the bar speakers. My head swirls a little from the drinks as I right myself on the table, and I cling to Evie's arm for support. From up here, I can't make out much in the shadowy sea of people.

"I'll start." Evie shakes out her red curls and croons the

lyrics as if she's the contestant fighting for a million-dollar prize.

"Dayyyyum!" I screech, caught up in the moment. Her confidence sucks me right in, so I don't hold back when the microphone passes near my face.

The two of us shimmy and sway through the song, our laughter mingling with the lyrics. During the chorus, she wraps her arm around my shoulders. I cling to her waist as we spin in a slow dance. Kiersten narrowly saves a glass from a perilous end by my foot. The enjoyable atmosphere sweeps me so deeply into its clutches, I forget all about fear, or panic, or embarrassment.

At the close of our sloppy rendition, the room erupts into more cheers. A round of drinks appears at our table, along with a group of three attractive men.

"Can I help you down?" The one in the middle—tall with light hair and sapphire eyes—extends his hand.

Evie shoos him away with a flailing limb. "Sorry, hunk. We're all taken."

"I'm still officially single last time I checked." I flutter my eyelashes one too many times to remain cute.

"Honey, I love you to death, but if Dane hears you say that, you'll be in trouble with a capital T."

"Trouble with a capital T sounds like fun." I giggle.

"What do you say?" The guy remains hopeful, and bless him that I don't have Evie's confidence to immediately say no. He doesn't know I intend to as soon as I get off this table with all my bones intact.

"She's with me."

I must be drunker than I thought because I could swear that voice belongs to Dane. His calm declaration instantly puts me at ease.

"Baby Daddy!" I shout.

Before I find my bearings, a pair of hands settle on my

waist and hoist me over the edge. Strong arms secure me to a broad chest, lowering me down a concrete torso until I feel the floor beneath my own two feet.

I squint one eye to peer into his handsome face and hook my thumbs into his belt loops. "Where did you come from?"

The quirk of his lips sends flutters to my abdomen. Rather than answer, he glides his fingers into the damp hair at the base of my neck, and without warning, he dips me. He follows me down, stealing my lips in a combustible kiss. I secure my flailing arms tight around his head while he devours my mouth, slipping his tongue in deep to taste the cheap vodka and sweet cocktails I've been drinking all night. After what has to be nearing a minute-long makeout sesh, he returns us to standing.

"What was that for?" I ask through the twirling in my head.

"I had to let them know you're taken."

The flutters in my stomach full-on flip flop. "Oh."

He brushes the corner of my lip with his thumb. "Any objections?"

"Not tonight at least."

"We'll work on that." He slides my hair away from my face. "Are you party animals ready to go?"

"This one is." A tall man stands protectively beside Cami. She gazes up at him adoringly and leans into his side.

"Whoa," I mutter, tipping my head to find his handsome face. "You're Cami's?"

He appears to bite back a smile. "I'm hers. You can call me Law. It's nice to meet you, Caiti."

"Remind me again on Saturday because there's a good chance I'll forget meeting you before then."

"You got it," Law replies.

"Rosie, if you don't get off that table, so help me God," Rhett growls, materializing from beyond our little circle.

"Hey, future hubby." Evie finger waves, a sassy smile firmly in place as she hops down.

"You look too damn good to be giving away my goods for free." Rhett hooks her around the waist and tugs her in close until their foreheads touch. I can just hear his question over the next singer belting out "Wannabe" from the Spice Girls. "You happy, baby?"

"Is Tommy still with Nathan's mom?" she asks a question of her own.

"He is," Rhett confirms, brushing his thumb along the column of her throat.

"Then I'll be happier when I'm home."

Rhett throws a hand in the air and tucks Evie close. "We're outtie."

"See you babes Saturday! Don't be late," Evie calls over her shoulder and allows Rhett to escort her safely from the bar.

"Us too," Law rumbles. "Can you walk, or should I carry you?"

Cami leans heavily into his side. "I'm good," she says through a yawn.

Kiersten hands a black envelope and pen to the server. "I'm good to go. I just need to drop the room keys at the desk to check out."

"We'll follow you home," Dane says. He finds my hand and entwines our fingers.

"Psh. I can find my own way," Kiersten argues.

"You're into your second trimester, it's a forty-mile drive, and you've been wrangling this wild bunch all night. It's after midnight. I'm making sure you get home safe."

Kiersten clasps Dane's bicep and passes by. "You're a good friend."

With the knowledge of everything he's told me, he's way more than a good friend. He's honorable and dedicated.

"Your people are lucky to have you." My voice slurs, and I totter on my heels.

"Mama, I just watched you dance on a table, and you suddenly can't walk two feet?" Dane's voice shakes.

"I'm tired," I snap without any heat.

"Not a problem." Before I can ask, gravity shifts. He lifts me up and over his shoulder.

"You're going to drop me!"

"Never."

The fabric of his tee stretches beneath my grabby hands. I curl my fingers around the waistband of his jeans. "Dane!"

A palm lands sharply on my ass. "Just relax."

Liquid heat pools in my lower abdomen. "I can't when your hand is that close." I wiggle from my perch over his shoulder.

He slips beneath the hem of my skirt and brushes his fingers over my center. I suck in a sharp gasp when he inadvertently directs pressure over my clit.

"Fuck, you're wet, Mama." He turns his head to murmur.

Recklessness infiltrates any remaining sensibilities. Or maybe it's the alcohol that has me throwing caution out the moment we step out of the bar. I slap his ass. "Speed it up."

Dane throws open the passenger door to his truck and flips me over his shoulder to land directly on the seat. He quirks an eyebrow. "Eager for something?"

"Just the long drive back," I emphasize the word long.

He grabs the buckle and leans across my body as he tugs it over me. The *click* is loud in the quiet truck. His eyes drop to my lips. We're so close I can feel the warm waft of his cinnamon breath.

"Let's get you home."

As soon as the door slams behind him, I lift my hips. My fingers work around the strings of my thong. I watch him move through the windshield as I shimmy my hips and tug the damp material from my body.

Dane speaks briefly to Kiersten. With a drunken flourish, I hang my panties from his rearview mirror before tucking myself into a ball on the seat, pleased with myself.

There's plenty of time for regrets in the morning after. Though, I know there won't be any.

A slight breeze intrudes the cab as Dane hops in. He throws the truck into reverse, backs from the spot, and positions himself behind Kiersten's car. I wait nervously for his discovery.

"Is this a confession for how wet you are or an invitation to see for myself?" The growled words give life to tingles.

"See for yourself." I open my legs wide and hike up my skirt.

"Fuck," he bites out, fighting to keep his attention on the white lines. His large palm settles on my thigh. "Is this okay?"

"Not quite," I purr and crook my knee against the door.

"Can I touch your pretty pussy?"

My head lolls back against the seat. The heat his question invokes nearly has me driving my own fingers between my legs. "Please."

He strokes his fingers deftly through the swollen folds. "I can smell how wet you are is. Is this for me?"

My affirmation transforms to a cry as he purposefully drives two fingers inside. My eyes slam shut, and my mouth falls open at the magnificent intrusion.

"That's it, Mama. I want to hear you."

I grip his wrist with both hands, not sure through my drunken haze if I'm trying to push him deeper or keep him from retreat. Either way, I want him to stay buried. He curls his fingers deep, brushing my G-spot with expert ease. I nearly convulse through the surge of pleasure. "Don't stop."

"Are you going to come all over my fingers?"

"Yes," I gasp, pumping my hips to ride his hand. Chasing my release.

His fingers tighten their grip around the wheel. "Fuck. Get there," he orders.

"Okay," I moan. His thumb brushes over my clit, sending me spiraling into a pit of pleasure.

"That's right, Mama. So beautiful," he praises while staying buried deep inside. The rhythm of his fingers slowly eases to still.

I'm spent after that. The effort it takes to roll my head to see his face nearly knocks me out. I watch his handsome features bathed in the yellow glow of streetlights as he swipes his tongue along his lower lip, his arousal evident. He slips his fingers from between my legs and pops them both into his mouth. His contented look emboldens me not to feel ashamed for taking what I want.

20

Dane

OPHELIA CHATTERS happily from her car seat in the back of my truck. The two of us have a very special impromptu outing planned this morning, and I'd be lying if I didn't acknowledge the nerves residing in my gut. My fingers remain crossed that today happens to be a good day because I'm bringing her to meet her grandma for the first time. I hope we can have a repeat experience.

Caiti ducked out earlier than usual with her laptop in tow, muttering something about an errand and working remotely from the coffee shop. The damn truth of it is she's hardly looked in my direction since she woke in bed with me this morning. It could be the hangover or something unrelated. Rather than putz around and try to decipher the secrets of a woman in a bad mood, I made an executive decision for our day. Ophelia and I will have our adventure, and once Caiti is back, hopefully in a clearer headspace, we can sit down and talk.

If she doesn't want talk, maybe she's interested in other things to relieve some extra tension. Her taste from last night still lingers on my tongue.

I park near the front of the lot at The Legendary since little legs accompany me today.

"We here?"

"We're here, princess. Hold on, and I'll let you out."

A cloudless blue sky looks down on us today. Sunbeams penetrate my black tee and heat the skin beneath. Once her little hand is secure in mine, we venture toward the front door, Ophelia skipping every third step.

"Hey, Nikki," I raise my sunglasses and greet the woman in scrubs at the front desk.

"Hey, Dane. She's on the patio with a volunteer today. Who's this cutie?" Nikki crouches down to toddler level.

"I'm Ofee'ya."

"It's nice to meet you, Ophelia." The two exchange a stinging high five.

"Got any suckers?"

"Ophelia," I admonish and wiggle her hand.

"I don't have any suckers, but if dad says it's okay, it's cookie day in the cafeteria." Nikki winks at me.

"Thanks, Nik."

Ophelia skips at my side to keep up. "I have cookie?"

"After we meet grandma, we'll have a cookie on the way back."

The sun's brightness highlights the beautiful day against the dim lighting inside. The pond shimmers a deep blue in the distance, a trio of ducks floating happily along the surface. Green manicured lawns welcome a relaxing stroll with a loved one. I knock my sunglasses back over my eyes in preparation of the blinding light once I slide open the back door. Ophelia shields her eyes with her forearm.

"Sorry, princess. We need to buy you a hat."

"A pink one." She tilts her head back. I bite back a laugh at her scrunched face, curled lips, and wrinkled nose. I halt our progress to give her my glasses, but before I can, she runs off.

"Momma, we meet Grandma and have cookies!"

I ram my glasses back on, blocking the sun to scan the occupied seats. Sure as shit, right on the end of the row, Caiti sits in an Adirondack chair, holding my mother's hand. The sweet sight hits me square in the chest. I've never had visions of introducing Ma to the woman I love, but here I am with a two-for-one-special. I can only hope the afternoon progresses smoothly.

"You do?" Caiti eyes me warily, a hint of guilt easily readable. Guilty for what? On my slow approach, she fills me in. "I swear I didn't know this is your mother. I've been volunteering here." Her voice remains uninteresting to little ears.

"Uh-huh. We get dem after." Ophelia turns to Ma in her wheelchair. Her pudgy fists smack Ma's knees. "Who're you?"

A wide smile splits Ma's face. "Corinne," she replies in a deep Southern accent.

"I'm Ofee'ya."

"Very nice to meet you," Ma says.

Ophelia tips her head my direction. "Dis grandma?"

"Yes, this is your grandma." Rigid muscles hold me captive while I await Ma's reaction.

"You my grandma." Ophelia points at Ma, who releases a joyful laugh.

"Am I?" The elation on her face pulverizes any remaining reservations for me. Caiti will never understand how grateful I am for this gift she's given. "I don't remember."

"Yeah, Ma. Ophelia's your granddaughter." The confirmation sticks in my throat.

Ma caresses one of Ophelia's springy locks. "You're a pretty girl."

"I sit wif you?" The big wheels capture her attention. I'm

sure she'll ask for a ride next, and I'll be happily tasked with pushing them along the concrete walking path.

"Oh, sure." Ma starts to struggle as if to make room.

"Hang on. I'll help."

Before I can stride forward, Caiti lifts Ophelia gently onto Ma's lap. "Sit nice, Ophelia."

Ophelia sits straight and grips the armrest with pride, the co-captain of her own ship. "Okay."

Caiti drifts near where I stand a few steps away, but not before I notice her swipe her cheek with her hand.

"Hey." I catch her arm. "What's wrong."

"It's nothing."

"Your tears are never nothing to me." I trace down her still damp cheek, noting the red rims. "Tell me."

"Not here." She avoids looking at me.

Fighting not to appear deflated, I speculate, "You regret last night." I wonder if I'll ever enjoy sex with her and not have her flee in regret the next morning before I banish the thought.

"This is moving a little fast, isn't it?"

"Not for me." A magnetic appeal inches me closer. "It feels as if I've waited a lifetime for you to appear without even knowing I was waiting for you."

Her breath catches, and she glances away. The breeze carries off her quiet sniff. "This morning..." Her voice is thick and clogged. "This morning, my phone sent me a memory of a collection of photos. I bought this phone as a fresh start two years ago, but I guess somehow a photo of Eric snuck through. I wasn't expecting to see it."

Especially not after sleeping in my arms. The unspoken part falls from her silent lips. The ache I feel for her loss threatens my ability to remain in my place. I want nothing more than to sweep her in my arms and hold her for eternity. "What do you need me to do?"

"It'll pass," she murmurs, keeping her voice low, I assume for Ophelia. "It's simply a reminder, like when I think of his birthdate or our anniversary. The pain isn't as fresh now. Still hurts, but I know I'll survive."

"Do you regret last night?"

Her dark eyes hold me captive. "I regret nothing with you, Dane. I just need more time."

"I'm not going anywhere." I hold my hands out to the sides. The truth is, I'm no longer certain what a future looks like without her. Not just as a co-parent. Despite my idle threat, I'd never remove Ophelia from her mother. I'd drop to my goddamned knees, kiss the ground she walks on, and beg her to stay, but I could never tear them apart. My own happiness goes long before either one of theirs.

But when I look at Caiti, I see meadows of fragrant flowers and quiet fishing on a sluggish stream. I picture more kisses under stoplights at twilight and walking Ophelia to the bus at sunrise. Slow mornings of lazy love-making followed by raspberry pancakes for family breakfasts. And at night, when the house is quiet, I dream of worshipping her delectable body and making her come.

The option to walk away evaporated the minute she showed up at my door with our toddler and pressed herself into my body for reassurance. We still have a lot to learn about one another, but she's everything I never knew I was missing wrapped in a pretty, sexy bow.

The rest is up to her. Because no matter how badly I want her, how much I crave the promise our future holds, I can never compete with the memory of her dead husband.

"It's okay to miss him." I fill the silence. "It's okay to miss him even while falling in love with me."

"I don't know how to fall in love anymore."

"That's how it happens. Little by little until you realize you're already halfway there. Then the rest is easy."

"You sound as if you speak from experience."

I capture her chin between my index finger and thumb, not permitting her to dodge my expression when I confirm. "I do."

She briefly nods but flits her attention away. I give her the temporary space. "They seem to be hitting it off," she remarks.

"It won't always be this easy. There will be many days Ma won't remember Ophelia or you. Heck, some days, she doesn't even remember me. And she can get upset."

"I understand. My grandma had a form of Dementia, so I'm a little familiar. Though I'm sure it's worse for you, being that she's your mom."

I run a hand over my hair. "She has early onset. I was only twenty when she started to notice the signs and saw her doctor. She actually ran her own therapy practice in the loft before I lived there. I moved in when we decided this was the safest place for her. It made me feel closer to her on the days I couldn't visit for long."

Her gentle touch seeps into my bicep. "I'm so sorry."

"This is part of why I didn't want kids," I confess. "It runs in families, and the thought of burdening a wife or a child when I'm no longer with it…" Fuck. Just speaking the fear into existence sends a spike of apprehension through me. What am I doing? Maybe I shouldn't be perusing her. Their distance might be the best thing for all of us. Except it's too late where my heart is concerned.

"You don't know that this will happen to you."

"You're right. And I don't think I have a choice anymore." I watch Ophelia babbling happily to Ma, who wears a matching smile. "It's not a strong enough reason to let you two go."

21

Caiti

"Come on, sweets. We're going to be late."

Ophelia swishes her puffy white dress at my side, waiting for me to lock up the car. "Wanna race?" Hopeful eyes full of unconditional love stare up at me.

"Okay, but you have to hold my hand so you don't trip and tear your dress."

Her little hand settles on her hip. "I be careful," she says in a deadly serious voice.

I will my racing heart to slow. The anxiety bubbles up from time to time, but nowhere near the daily occurrence from when I first arrived. I only hope it remains in check while I sort through the next steps.

"Ready...three...two...one!"

She races across the blacktop, leaving me in her puny dust. I trail at a moderate jog. Exertion isn't on the maid-of-honor checklist, and the rules say I have to let her beat me. I also refuse to sit for another half an hour while someone remedies my windblown curls.

"You're too fast!" I call, thankful she made it to the sidewalk in one piece.

"I win!"

"Let's get inside and see Auntie Evie in her pretty dress."

Ophelia dances at my side. "I tell Aut Ebie I win."

"You sure can."

We enter the small non-denominational church. A short entry hall separates us from the aisle and rows of pews Evie will walk down to her happily-ever-after. Tears begin to gather in the corners of my eyes at the stunning image in my head. Happiness bubbles inside me. I hope I can keep it together through the short ceremony. Nobody wants to be the blubbering mess in all the pictures. With what I have planned, it'll be a miracle if I escape unscathed.

Girlish giggles alert me to our destination. With a sharp rap on the wooden door, Ophelia and I enter into a tulle and lace explosion.

Hot tools line the windowsill next to Evie. Cami works through her thick locks, curling sections and pinning pieces in a half up-do, while Evelyn wields a fat powder brush on Evie's face. Three pizza boxes lay messily across a white folding table in the center of the room where Kiersten has taken up residence.

"We've finally made it," I sing upon entry. They smile and wave in greeting.

"Come have lunch, Ophelia. Are you ready for your big job today?" The blonde commands control of my wild toddler so easily. The pizza bribery definitely helps.

"I wif Tommy?"

We've been practicing down a pretend aisle in our kitchen all week. As long as she doesn't have a sudden case of shyness, she'll nail her task.

"Yes. He'll be here soon, and you can practice."

Ophelia climbs onto a metal folding chair, her diapered butt and ruffle high in the air. "I love Tommy. I marry him when I big."

"Awe, I can't wait to tell Rhett," Evie sighs.

"You can't marry Tommy, baby. He's your cousin," I respond. As if she has any understanding of what that means.

"Not by blood." Kiersten pins a white bow on the side of Ophelia's hair.

"Close enough," I mutter.

I fix Ophelia a small plate but pass on my own attempt at lunch. I'm too nervous to eat. My stomach simmers in anticipation of what's to come. In an attempt at distraction, I find my dress hanging on a rack in the corner and swiftly change, discarding my clothing in a duffel bag.

"Is it just me or is this shorter than I remember?" I tug at the hemline, eyeing the thigh slit with unease.

Kiersten smacks my hand away. "You're going to rip it if you're not careful. It looks great. You're beautiful." She moves to discard her empty plate in the trash.

"Can we get a little assistance here?" Cami calls across the room. She unzips the huge black bag encasing Evie's gown.

"I'm on it." I hold up one side while Cami takes the other. Together, we remove the dress from the hanger and hold it open for Evie to step into.

"Thank God we don't have to lift this over your hair. This thing weighs a ton," Cami teases. I hold the back sections together, and she zips Evie inside. The material molds effortlessly to each of her plus-sized curves, proof the tailor did a terrific job. Evie's not once worried about her weight, but last week she began to doubt the fit of her dress to the point she wanted to try it on daily just to make sure it still fit.

"Be thankful you don't have to wear it. At least it's not as heavy as the full ball gown I originally tried on before I found this. The damn thing was gorgeous, but I wouldn't have survived the reception." Evie tucks herself in on top.

"You're absolutely stunning," I breathe, the lock on my emotions already slipping.

"Don't you start that." Cami shoves a tissue in my hand. "We don't have time to fix all our makeup, and if you start, then Evie will start, and Kiersten's hormones will be unleashed to their full effect, and then I'm screwed cleaning up the mess."

"Got it. I'm good." I snatch the tissue and wave them off.

"Momma, I all done." Ophelia shoves her plate away, red sauce evident on her face. "I pway wif Tommy?"

"I'll take her," Evelyn volunteers and scoops Ophelia into her arms. Delighted squeals ring around the room. I wipe the little girl's face with the tissue in my hand and bid them goodbye.

Two down, two to go.

"Are the flowers here?" I ask the room. I may be the maid of honor in name, but the other girls were kind enough to distribute my duties. Although the distraction would have been nice, there's simply been too much on my plate with this extended visit and a strained workload.

"They're here." Kiersten answers while clearing away empty pizza boxes.

I lower my shoulders from my ears and release a deep breath. "If you two are ready, do you mind giving us a minute alone?"

"Sure." Cami fixes a soft smile in place and pats my forearm as she passes. "Gives us an excuse to spy on our men."

"Nathan wears just about anything well, but seeing him in a suit?" Kiersten fakes a groan. "He's downright yummy."

My nose scrunches. "Thank you. It'll just be a minute."

The door closes softly behind them.

"Not going to lie, when I pictured having a minute alone before my wedding, it wasn't you standing in the room." Her attempt to lighten the mood falls slightly short at the concern marring her brow. "What's going on?"

I move close and take both her hands in mine, steeling myself with a cleansing breath. "I don't want to draw this out and send us both down the aisle a blubbering mess."

Her gaze flits between my eyes. "Okay?"

"Eric should be here with you. I know he was supposed to be the one walking you down the aisle someday, and I know you're strong enough to walk alone." I fiddle with the clasp around my neck. "This doesn't even come close, but I want you to have this."

She gasps, her palm flying to cover her mouth as tears glisten in her eyes. "Caiti…no. I can't," she chokes out.

I pull her hand from her mouth and wrap her fingers around the vial of Eric's ashes. "You need to. This belongs to you more than me."

She moves her attention between the vial and me. "What does this mean?"

Every cell in my body fights to hold back the wave of tears. "It means I'm letting him go."

"Caiti…" Heartbreak scores across her face.

"No. We aren't doing this on your wedding day. I just wanted him to be with you. Not some flower stuck in your bouquet as a memorial. Tangibly, he's here with you."

She's quiet for a moment. The words sink in deep between us. "You know, when I told Rhett about my parents' death, I struggled too. One of the biggest reasons I didn't want to live in Germany with you and Eric is because it felt like leaving them behind. Do you know what he said?"

My lips remain sealed, and I shake my head.

"He reminded me I carry them everywhere inside me. That it's impossible to leave them behind. Eric's there too. So if you need this…" She shakes her fist with the vial clenched inside.

"It belongs with you." I hold my voice firm.

"Do you love him?"

It takes a moment to realize she's no longer talking about Eric. Guilt forces me to glance away. "Isn't it too fast?"

"I'm only going to be sappy because it's my wedding day, but your heart will tell you exactly what it wants. You just have to be willing to listen."

"My heart was once promised to someone else. I don't know how to move past that."

"You don't force it." Evie grips my shoulders, the vial pressing into my skin. "You passively accept whatever happens, and when you're ready, *if* you're ready, you'll know."

"I think I know," I answer hoarsely.

"Then you should know not to let that go. I knew my brother pretty well. We'd been through a lot together. I can state with confidence that he wouldn't want you to be alone."

"I love you, Evie. You'll always be my sister." I dash away a stray tear with the back of my hand. She jerks me into an impossibly tight hug.

"I love you too. Thank you for this gift. Help me put it on?"

"You want to wear it?" The gold chain doesn't necessarily go with her dress.

"Of course." She presents her back and waits.

I loop the two ends around her neck. "You know, I almost dumped him over the cliff on the hiking trail you brought us to. It felt romantic at the time, but I'm really glad I didn't."

A watery laugh bursts from Evie. "That was a good day," she sighs. She and Eric bickered the entire hike about how she should come home with us and stop stubbornly living out of her car. Obviously, Evie won the argument.

The clasp hooks into place. She spins around, holding a hand to the vial centered on her chest.

"Are you ready to get married?" I hand her a simple bouquet of pink roses. Three are orange to represent her parents and Eric.

"I'm ready to run down that aisle and march straight off to our honeymoon. Unfortunately, our guests would be disappointed, and we aren't actually leaving for another month."

We link our arms.

"Let's start with step one. You put enough money into this to at least see through the ceremony."

The rest of our wedding party mingles in the foyer when I poke my head out. Evie remains in the room, wanting to keep her appearance a surprise until the very last second. The pairs queue up. Evelyn heads the precession as a junior attendant, walking beside Evie's blind and deaf pit bull, Ghost. Behind her is Kiersten paired with Cami's husband Law, followed by Cami and Dane. Nathan stands beside him chatting away. As the best man, he'll be my partner down the aisle. Ophelia and Tommy sit with their heads bent together on the floor in the very back.

I linger a little too long over the image of Dane in a suit. The man looks hot in a pair of jeans and a tee but cleaned up...*my god*. The tailored fit showcases his muscular stature. The rounded glutes and lean quads. The white shirt tucks into a trim waist hidden by an opened coat. Someone should tell him to button up before the precession starts because if I have to go over there, I'll have a hell of a time not convincing him to just take it all off.

The music trickles in quietly at first. Conversation beyond the church doors gradually ceases. Evelyn begins a slow march down the aisle, kicking off the event.

"It's starting," I whisper to Evie. The rapid thump in my

chest urges me to practice deep breaths. If I have an attack right now, I'll be mortified. My anxiety has been increasingly better as I put in the effort to practice strategies for calming myself and fighting the fear. Still, I'm definitely not out of the woods yet.

I push the breaths into my belly as I work on loosening my neck, shoulders, and chest. The tense muscles contribute to the sensation I'm short of breath, but it's a lie. The next pair moves down the line.

"Are you ready?" I ask my sister to distract me from my inward thoughts and feelings.

"I'm ready." She rests her chin on my shoulder and peeks out the door with me.

Cami and Dane are next. I reach down to my side and find her hand. "Love you."

"Love you too." She squeezes me back. "I'm so glad you're here."

"Let's get you married."

With only Nathan and the kiddos left, we finally emerge from the room. His face splits into a massive grin upon seeing his best friend's fiancée.

"You're gorgeous, Evie. Rhett's so going to cry, and I'm going to win the bet." He links arms with me.

"You bet on whether my husband will cry when he sees me for the first time?" Evie attempts a stern face but fails. "Why wasn't I allowed in on this?"

"That just wouldn't be fair."

Her retort is lost as we begin our unhurried trek. About fifty guests witness our advance, various smiles in place. Cameras aim from all directions, sending my heart racing again.

"Nathan." I stutter a step, anxiety stealing rational thought in an instant.

"Look up, honey. Don't think about anything else."

Confusion wrinkles my brow, but I follow his suggestion. My heart gives a hard thump, mimicking a dead stop. Dane stands at the end of the aisle, one space beside the groom. He has his hands cupped in front of his waist, and his awed expression steals my entire breath.

He rocks back and forth on his heels, an intense energy emanating from him while a classical wedding melody floats around us. His stormy gray eye contact nearly roots me to the damn spot. Only Nathan's measured steps keep me moving steadily down our path. The urge to run down the aisle erupts even though this isn't my wedding. A piece of me longs for the comfort of his embrace.

As we near the end, Dane flashes a half smirk and a wink, almost like he can read the uneasy sensations soaring through me. Luckily, I don't have enough time to dwell. Tommy and Ophelia skip down the aisle, stealing hearts and laughing along the way. Then the music changes. Guests rise in unison and turn toward the back to wait for Evie to appear.

The room expresses a collective gasp. She floats down the aisle, her mermaid skirt swishing around her knees with each leisurely step. The smile gracing her face is pure radiance. I take my eyes off her, intending to check the status of the men's bet. Rhett's tears only capture my attention for a second before my gaze finds *him*.

He watches me unabashedly in a room full of people, their full attention is on the bride and groom. His heated stare infiltrates the cracks exposed in my healing heart. The organ jumps as if it's trying to flee straight to him. Tension ignites as he traces down my body like I'm a present waiting to be unwrapped. The large bow at my side certainly adds to the impression.

I subtly shake my head to scold the tempting man. He's distracting me from my maid-of-honorly duties. Ignoring him proves challenging as I watch my sister take the final steps to her forever man.

Rhett dries a solid tear with his shoulder before cradling Evie's face in his hands. Without preamble, he takes her lips in a swift kiss.

"If you can hold on for just fifteen minutes, I'll let you know when it's time for that part," the minister jovially reprimands. The guests chuckle along with him.

"I just couldn't wait." Rhett brushes his thumb across Evie's lips to fix her smudged lipstick.

"That's okay," she breathes with stars in her eyes. These two are damn near perfect for each other.

22

Dane

GODDAMN. *Goddamn.*

Dress pants do fuck-all to hide a hard-on. The moment I saw Caiti appear at the end of the aisle, my dick turned to stone. The slit on the side of her dress rode her thigh with each step. I know I'm not the only man in the place who noticed. Though it has nothing on the little plunge on her neckline between her breasts.

Standing in front of the church, a place of holy worship, does nothing to curb my indecent thoughts. Anyone recording the ceremony won't miss the constant glances Caiti and I share behind the happy couples back. I'm pretty sure Nathan's going to develop a crick in his neck for the number of times he's looked at me over his shoulder.

If he's checking to see if I noticed her, the answer is a resounding *fuck yes*. I noticed. He acts as if he hasn't been sneaking glances at Kiersten's ass this entire time.

Caiti's heated stare acts as a magnet. What feels like an

hour later, the minister finally pronounces our friends as married. With a rowdy applause, the two seal their status as Mr. and Mrs. Senova. Rhett dips Evie low in a deep, fervent kiss. A bolt of jealousy strikes fast, nearly bringing me to my knees. I'm happy for my friends. Ecstatic even. But the knowledge does nothing to ease the sudden pang for something I never thought I wanted.

I'll take her however I can. The sacrifice would be worth it.

The happy couple marches down the aisle, arms linked together. When they near the end, Caiti sends Ophelia and Tommy. Nathan's mom, Regina, waits near the back of the church to gather the remaining little ones, her arms already full with Kiersten and Nathan's two sandy-haired boys. She and her two friends volunteered for babysitting duty, so we pitched in to rent them a hotel room. Which means I'll have Caiti all to myself this evening.

Caiti delivers a sultry glance my way as she meets up with Nathan. The lust-filled look sends possession through my veins. We've been dancing on a perilous edge. Maybe it's desire or a correct interpretation, but I can almost assume her thoughts are on the same page.

"You're going to miss your cue," Cami mumbles and hooks my arm with her elbow.

"Sorry." I can't stop the grin stealing over my face.

"Uh-huh. You two are smitten."

"Who uses the word smitten?"

"I guess I do." Cami hangs on my arm until we part ways at the end. She pats me on the chest. "See you at the reception."

The reception is in a local hotel ballroom just across town. Evie and Rhett are off to take couple's photos. With Ophelia taken care of and dinner over an hour away, I have some time to kill.

I weave through mingling guests, offering a wave at acquaintances and friends as people are ushered to make their way to the reception. I duck into the groom's room to gather my bags. The place is oddly empty. Seems I'm lagging behind the rest. The couples have already paired off to begin the festivities. If only a certain someone would come around to the idea of us, I might not be feeling peculiarly left behind.

With the blue duffel slung over my shoulder, I drag open the wooden door, intent on finding her. Before I can get a foot over the threshold, a palm hits solidly in the center of my chest and shoves me back in. The door bangs shut behind us, the telltale *snick* of the lock not far behind.

Dark eyes burn into mine. Caiti's arm remains behind her back on the knob as if she's entertaining second thoughts. Rather than approach, I hold steady, excited to see how this plays out.

Reaching forward, her fingers curl around my tie and yank me off balance. I crash into her, my palms slapping the door on either side of her head in order not to crush her slender body beneath mine. Her tits smash beautifully against my chest as she tugs me lower to bring our mouths together.

Tender licks stoke a fire burning in my blood. Her kiss is fire and passion rolled into one. She releases my head to shove at the jacket on my shoulders without a word. The heavy material easily slips down. I drop my arms behind me to shirk it off, where it falls silently to the floor. She moves to the buttons on my shirt next.

With enough foresight not to yank and send the buttons flying, my fingers join hers in a race to get them undone. She abandons the mission. A tickle clenches my lower abdomen as she finds the material tucked into my slacks and rips it loose. Nimble fingers skim over the bare skin, over the contours and dips, and around my back. I finally pop the last button open and shrug the shirt off to join the jacket before ripping my simple white tee over my head, pausing only a second before diving back into her delectable mouth.

Caiti moves down to my belt, button, then zipper of my slacks. She hastily frees the material, and as she shoves everything down my hips, she wrenches from my kiss and falls to her knees on the aged carpet.

"Caiti." A guttural groan chases her name as she wraps puffy lips around my aching cock. One palm remains on the door for balance while I thread the other carefully through her styled locks to hold the back of her head. She works me eagerly, her head bobbing a rapid rhythm. I fight between watching her and closing my eyes as her lips slide expertly up and down my shaft.

"Fuck, Mama. Just like that. *God*," I pant. "You suck me so, so good, baby. You know just what I like." She nearly has me begging for mercy in the first two minutes. My balls tighten, and I grow impossibly hard as more blood rushes south.

"Hold on," I growl, not ready to come, and hook her beneath the armpits. She releases me with a gasp as I lift her and pin her against the door on tiptoe. My knee slips between her thighs. "Hike up your dress, beautiful. Show me your pussy."

"I wasn't done," she gripes, her hands digging into the material just beneath her hips. With a sharp tug, she reveals the hidden trove between her thighs.

"Where're your panties?"

"They slipped off somewhere." With a finger beneath my chin, she directs my mouth back to hers in a scorching kiss, conveying exactly what dirty things she has in mind.

I drive my knee between her legs, resting her bare pussy right on my thigh. "I want you to use me to get off," I mumble against her sinful mouth. My bare skin feels everything beneath her. The pressure she uses, the wet warmth as she grinds herself down. "That's it, Mama."

Her moans transform into high-pitched sighs the closer she gets. Fingertips curl into my biceps with bruising force. With a sudden jerk, she rides out her pleasure, her liquid coating my leg as she shatters in my arms.

I pin her to the door and drop to my knees without giving her time to recover. The scent of her orgasm permeates the small room, and I'm dying for a taste. Hooking an arm around her back, I drag her pussy to my mouth, throw one leg over my shoulder, and feast on her sweet pleasure.

"Ah, Dane!" she cries, shoving her hips against my tongue.

I nip her inner thigh. "Shh. We're in a church." I steal her retort with a flick of my tongue against her swollen clit.

"I need to come again," she pleads in a breathy whisper.

I suck the peaking nub into my mouth and twirl it with my tongue. "Beg me," I answer wickedly, bringing her close to the edge.

"Please."

The easy out isn't enough. I slow the speed of my tongue into gentle strokes.

"Dane, please make me come."

She's earned light flicks, but I know she can do better. The memory of her screaming in my bed so long ago lingers as proof.

She threads her fingers through the hair at the back of my head, shamelessly fucking my face. "Lick me, please. I need you to make me come."

"So beautiful," I croon, diving in to finish the task. Her filthy words have precum leaking from my tip, so I fist myself in preparation to drive home between her sexy, lean legs. Right as she reaches the peak, I surge upward, catching her thigh on my hip and burying myself deep.

A scream startles from her, and I swallow the noise with my mouth.

Knowing it's only a matter of time until we're discovered, I hammer into her against the wooden door. Her forehead rests on my shoulder, the sweat dampening my skin. I cradle the back of her neck with one hand and use the other around her waist to lift her up and down my steel cock, impaling her deeply with each solid thrust.

"I'm going to come inside you," I groan into her hair. Just as the first twitch signals my orgasm, I bury my face into her neck. "Fuck, you feel so good. I'm going to fill you up."

She mewls and writhes in my hold, chasing a third orgasm as her pussy squeezes my cock.

For several long breaths, I just hold her as we come down, neither of us bothering to move yet.

"I think I'm dead," she mutters into my neck.

"Me too."

She slowly lifts her head, her hair a wavy mess, and I catch her grin. "Thank you."

I help her lower her feet back to the ground. "I should be thanking you."

A chill sends goose bumps over my skin. I realize all she has to do is hike her skirt back down while I'm still fully nude. I tag my shirt from the floor.

"A mutual thanks, I guess," she teases.

"I don't know how I'm supposed to see you in that dress for the rest of the evening and not want to do this all over again."

Caiti bites her lip and nods as her gaze rakes down my body, pausing at my still-hard cock.

"Caiti." Her name is a warning. "If you keep looking at it like that, we'll never make it to the reception."

"You're right." She holds her palms up and backs toward the door.

"Find some damn panties," I growl. "Before someone sees my come running down your legs." The thought fills me with possessive heat.

"I'll meet you there."

Then she's quietly slipping back out the same way she entered.

23

Caiti

THE LATE SUMMER air shuttles a warm breeze across my neck. Even as evening settles, I still feel the heat of the sun. My feet carry me lazily through a quiet neighborhood a few blocks from Main Street as I walk for my mental health. I started with a new therapist today, and she suggested daily walks might help with the lingering anxiety. Since living here and having Dane to watch Ophelia, I have more time to focus on myself. Self-care and all that, except I'm not into bubble baths.

Our first meeting was virtual and only introductory, but I like her. She gives me total April Ludgate vibes from the show *Parks and Recreation*. Her sarcasm and advice make me feel like I'm gabbing with a girlfriend and not being psycho-analyzed on a therapist's couch. Even though I technically am.

I hate to admit it, but the fresh air has cleared some cobwebs in my head. Decisions come without examining all possible tangents, and since the wedding, I feel settled. Arrow Creek is full of all the things I've been missing. Most importantly, this is where Dane is. But the friendships are an added bonus I don't take lightly.

Colorado was once my home, but it won't be for much longer.

The thought adds a skip in my step. The time feels right to rush home and tell Dane. We've become so close in such a short period. His comforting presence is more than I could have ever asked for when I showed up just over a month ago. I smile at the old arguments I'd have with myself about how to convince him to hear me out. None of them came to fruition. He took the role better than I could have ever imagined.

Headlights bathe over me from behind. A spike of anxiety strikes unbidden but not unwelcome at this stage. I'm learning to live with the sensations and not add a layer of fear to the alarm bells my body rings from time to time.

The whirr of a window rolling down forces me to check over my shoulder. Relief chases away the fear at the familiar truck now moving beside me. "What are you doing here?"

"Get in." Dane taps the outside of his driver's door through the open window.

I roll my eyes, the motion concealed through the yellow streetlights. "I'm almost home. You didn't have to come find me."

"Nobody can see you out here, Mama. If you want to walk at night, you need to wear something reflective. And bring a big dog."

My heart flutters at his concern. "We don't have a big dog."

"I'll buy one." He taps the outside of the door again. "Come on. The guys are watching Ophelia for me, and if I don't hurry, she might wrangle them all into a tea party."

The thought of Ophelia sitting down Law, Nathan, and Rhett for princess tee is an amusing one. "They might enjoy her tea more than the beer you're serving."

"If I don't rescue them, they might need to drink free on me all night, and I can't afford that."

I guess my mental health walk is over for today. The butterflies soaring in my stomach tell me that's okay. Happiness wells inside like a bubbling fountain. "Fine. But I have to be alone sometimes. My therapist said so."

"Sure. During daylight hours."

I heft myself into his big truck and throw on my seat belt before he pulls away. "What are you guys supposed to be up to tonight?"

"Late bachelor celebrations. I offered the guys a free round."

The thought of the wedding sends a clench through my core as the memories of being nailed against a church door stream through my head.

"Knock those thoughts off, Mama, or I'm going to have to call for a rain check." Dane's possessive growl does nothing to slow the dull throb between my legs.

"We aren't shrugging off your friends for sex. Not tonight anyway."

He clicks the blinker and makes the left toward home. "I also wanted to ask if you're able to watch Ophelia on Wednesday. Rhett wants to take one last canoe trip down the river this summer, and the other guys have to work."

I brush my damp palms against my knees, still fighting the delicious ache. "Uh-huh. That's fine."

The truck halts in the middle of Main Street. Dane slams the shifter into park with a growled, "Goddammit." He leans over the seat, yanks me to him, and takes my lips in a bruising kiss. His tongue flicks the seam of my lips, seeking access. I open easily and practically crawl across the middle to reach him. My hands find his hard chest, skating down his sides to reach the waistband of his jeans. Dane wrenches away with a huff.

"I can't fuck you in the middle of Main Street."

"Are you sure?" I ask sweetly. Memories of his fingers doing that exact thing in this exact seat push my taunt further.

"If you can manage not to get yourself off while I'm gone, I promise to make it worth it when I get home later."

Unconsciously, I squeeze my thighs together.

"That is if you can quit squirming in that damn seat and not force me to get you off now."

"I can't help it." I don't know if it's the three years without sex or just this man, but I mean every word of that admission.

Dane punches the gas pedal. "I used to think it was me."

"What was you?"

"For three years, I've dreamed of that night, and sometimes, I felt sick, like there was something perverted about me that I couldn't stop reliving the best lay of my life."

My throat tightens at his confession.

"I understand now it's just you. You make me unable to think of anything other than all the things I've done and could do with you."

I close my eyes tight. "It's not just you. I've thought of that night too." Guilt leaks into my voice. I know he doesn't miss it when he gently says, "Baby."

"I'd slip into the tee I stole, and I'd get off to the memory."

"You're killing me," he groans as he slides the truck into a spot at the curb outside his apartment. The shift and twist of the key fill the silence.

A man pacing on the sidewalk in front of Dane's porch attracts my attention away from the awkwardness welling inside me.

"We better get inside. The sooner I get this round of drinks over with, the sooner I can get back to take care of you." The way he says *take care* ignites filthy fantasies.

"I think that sounds good."

"Put Ophelia down early tonight," he orders.

"Agreed."

Dane gives me a heated stare, but his attention flicks over my shoulder to the man on the sidewalk. "Don't get out until I'm there."

He hops down and circles the back of the truck in order to keep his eye on the interloper. I unbuckle, ready to jump out as soon as the door creaks open. Dane threads our fingers together, me on the side farthest from the man, and he keeps me slightly behind his back.

Something about the figure looks familiar. The height, and maybe the gait. I can't shake the feeling that I've seen this person before. He glances in our direction before muttering something and retracing his steps.

"Bar entrance is that one, buddy." Dane throws his hand in the general direction, though it's not necessary. The signage and fence clearly demarcate the property from this one.

This time, when he scans us, he tugs the nondescript ballcap lower over his head, but he's not quick enough. I recognize the deep-set eyes and the shape of his jaw.

"It was you?" The incredulity in my tone echoes above the music filtering outside from the bar.

My boss, Jason, freezes as if he's contemplating running. I try to pull my hand from Dane's and advance, but he keeps it firmly in place. "How could you do that to me?"

"I just wanted to talk to you." His answer shakes, revealing him for the coward he truly is.

"So you pick up the phone and call me." Anger strikes hot

and fast. The terror he brought me over the last few months threatens to unleash. "You harassed me. You stalked me!"

Jason swipes the hat from his head and steps closer. Dane shoves me behind him with a hand to my belly. With a wide stance, he positions himself between us. "Close enough," Dane objects.

"I didn't mean any harm, I swear."

"You're sick! You're married! I've met your wife." Once I begin, I can't stop screeching into the dark night, drawing stares from customers at patio tables. I'm beyond the ability to care as I think back on all the mornings of paralyzing fear. Of all the ways he limited my life. "I couldn't even take my daughter to the fucking park in case you were watching me. Of course I didn't know it was you at the time, and that makes it a hundred times worse!"

"I think it's time you go inside." Dane tries reasoning with me.

"How did you find me?" I demand.

"I'm going to go." The coward begins to retreat.

"No!" I shove around Dane's back. He grabs me by the shoulders and pulls my back flush against his chest. "Tell me. I want to know how you tracked me down across the fucking country so you can never do it again."

"Let him go, Caiti. He won't be a problem ever again." Dane's attempt to placate me falls flat.

"You can't know that, but I do. And he's undeterred if he's willing to hop a plane and fly across the country behind his wife's back. He doesn't plan to stop harassing me." I think of the things he knew about me. The things I told him, thinking I was confiding in a friend about my fears, and I get angrier. "Do you normally find widows with children to prey on? Is that what gets your rocks off?"

"Caiti," Dane tries again. I'm not sure if he's trying to drop it or if he just wants me out of the vicinity while he beats this guy's ass, but I'm not leaving.

"He's not scared of you, Dane. He's not going to stop!"

The door to Dane's loft flies open, followed immediately by a fury-filled threat. "He'll stop."

Law stalks across the porch, blocking me from Jason with his arms crossed over his wide chest.

My heart slams against my ribs. Nathan and Rhett follow close behind, positioning themselves the same. I can no longer see Jason through the mountains of muscles surrounding me. If I've had any remaining questions about where I truly belong, they vanish in a puff of smoke.

"She's well protected here, but you're not welcome," Nathan says.

Jason slips on a rock as he moves back. "We can talk during work hours tomorrow and straighten this out."

"There's nothing to straighten out," Rhett joins in, thrusting his finger in Jason's face. "If you so much as send my sister an emoji, I'll come after your ass."

The sentiment springs tears to my eyes, but something Jason said triggers a light bulb to go off. "The laptop," I whisper to myself. I spin on a heel and dash into the apartment, hoping there isn't any blood shed before my reappearance.

Evie intercepts me at the top of the steps, her face etched with concern. "What's going on out there? Are you okay?"

"Yes. I just need to take care of one more thing." I locate my travel bag and grab the entire thing. Flipping the computer end to end, I find what I'm looking for on the bottom. "That bastard!"

Ignoring Evie's calls for me to wait, I race back down the steps and burst into the cool evening air. With steel infusing my spine, I march straight to Jason, bypassing the wall of intimidating men. I suppress the urge to bitch slap him across the face with the sleek electronic device, and instead, I push the computer into his chest. He barely gets his hand around it before Dane yanks me back into his arms.

"I quit. It isn't really company policy to have the equipment fitted with a GPS device, is it? You made that up to track me while I was working. That's how you found me here. I quit. I fucking quit! I'm not coming back to your company, and I'm not returning to Colorado. Get the fuck out of my life."

Red and blue lights flash around us as I finish my livid speech. My shoulders rise and fall so quickly that Dane places his hands on them in a bid to calm me down.

His mouth touches my ear. "Are you having a panic attack?"

I shake my head, not wanting to probe my feelings and too busy watching two officers climb out of the cruiser to respond.

"We have a report of a disturbance here."

Either Evie or the customers of Calypso's have our back, another reason for me to love this town.

The group splits up, immediately relaying the information of the past fifteen minutes to the two officers. Another cruiser shows not long after and loads Jason into the back in a pair of handcuffs.

"He shouldn't be a problem any longer." The badge across his navy uniform says Stryker. The officer reveals a dimple with his gentle smile, and his baby blues flash. "You're safe here."

"Please tell me he finally messed up." I hold my breath in wait for confirmation.

Office Stryker nods. "He should have stayed in Colorado. Crossing state lines to stalk someone is a federal crime."

"Thank you." I take the card he offers between two

fingers. Dane tucks me into his side, and Officer Stryker walks away.

I roll my shoulders to remove some of the tension residing there. "I'm sorry your night was delayed. You guys should head over to the bar."

"I'm not. I think our timing was perfect. I don't even want to consider what he was planning on doing."

"So let's not."

"Agreed." Dane places a soft peck against my lips. He strokes gently down the loose hair framing my face. "Did you mean it?"

He almost sounds nervous, and I know what he's asking even without specifying. Hope shines in his gray eyes.

"Yes." My answer floats away on the wind.

"You're staying," he confirms and grips my waist.

"It's stupid to consider any other option."

24

Dane

THE LAST THREE days have been beyond my wildest dreams. I can only hope Caiti and I continue moving in the right direction because the glimpses she's given me of a future could sate me for the rest of my lifetime. I stretch out on my bed beside the woman occupying my every waking thought, taking in the sweet scent of cherry blossoms. I press a swift kiss to her forehead before rolling off and out and moving silently to the dresser to dig out clothes for today's canoe trip. After slipping on a plain blue tee and a pair of shorts, I turn back to my sleeping beauty.

She mumbles something in her sleep and rolls over. The tee she's wearing rides up, giving me an uninhibited view of her tight ass in nothing but cotton panties.

If Rhett wasn't such a good friend, I'd skip our adventure, call in a friend to pick up Ophelia, and crawl back in beside her. Fighting the temptation to do just that, I slip quietly from the room.

The coffee pot starts to trickle so I can fill a thermos, the smell instantly perking me up. I pull out my laptop to search for airline tickets. With the situation concerning her boss finally squared away, we have new plans to accomplish. Starting with getting the rest of her stuff, putting her house on the market, and moving her fully to Arrow Creek.

Caiti doesn't know it yet, but I already have a call in with a real estate agent to find us a more suitable home. Living above my bar has had a lot of perks over the years. Namely the nonexistent commute. But it's time to move on.

Images of raising a family in a house with a yard take precedence. I'd drive fifty miles each way if that's what she wanted.

With a few clicks, I have two tickets booked for next week. I might be moving fast, but the sooner her stuff is here, the sooner we can cross our list off. If I had my way, we'd have a place and be living together officially by next week, but I understand she might need a little more time.

As long as she realizes she's not alone in this, she can have all the time she needs.

I gather the confirmation sheets from the printer in my living room and set them on the bar. She'll see them when she wakes and hopefully have enough time to sort her feelings before I return this afternoon.

I pour myself a thermos, grab the small bag I packed last night, and lock the door behind me, shutting my girls safely inside. When I emerge in the early morning sunlight, Rhett's Jeep idles at the curb.

"You look like a lovestruck schmuck." He laughs when I climb in the passenger seat.

"So you confirm you know what one looks like?"

"Touché. Welcome to the club."

I'd never admit it, but it's a club I'm happy to be a part of. "We lucked out on the weather today." The forecast predicted rain earlier in the week, but it's starting out as a cloudless day. Pale blue sky begins to overtake the peach hues.

"Wind might pick up later, but a few hours in the sun on the river is just what I need." He takes the highway out of town to the river entry about ten minutes away.

"Everything okay?" Something in his tone hints at restlessness.

He scrubs his forehead before heavily dropping his hand. "Evie's struggling, man. I'm worried trying to have a baby will throw her into another depression."

"Another?"

He nods, his voice turning serious. "When she left her ex, she explained how she spiraled. Now I'm nothing like that fucker, and I'll do everything in my power to help her, but I can't deny I'm scared."

Hearing my best friend admit he's scared slices me straight to the core. "I'm here for you. We both are. If you two need anything, you call."

"Evie told me about Caiti's panic attacks. As much as that sucks for her, I hope it makes Evie feel less alone. Even if she doesn't want to talk to me, she should talk to someone about her feelings."

"Caiti's moving here, so I'm sure she'll keep an eye on her."

Rhett flicks his attention to me for a split second before returning to the road. "I'm thrilled to hear that."

"I am too." I can't contain the flash of teeth the thought provokes.

"On a happier note, thanks for helping with Tommy for our honeymoon. If you two need us to repay the favor, just give me a call."

"You can count on it." The gong of wedding bells rings in the back of my mind. How long is an acceptable amount of time before I ask her to marry me? I don't doubt she has feelings for me, even if she's yet to admit them. They're more than evident in her actions. I'm simply waiting for her to come to terms with the fact she might love me back.

Because I do love her. I said I'm falling, but I realize I've already fallen.

Gravel crunches beneath the tires as Rhett turns into the pebbled lot. We work together to move the canoe from the roof rack and carry it to the entrance to the river.

"I'm really glad we made this work," I remark. My keys, phone, and wallet all find a home in my small pack, along with a couple of snacks. We used to get out almost once a week before the women started picking off our men one by one. This is only the fourth time out all summer.

"With all the weddings and babies and kids, we need to start scheduling this shit."

"Is this who we are now?" I laugh. "Family men with schedules to maintain?"

Rhett looks like he doesn't give a shit in the slightest to be that type of man. "Absolutely."

I slip a life jacket over my head and toss one to Rhett. "Ready?"

"Let's go."

We set off. Rhett rides up front, and I steer from the back. Our canoe sluices through the water. This part of the river is a placid glide. Images of taking Caiti and Ophelia for a ride fill me with a sense of belonging. I want to share my life with them. All parts of what makes me who I am.

An eagle soars overhead, giving us a rare show when it dips into the flowing water and pulls out with a fish clutched in its talons. We move further down the river with sparse conversation. Each other's company and nature keeping us occupied.

Small rapids pick up, prompting me to pay closer attention. We've been down this part of the river many times. Rocks lurk just beneath the surface.

"We're picking up speed. Keep an eye out ahead," I call to Rhett.

"I'm on it. Rock at twelve o'clock."

With steady pressure from the back, I steer us out of the way.

"You're really good with your shaft," Rhett jokes.

I pretend to fan a blush and blow him a fake kiss. "Thanks."

"We should go further upstream next time and bring the girls."

Sweat beads on my forehead from the high sun. I swipe my arm across the damp skin. "I thought that earlier. We should plan an entire camping trip. Bring the kids."

The canoe jostles beneath us.

"We must have hit a rock," Rhett surmises.

I tighten my grip on the paddle. "If you'd quit talking about my shaft and pay attention…"

"Another one!" he calls out. "Twelve o'clock."

As I move to execute another slight turn, I stick my paddle in just right that the blade wedges between two rocks. "Fuck! My paddle's stuck!"

Before I have time to think, I react in an attempt to free it. The canoe keeps moving, the current pushing us down, and I overcorrect. The motion yanks me in.

"Dane!" Rhett's shout gets lost in the rushing water.

The current tugs me under, throwing me against rock and debris. My head slams against something, stunning me and clouding my perception of up and down. Water rushes in my nostrils. I pop above the surface with a choking gasp, the life jacket barely keeping me above water.

My heart races as I'm jostled beneath the surface again. When I resurface, the canoe with Rhett has disappeared. My lungs burn with the need for air. I fight back the rising panic. This river can be a monster and has me firmly in its grasp.

A strainer appears to the left, a collection of tree limbs and debris caught in one spot, but it's too far for me to grab. Something hard beneath the surface slams into my knee as I'm dragged past. I swallow a mouthful of water as the river tows me beneath the surface again, twisting me around and around, and thrashing me against the rock bottom. I'm caught in a spin cycle I can't seem to break out of.

The need to breathe serves a warning I'm running out of air. But before I can break through the surface, my foot wedges between two rocks, locking me in place.

Caiti's face flashes through my mind, the love stark beneath those thick lashes. The thought of putting her through another unimaginable loss demands I fight harder. I can't leave her. I can't leave Ophelia. I can't do that to her so long as I can help it. They need me as much as I need them.

But the river is stronger. She's as powerful as her beauty, and with as much knowledge as I have out here, the river's smarter. The harder I fight, the quicker I tire. Bubbles leak from my sealed lips.

For one single second, between the fight and fear and demand for air, the terrifying thought enters my mind. I might actually die out here.

25

Caiti

"I swear you walk around with hearts in your eyes all of a sudden. Dane must be giving you the goods regularly." Evie remarks, nudging my shoulder with hers. We're walking down the street to the cute preschool she and Rhett brought Tommy to for a tour. Ophelia twirls around my arm happily at my side, dancing with her shadow from the sunshine. Now that the decision to move to Arrow Creek is final, I don't want to waste any time establishing ourselves here.

The two plane ticket confirmations left on the counter this morning also felt like a sign. Just another way Dane's showing he's all in with my sudden arrival. He's only been gone a few hours, but I already can't wait for him to return home so I can thank him.

"I do not," I scold with a smile. "And the rest is none of your business."

"Let me be happy for you. I haven't seen you this way in so long."

Since before Eric died. The truth rings out in my head. I abruptly stop us and fling my arms around her shoulders, squeezing tight. "Love you."

Her return hug is equally fierce. "Love you too. Now that you're here to stay, we'll have to schedule regular girls' night out. Kiersten will be pissed while she's still pregnant, but after she pops those kids out, she'll be desperate for a drink."

I'm about to laugh, but I catch sight of her face. The talk of kids instantly taints her mood. "Hey. Do you want to talk about it?"

"Nah." We resume our trek down the final block. "It is what it is. This is my lot in life, you know?"

"You don't know that. Don't give up hope yet."

She shakes her head. "I haven't. I'm so lucky to have Tommy around. He's like my own. But I love Rhett so much, you know? I just wish more than anything I could give him that part of me."

"I wish I could tell the future. Whatever happens, I'm here for you."

"Sometimes, I think I could kiss Dane for bringing you back to me."

I scrunch my nose at her. "Please don't."

The rock of a diamond on her left hand flashes brightly in the sun. "Don't worry. He's all yours."

Our unit reaches the chain link fence separating the kids playing outside from the sidewalk and street. "Look, Ophelia. We're going to see if this is your new school."

"I don't want school. I want Daddy." She throws my hand and crosses her arms tightly over her chest.

"Uh-oh. Someone might be nervous," Evie whispers beside my ear.

Ophelia's sudden change in demeanor surprises me. She's extremely outgoing on even her worst days.

"Daddy will be home later, and you can tell him all about it."

"No!" She pouts.

"Hey Ophelia, did you know Tommy went to this school?" Evie crouches to her level.

The little diva drops her tight pose and cocks her head. "Tommy?"

Any mention of her bigger cousin immediately gets her attention.

"Uh-huh. Want to meet his teacher? I bet Ms. Laura is here today." Evie flashes me her index and middle finger in an X.

"Okay. I go wif Autie Ebie." She runs around my legs to take hold of Evie's outstretched hand.

"Thanks," I mutter, never one to begrudge a little assistance with the Terrible Twos.

"You can pay me back with a cocktail."

"What's cocktail?" Ophelia asks.

I send a glare to my loose-lipped sister. "It's a grown-up word, honey."

Ophelia twists her head to look up at me. "Is it a bad word?"

Not wanting to enforce a lie, I let my shoulders drop with a quiet sigh. "No, it's not a bad word."

Evie opens the front doors, revealing a playroom with a group of kids and a mass of toys. Ophelia's eyes grow round, and she drops Evie's hand. "Okay. See you tail-cocky!"

I nearly choke on my own spit at her chosen farewell.

"This is your fault." I poke my finger at Evie.

"Oops. Sorry, tail-cocky."

I move through the open door, trying to hide my grin. "This is nice."

There's an office to my left and restrooms to the right, but straight ahead is a large, open space. Kids in the two-to-four age range wander in various states of play with toys littering the floor around them. The hallway between the rooms is lined with a rainbow assortment of backpacks, coats, and cubbies at waist height for the little kids.

Noticing the newcomer, a woman around my own age approaches with a warm smile. Brown hair with reddish highlights is pulled back into a low ponytail that swishes with her bouncy steps. "You must be Caiti." Before I can greet her, she does a double take. "Evie! What are you doing here?"

The two exchange a brief hug. "Caiti's my sister."

"How cool. Well, we're excited to have you here. I'm Laura, or as the kids call me, Ms. Laura. We spoke on the phone."

"It's nice to officially meet you." We exchange a customary handshake. Her friendly reception already puts me at ease. "As you can see, Ophelia's ready to fit right in. I'm the one who's going to have a hard time saying goodbye."

Laura laughs. "That's usually the case. The parents struggle more than the kiddos do. I have three of my own, so I can say from experience it's okay if you need to sit in the car and cry the first week. It'll get easier."

"Luckily, I live just down the street, so I can cry on my walk home," I joke back.

Evie's phone rings, interrupting the greeting. Her forehead creases when she looks at the screen. "One sec. Go take a look around."

"Let me give you a tour. The bathrooms here are outfitted for our littles, so we can work on potty training without having to help them on and off a large toilet."

Even the sinks and hand dryers are set to kid height. I can only imagine how awkward it is using as an adult. "I love it. We haven't started working on that yet. I was waiting until she showed signs of being ready."

"I totally agree. No rush yet." Laura leads me farther

down the hall. "We have coat hooks and boot trays for wet winter gear. Each spot is labeled so there are no mistakes in taking home the wrong jacket."

"Great."

"And here's our infant room on the left and our one-year-olds on the right."

I peer through the glass window at the line of cradles. Two aids smile and chat as they bottle feed tiny babies. Recalling Ophelia being that small brings a sense of longing. Imaginary or not, the sight invokes warmth in my lower abdomen. I clutch a hand over the ache. "I think the baby fever is already starting."

"You're telling me. How do you think I ended up with three?" Laura whispers conspiratorially.

Evie sidles up to us, her pallor and expression sending immediate concern rocketing through me. "Laura, would you mind watching Ophelia for just a few minutes?"

The woman's brow knits in concern, her eyes assessing. "Sure."

"What is it?" I nearly hiss as panic grips me. It feels as if I'm balancing on the edge, and her words are about to push me over. She grabs my arm and tows me back out the door and onto the sidewalk.

"Rhett called." Her eyes immediately well with tears. "Caiti, honey, Dane fell out of the canoe when they were going over some rapids."

A roaring buzz soars to life inside my ears, and the world seems to tip around me. I realize I'm holding my breath and force myself to inhale slowly. I take her wrist in a crushing grip. "Tell me what happened."

"I don't know." She shakes her head. "They haven't found him yet."

My hands fly to cover my mouth. "No. No, I don't believe it."

"Rhett says we should meet him at the launching site. Rescue is there now."

"Why aren't they doing something?" I argue stubbornly. I refuse to believe something is wrong. "I'll go find him my damn self."

"Please listen. I need you to keep it together, okay?"

"I am keeping it together." A snarl wells up inside me. What does she think I'm doing? I haven't run off yet. I haven't fallen into a useless heap on the cracked concrete. I need information so that I can be productive. I need someone to tell me how to get to him.

"They're doing everything they can. I'm going to get my car and take you to the site."

As if I snap back to the present moment, I remember where we are. "Ophelia," I breathe, whipping my attention to check the glass doors. I can just make out her little form waving a book above her head. She hasn't even noticed we're outside. "She can't know he's missing."

Evie clutches my shoulder. "I've already called Cami. She's on her way to take her so we can go."

Reality sets in, slowly like a distant train. I can see it coming down the tracks, but it hardly seems to be moving until it's right in front of me and racing passed. That's how the trembles begin. Numbness overtakes my hands, prickling to life until it spreads up my arms until they're without feeling too. "I think I'm going to be sick."

"Breathe. Keep it together. If you can wait here, I can go get my car from your house. It's just down the road, and Cami will be here any minute for Ophelia."

I feel the motion of my head nodding, but it's as if someone else controls it. "Okay."

"Wait here," she reiterates, already moving away.

"Okay," I respond again.

After a few steps, she turns and takes off at a jog, punctuating the seriousness of the situation. Dane fell into a river. Dane fell in a river with rapids and is missing.

My Dane. Ophelia's father.

Old cracks in my heart renew. The barely healed scar tissue splits down the seams. This can't be happening to me. Not again.

I pull the glass door open just enough to attract Laura's attention. She moves quickly down the hall away from the children. "Is everything okay?"

"There's an emergency with Ophelia's dad. Evie's grabbing her car from just down the street, and then a friend is coming to pick up Ophelia. I know this is a lot to ask, but I don't want her to see me and wonder why she can't come with me. Do you think you can facilitate her going with my friend Cami? I'll wait out here until you do."

Laura's already nodding her head before I'm finished. "Yeah, of course. I hope everyone's all right."

I brace against a tremor. "Me too."

The arrival of my friends saves me from further small talk. Cami jerks to a halt at the curb in a sporty SUV, and not a moment later, Evie steers her white Lexus behind her.

"That's Cami."

The petite brunette races from her car and intercepts me. I nearly crumple as she enfolds me in a constricting hug. "He's going to be okay." Seeing all I can manage is a nod, she lets me go. "I've got Ophelia. Don't worry about her. Have Evie keep me posted."

"Thanks, Cami." The constriction in my throat steals my voice.

Mechanically, I run to Evie's car, climb in, and buckle, hardly noticing when she takes off.

Trees whip passed my window in a green blur. Fence posts eventually give way to emerald fields. My heart mimics Evie's lead foot on the gas, its galloping rhythm refusing to slow down. The sensations rise, much like they had the first day I arrived in town, and all my tricks and tips to slow them down are useless in the face of immeasurable fear.

My chest burns as if a candle resides beneath my ribs, and someone else controls the flickering flame. I can no longer avoid the thought of Dane thrown in a river, unable to breathe as he's forced underwater, triggering thought after intrusive thought. Images of him drowning fill my head.

"I can't lose him," I choke out. "I can't go through this again." My loud voice fills the confines of the car where the only other sound is the tires racing across the asphalt.

"I know," Evie answers. Even though she isn't as close with Dane, I'm sure memories of losing her brother are surfacing for her in light of my distress.

"Fuck." A rare curse spills from my trembling lips.

Flashing lights up ahead announce our destination. Police cars and SUVS, some with trailers, fire trucks, an ambulance, and park ranger vehicles all line the side of the road near the boat launch. My stomach pitches into a free fall. Several uniformed people mill around, turning to look at our decelerating vehicle.

"Why are they standing there?" I palm the window, trying to read expressions in an attempt to glean information as they drift passed. "Evie," I half beg, half sob.

"I don't know." Her answer is sad.

The moment the shifter hits park, I fling my door open and scramble out. I spin in a circle, looking for someone to help. Across the gravel lot, I spot Rhett, a silver blanket wrapped around his shoulders and a distraught look on his face. A Styrofoam cup dangles forgotten between his knees. Beside him, Law stands rigid with a matching expression. Without waiting for Evie, I take off toward her husband in a desperate search for the answers only he has.

"Caiti." His rough utterance of my name stutters my steps. A piece of hope peels away. "I'm so sorry."

"Did they find him?" I ask, bracing for an answer I'd never be prepared to receive.

"Not yet." Rhett's voice is hardly a whisper. Guilt lances through his usually lighthearted features. "They're searching with watercraft and drones."

"What happened?"

"I don't even know. We've been down that river so many times. Yes, it's fast, but it's not like we needed a kayak or a raft. We should have easily made it. All I heard was him shouting something about his paddle, and then the canoe rocked so hard I almost flew out the front. I saw him for a second, but then he was gone."

"You couldn't get to him?"

Rhett shakes his head. "It's incredibly hard to paddle a canoe solo like that. All I could do was ride it until it spit me out in milder waters."

A shudder races through me with the new information. "You're wet." I notice the way his wrinkled clothes cling to his skin beneath the blanket. "Did you fall in too?"

"I, uh…" Rhett glances away and jams his index finger and thumb into the corner of his eyes. "When I made it back to the shore, I ran back up the river to try to find him. I slipped over a steep edge and fell in but was able to make it back out," he says this with disgust as if he shouldn't have been able to escape so easily.

I can't bear to see the blame he holds for himself. I move on instinct and pull him into a tight hug without much contemplation. "I'm so glad you're safe," I murmur. A sudden tremor wracks his body when I brush his damp hair and back away.

"Rosie," he grunts. Evie runs straight into his awaiting arms with a sob. They tip their heads together, murmuring a private conversation I can't bear to hear. I move a few paces away until I can see the amber river. The surface appears peaceful here. Not capable of claiming the life of the man whose every action embodies the difference between surviving and living.

A twig cracks beneath Law's boot. "Dane's tough. Always has been. Knowing he has you and your little girl waiting on him, he's not going to go down easy. More than likely, he's sitting on a shore waiting to be rescued, or he's in the woods somewhere trying to walk back to town."

"Yeah." The energy to muster a better response is nonexistent. As I gaze out at the water, I wish I had a way to go find him. "I feel so helpless."

"Do you want me to bring you somewhere? We can wait at the bar until there's news."

Law's sweet offer provides little warmth to my frozen core. "I'm not going anywhere," I state with finality.

"Okay. Me neither."

The two of us stand silently, side by side. I don't know what Law's thoughts look like, but supplicant prayers swirl in my head. When I shiver, he wraps his arm around my back, and I lean my head on his shoulder.

The sun moving overhead marks the passage of time. Friends begin to arrive. First, Nathan and Kiersten appear after securing a babysitter. Duke from the bar shows up with his partner, Ronnie, and he announces they have closed the bar to customers. Regulars who have heard the news through the rumor mill gather, some bringing replenishments to rescue workers.

As I look around at the worried faces, I feel anything but comfort. Because as the hours tick past, the thoughtful vigil begins to look more like a funeral.

26

Caiti

A BLANKET IS WRAPPED around me from behind where I sit on the gravel. Various people have offered to give me a ride back into town and stay with me so I'm not alone, but I've turned each of them down. Duke even offered to provide unlimited shots on the house if I wanted to sit in the bar, but just as I told Law hours ago, I refuse to leave. Not until there's news.

Perimeter lights have been set up overhead, and a white tent sits in the far corner of the lot near the river. Anyone who wasn't myself, Evie, Rhett, Kiersten, Nathan, and Law was ordered to go home. We've been relegated to the other side to stay out of the professionals' way. Fine by me. Drag me kicking and screaming back into town for all I care because I'm not leaving until he's found, so if they need me to stay off to the side, I'm okay with that.

The closer we get to sunset, the edgier I become, waiting for the news the search has been called off for the night or indefinitely. For the moment they decide he's likely no longer alive, and the rescue becomes recovery.

My heart aches with all the things left unsaid between us. The moments I already kept him from experiencing the last three years and everything he's supposed to do now that we're together. Ophelia's counting on him, and so am I. Regret simmers just beneath the surface for time lost, and time we might never get at all. I don't know if I'll be able to forgive myself if we experience the unimaginable. Hope tries to leak from my grip like sand between my fingers, but I close my eyes and hold on.

"Can I get you anything?" Kiersten drops into a slow squat beside me.

"You're too far along to be doing that. You're going to get stuck." The gentle tease surprises even me. The moment is far too serious for jokes, but it feels right with my newer friend.

"I'm only in my second trimester."

"With twins."

She makes a face and drops to her butt. "I don't want to admit it, but you're right. My husband's going to have to help me up."

A fragile smile graces my face for the first time since Evie delivered the shocking news.

"I brought you this." Kiersten digs a water bottle from her coat pocket. "I know you're not hungry, but you don't want to get dehydrated."

"Thanks." I accept her thoughtfulness.

"Take a sip."

I cut a sharp glare in her direction as I unscrew the cap and take a swig. The cool liquid soothes my dry throat. "Happy?"

"No." She tucks her palms together between her knees. "You can stay with us tonight if…they kick us out. So you aren't alone." Her pause reveals more than she intends. The unspoken words float between us.

If he isn't found.

If they call off the search.

If they recover his body.

Vomit rises in my throat. "I should probably check in with Cami before I do."

"I have. Ophelia's already fast asleep in Evelyn's room, and she's happy to keep her as long as you need."

Rather than argue for the umpteenth time, I acquiesce. "That'd be nice then. Thank you."

"Good. We'll wait for you then. Do you want to be alone?"

I nod my head. "I'm not good company right now." Not only do I have nothing to say, but the only person I want right now is the one missing.

"I understand."

Kiersten moves to stand just as a radio in the distance crackles to life. A staticky voice penetrates the air. With all the people moving around in the distance, I can't tell who it's coming from.

"What'd they say?"

"I don't know." Kiersten waves her hand at her husband. "Hey, Nathan!"

He jogs over, ready to do his wife's bidding at a moment's notice.

"Something's happening." She flicks her wrist in the direction of the tent. "Do you think they'll give you some information?"

That's right. He's a paramedic. Shrugging off the blanket, I hop to my feet without thinking and seize his arm. "Please," I beg. "They were just talking on the radio. I need to know something."

"They wouldn't talk to me earlier, but let me see if there's a face I know."

My hand drops from his arm as his long strides take him out of range, and I send up a silent prayer. Rooted to the spot, I can't take my eyes from his back. He weaves through people with ease. Whatever he's saying lets him pass by unhindered until he blends in with the group.

"Help me up." Kiersten's untimely request distracts me from seeking out her husband.

I offer her a solid hand, and together, she regains her footing.

"Thanks."

Nathan reappears at the edge of the white tent.

"Kiersten," I stammer with a mixture of cold and fear.

"Hang on, honey. I'm here." Her arm folds around me. I reach up and grip her forearm across my chest.

The desperation to squeeze my eyes shut and block out what he might say nearly overwhelms me. When he takes off in a jog, my knees nearly buckle. "Oh my God."

"Hold steady. Just breathe."

I drag in a lungful of muddy, damp air through my nostrils, releasing the breath just as Nathan reaches us.

"They've got him," he chokes out, leaning over to clutch his knees.

"He's alive?"

Nathan lowers himself into a squat, overcome with emotion. "He's alive. They don't know what condition he's in, but he's alive, Caiti."

Dane's alive.

Oh, thank God.

A man runs toward us from the direction Nathan came. As he gets close, I recognize him as Officer Stryker from the other night. Dealing with Jason seems like a lifetime ago, not merely a few days.

His observant eyes scan the group. "They're bringing him up now."

All information is relevant, and the fact he's being brought up doesn't fill me with happy feelings. Dane would march on his own two feet from the riverbank with a smirk on his face and make a joke for scaring us in an ideal world.

But I'll take him any way I can.

The paramedics prepare a gurney and bring it near the river's edge. The minutes seem to pass by without a single breath. The people who've spent most of their day trying to help await to see the results of their hard work with the rest of us. The members of our little group cinch tight together.

There.

At the water's edge, a group of men appears, carrying a sort of rescue sled between them. A heap of metallic blanket reflects the perimeter lights as they transport him across the open space. The people around me break out into thunderous cheers. They transfer him to a gurney, but I'm fixed to the spot.

I should run to him, but I can't seem to remember how to move. Or breathe. Or think. I run on autopilot.

The only thought on a repetitive loop is Dane's alive.

27

Dane

I'M ALIVE.

I can't seem to stop shivering. A day stuck in a river will do that to a guy. If my ankle didn't hurt like a bitch, I'd put up a bigger fight about being carried up the embankment, but I can't have it all my way. One thought forced me to keep my mouth shut and let the rescue workers do their job, and that was getting to Caiti as fast as possible. Any argument I'd probably lose wasn't worth further delay.

The fight begins when they transfer me from their sled to the gurney. I'm close enough that my heart beats faster just knowing she's near.

"You need to lie down."

"I can sit just fine." I throw off the hand on my shoulder. "Take me to the hospital or stab me with an IV. I don't care. But I need to see if she's here."

"Ah," the medic responds knowingly. He adjusts me into

an inclined seated position. "Fine, but be a good patient and stay put or I'll bust out the restraints."

"I'm already buckled in," I snap. Exhaustion threatens to whisk me to slumber, but not before I check on my girl.

Her stricken face materializes in the small crowd of my closest friends. I briefly wonder if the medic will make good on his threat because I'm half a second from jumping off and running toward her. Only knowing my ankle might be broken keeps me from the foolish decision.

Instead, I call her name. "Caiti."

If she hears me, she doesn't show it. The rapid rise and fall of her shoulders indicate the probability she's stuck in a cycle of panic. Hesitant steps bring her closer, the first signs of life from her, before she breaks out in a run.

There's my girl.

I open my arms, the blanket surrounding me crumples. I'd haul her ass right up on this gurney with me if I wasn't surrounded by so many people. The sight of glistening tears in her dark eyes breaks my heart and fills me with guilt. I can't believe I put her through this.

She stops short, a good six inches from where I need her to be. A look of uncertainty crosses her face. "I don't want to hurt you."

"You're hurting me more by being so far away."

Haltingly, she moves into my arms. She cradles my face, the touch warming my skin faster than any blanket could. My eyes shutter closed. I lean into her palm, relishing the instant comfort the contact brings.

"I'm okay, Mama."

A rough hiccup breaks loose. Obviously, she's fighting the breakdown, and I don't want to make it worse by forcing her to express her emotions for all these people to see.

"Can she ride with me to the hospital?" I ask the medic who threatened to tie me down.

"If she can buckle up and stay in her seat."

"She can," I confirm sarcastically.

I'm loaded in first, and Caiti climbs in behind me, followed by the paramedic. The doors shut, securing us inside.

"Hey." I stroke a crooked index finger along the back of her hand. The uncertainty in her eyes tears me up inside. "I'm going to be just fine."

Her expression remains unconvinced.

"It's just a messed-up ankle."

"What happened out there?"

I'm momentarily distracted by the squeeze of the blood pressure cuff. "I don't know how much Rhett told you, but I was thrown from the canoe and washed down the river." I save her the worst details, of the number of times I was pulled beneath the surface. She doesn't need to know how many ways I nearly drowned. "I was able to make it to the shore, but it was at a rocky embankment that I couldn't climb. All I could do was hang on and slowly work my way downriver until I could pull myself out. By then, I was so exhausted I could only wait until they found me."

"I don't know what to say. This was—"

"Horrible, I know." I fill in her sentence through chattering teeth. I'm probably hypothermic, but it's hard for me to care.

"I was going to say it was the scariest day of my life."

I'm stunned as she reveals so much with such a simple sentence. "Mama..."

"When Eric died, there was no waiting. No helplessly sitting around for news. He was there, we went to bed, and he was gone. This, though, spending hours not knowing what happened to you, if you were hurt or if I'd ever even see you again, it was a pain so unimaginable, I questioned if I could even survive it."

I feel her emotional retreat like a physical barrier between us. "You survived it. You're so much stronger than you believe. I'm here." I force her hand to my chest to feel the life thumping within me. "I'm safe."

"I can't go through something like that again."

"You love me." I speak the truth she's too scared to admit. It's as clear to me as the sky is blue. I press my hand against the back of hers.

Squeezing her eyes shut, she shakes her head. When she opens them again, they shine. "I can't. It'll kill me."

"You love me, Caiti," I repeat, praying the words sink in. "You love me like Ophelia loves me."

A startled laugh bursts free, followed immediately by a sob. "It hurts to love you."

The monitor on my finger picks up my increasing heart rhythm. "It's supposed to hurt a little bit. That's how you know you're doing love right."

"I don't want to lose you."

I pull her hand from my chest. The warmth remains like a brand. I bring her hand to my lips and kiss each individual fingertip. "I can't promise you never will. But I can promise I'll make the time we spend together worth it."

She seems to think for a minute. The ambulance slows as we near our destination.

"I think I've known that I've loved you for a while, but I've been too scared to admit it."

"I know," I tell her honestly. "I loved you enough to wait until you were ready to say it."

Caiti cracks a smile. "Oh really? You seemed pretty insistent right now."

"Because," I begin, bringing her hand to cradle my cheek, "the only thing I thought about in that water was getting to tell you I loved you just one more time. I thought maybe, like me, you wouldn't want to waste another minute, but you just needed a little nudge in the right direction."

Keeping her one hand in place, she strokes over my still damp hair and down the other side of my face to hold me steady in her palms. "I love you, Dane Blackwood."

"If it takes a near-death experience to finally hear you say that, I'll have to plan tomorrow's excursion."

"Too soon for jokes," she mutters, her eyes dropping to my lips a second before she leans in. She suffuses me in warmth with a simple kiss. The braking vehicle prompts her to pull away.

"I love you too, Caiti Harris."

And if I have my way, she'll be Caiti Blackwood within the year.

28

Caiti

MURMURING VOICES ROUSES me from restless sleep. The hard plastic chair beneath me creaks as I maneuver into an upright position. The sterile smell of antiseptics wafts into my nose. Through blurry eyes, I take in the three people staring at me and tame my wild hair into an acceptable mess without the use of a brush. Dane's thumb strokes over my hand where our fingers lay entwined on his crisp hospital bed. The deadened sensation in my limb is almost enough to have me pulling my hand back. *Almost.* After yesterday, I wouldn't mind making the attachment permanent.

"Sorry," I mumble through a yawn. "What time is it?"

"It's just after nine in the morning," a woman in purple scrubs informs. I don't know if she's a nurse or a CNA. Exhaustion steals my ability to care.

"Did you sleep?" I ask Dane. His tender smile settles some of the flutters in my chest, the remnants of my morning anxiety.

"A little. I mostly watched you." He averts his gaze to our hands. Words unsaid hang in the air between us. Yesterday's events will affect us, probably for a long time.

I should feel shy knowing he watched me sleep, but all I can seem to muster is the love I finally set free. "We'll get you some rest at home."

Dane's gaze returns to mine, downright hot and needy. A thousand promises swirl in the deep depths, communicating the last thing on his mind is rest.

My hand settles at the base of my throat, the nervous habit coming up empty when I clutch for the vial no longer there. I relax my shoulders and release a solid breath. Dane doesn't seem to miss the motion, a small furrow marring his brow.

"I was just telling him the good news that we're letting him go." The woman smiles at me and begins unstrapping wires from Dane's body. "I'll remove this IV, and we'll start the discharge paperwork."

"That's great. Thank you," Dane answers, his eyes not leaving mine.

"There's a bag here with some fresh clothes. Nathan dropped it off after you arrived last night." I rush off to the tiny closet, retrieve the black duffel, and set it in the bathroom. "Can I help you?"

Dane chuckles. "I have an ankle injury, Mama. I think I can manage."

He eases off the bed, and I rush into his space. The need to do something productive wells up inside of me after feeling so helpless yesterday. His hands settle on my hips, warm and weighted, slightly depressing my flesh there. He tucks his chin into his chest. "But if you want to join me and close the door, I won't oppose."

Heat suffuses my cheeks. I slide my hands up his arms to

settle on his hard chest. "Hurry up and change so we can get home," I utter and loop my wrists around his neck.

He's off like a man on a world-saving mission. Faster than I would have assumed with only one decent leg, Dane's dressed, ready, and fighting the young guy working discharge about taking the wheelchair downstairs. After hearing hospital policy reiterated three times, he seats himself, rather grumpily though I find his scowl cute, into the chair, allowing the poor guy to push him to the curb.

The first step into a new day filled with sun and warmth feels like the first day of a brand new life. One I'm more than ready to start with this man by my side.

Irritable tension rolling off Dane during the ten-minute drive back to his apartment is tangible. Even though I'm in the driver's seat, his hand sits possessively on my upper thigh. Need wells inside of me from the proximity. Depressing the gas pedal evenly becomes a chore. His desire to take care of me and do manly things like drive his woman around push him to the edge. How he'll ever manage to stay off his foot and rest is beyond me. The man is a machine on an average day. Give him a challenge, and he won't quit until he defeats the task.

Walking into Dane's loft is like a welcome home. A few of Ophelia's toys are scattered across the floor. Dirty lunch dishes remain in the sink where I meant to load them into the dishwasher after our walk to the preschool. In many ways, it feels like a lifetime has passed between that hopeful moment of new beginnings and this morning at the hospital.

"Let me take you to bed," Dane grunts. Dark circles ring his lower lids. His furrowed brow sends a pang of worry through me.

"I think it's the other way around, big man. Let me help you." I sling his arm over my shoulder, settling into the warm weight and the length of his torso pressed against mine.

Feeling him close, his comforting smell, hearing his lungs working, I can breathe easier. I gingerly wrap my arm around his waist, curling my fingers into the elastic band of his sweats. "I've got you."

He presses a lingering kiss to the top of my head. "I know you do."

When we reach the bedroom, he crawls straight to the center of the bed, settling down with an arm slung across his eyes.

My strong, beautiful, brave, selfless man...I think I know what he needs, but I don't want to overstep. I toe off my shoes and settle on my knees beside him, tracing my finger along the coarse hair covering his other arm. "I'm here."

He flips his hand around and latches onto my wrist, his grip nearly painful. "Come here," he grunts, his voice gruff. I squeeze tight against his side as the first heaving sob wracks his body.

"Fuck." His arm leaves his eyes long enough for his fist to drive into the mattress at his side. "I fucking need you, Caiti."

"I'm here." I get out before he's hauling me up and settling me on his torso. A hand tangles in my hair, and his mouth crashes against mine. A desperation from the depths of his soul pours into me, filling me up.

He breaks away, a confession on his lips. "I need to feel you."

I breathe life into him and swear promises with my kiss. I swallow his sharp cry of distress down my throat as I let him release everything pent up for the last twenty-four hours. "I'm here," I pull away to mumble. He doesn't let me get far before he drags me back against him.

Dane grabs the hem of my shirt, the tug signifying his intentions. I lift my chest, allowing him to yank the cotton straight over my head. With a flick, my bra unsnaps, and he tears it away. Then he draws my small tits straight to his mouth and sucks a sensitive nipple between his lips.

I grind against him, the ridge of his hard erection the perfect friction against my clit. His other hand starts shoving the material of my leggings down. I lift up in my straddle to shimmy them off my legs. Once freed, he takes me to my back in his bed and shoves his sweatpants down his hips. His dick is beautiful and thick, and I clench at the sight.

Taking him into my hand, I pump his hardness twice before I lose contact. He descends my body. His mouth trails kisses along my sternum, pausing to dip his tongue in my belly button and trace the stretch marks along my lower stomach before continuing his rapid descent.

He doesn't bother with pleasantries before reacquainting himself with the most intimate part of me. Without preamble, his mouth is there, attacking, licking, sucking, probing. My fingers sift and clutch the dark strands of his hair to guide him where I want him most as my hips rise from the bed to greet him.

"I want to consume every inch of you." He eases two thick fingers inside me in a delicious stretch. My neck arches on the pillow behind my head. "I want to drown in you until I'm forced to come up for air."

As if to prove his point, he redoubles his efforts, driving me to the brink in half a minute. The orgasmic climb is straight bliss beneath his skillful hands and mouth. Even though he's the one who needs taking care of, he still proves his selflessness by attending to me first.

"Dane, baby, I'm going to come." I barely have time to gasp the words before he tips me over the edge of pleasure. My stomach clenches, waves wracking my body in tremors.

"That's it, pretty girl. Come all over my tongue and show me who you belong to."

He swipes through my slick center once more before

crawling directly up my body. Without further distractions, he takes his hard dick in his hand. I hitch my calves around his trim hips and dig my heels into his ass. With one hard thrust, he glides deep and seats himself fully inside.

"Ah!" I cry around the stretch and the slow, even pace he sets. His hand seeks mine at my side, and he threads our fingers together, planting them in the mattress above my head.

"I'm yours." Dane rests his forehead against mine and declares quietly. "I have been since the minute you showed up on my doorstep with the beautiful baby we created together."

"Dane."

"And you're mine." We're connected in all the ways two people can be, and still his gaze feels like it reaches deeper inside. "Please, tell me you're mine."

I caress his stubbled cheek, my thumb running from his bottom lip down his chin as I whisper with tears in my eyes, "I'm yours."

The animalistic rumble he emits vibrates against my chest. He crashes his mouth to mine in a soul-branding kiss. I hold him to me, his languid thrusts increasing to drive us both closer to the edge, until we fall over together into bliss.

Our heaving chests ease to normal. Dane slips from between my thighs, only moving far enough to shift his weight to his side. Most of his torso still covers mine like a warm blanket I wouldn't mind curling up with each night to sleep beneath.

I stroke the back of his head, where he rests his cheek against the center of my chest. "Are you okay?"

My question breaks the silence. He props his chin on the back of his hand against my sternum. What he says next catches my breath and spills tears from my eyes.

"If I could go back in time," he starts quietly, "I'd shake

Eric's hand and thank him for taking care of you. For keeping you safe and happy and loved beyond measure until it was my turn.

"It kills me you had to go through losing him for me to have you," he goes on. "And if I can do anything to ease that for you, all you have to do is ask."

"I don't know what I did to ever deserve being lucky enough to be loved by two amazing individuals."

"It's just you, Mama. Luck has nothing to do with it."

I pull him to me for another kiss that lasts long, sweet minutes. I part with heavy eyelids and a lazy grin. "Don't think I missed you evading my question."

"I'm better now." A serene smile crosses his face. He brings my hand clenched in his to his lips. "With you and Ophelia, I'm finally whole."

EPILOGUE

Caiti

Four weeks later

"How many more boxes do you think you need?"

I scan my bare surroundings at Dane's question. The remaining pile to pack dwindles fast. We sold my house in Colorado and used the profits for our down payment on a family home. Today is officially moving day. "I think two."

He plops a kiss on the crown of my head. "I'll be back with two."

"Careful with your foot on those stairs!" I call after him. He's still in a walking boot after the incident on the river. The bones weren't broken, but ankle injuries can be difficult to heal, and he's experienced some lingering effects.

The man takes it all in stride. The next day, it was outwardly impossible to tell he'd nearly died, something he later confessed in the quiet dark of our bed, but I could tell it affected him. His touches lingered far longer than before as if he needed constant connection. As soon as he was discharged from the hospital, our relationship status was no longer in question. He claimed me so thoroughly that night if I truly had any remaining doubt about loving him, he washed it away with his own bare hands. And lips. And tongue.

I blush at the memory. Carefully wrapping the framed picture of him and his mom in bubble wrap, I set it aside. The next frame holds a photo of the three of us—Dane, Ophelia, and me—down at the Swinging Bridge taken two days after his accident when we finally retrieved Ophelia from Cami and Law. She missed her daddy fiercely when we picked her up, and I'm eternally grateful that she didn't have to experience something I could never cushion her from.

"Look who I found." The sound of Dane's voice draws my attention from the wrapped breakables to the doorway of his room. He gallops in with Ophelia squealing from high on his shoulders, her hands wrapped around his forehead and a wide grin displaying her white teeth.

"I widin Daddy!"

A laugh bursts out of me. "You are. Just like a cowgirl."

"Giddup!" She pulls his head back like a lever to control his speed. He flips her from her perch into his awaiting arms and dips low in a fake plunge. "Don't dwop me!" She squeals.

"Never!" He kisses her on the cheeks with a loud smack. "Are you ready to see the new house?"

Ophelia nods, a crease across her brow. I think the idea of moving is beyond her comprehension. We've enlisted all of our Arrow Creek friends to help us move, and her bedroom went first. We wanted all her stuff ready to greet her to ease the transition. Kiersten took her for some ice cream so she didn't have a meltdown when her entire room disappeared.

"How about you, Mama?"

"This is it." I gesture to the pile before me. "Just waiting on the boxes."

"Sorry. There was a minor distraction." Dane flashes me a sexy grin in apology. "Hey, Nathan. Grab two more boxes, and we'll be good to go."

A moment later, Nathan steps into the room, extending the requested boxes my way. "You are a Tetris master with these packing skills, Caiti. I thought we'd be around all day moving your stuff."

"I can't even count the number of times I've moved in my life. I have it down to a science."

"Well, you could make a career out of it. Just saying."

Professional packer? I file the idea away for later. Even though I quit my job on the spot, I'm not without money. I had a sizeable savings of my own, and that's not even including the life insurance money I've barely touched. The plan is to take the time I didn't have the last three years to focus on transitioning Ophelia and me into our new life. Once she's settled and my anxiety is a little more stable, I'll begin the search for something to fill my time.

The guys chat while I pack up the remaining items, wiping the sheen on my forehead when I finish. I gaze at Dane and our friends proudly. "That's a wrap. We're officially ready."

"All right. I'll take these and see you guys there." Nathan scoops up the remaining boxes and hauls them from the room, leaving Dane, Ophelia, and me.

"You want her to ride with me or you?"

I don't have to hesitate before giving my answer. "I'll take her this time." I've slowly regained my confidence driving with Ophelia in the car, and now I never pass up an opportunity to practice. I stand and take my little girl's hand.

"I'll be right behind you." Dane presses his lips to my forehead.

The drive to our new home is about twenty minutes. A much longer commute to the bar for Dane, but not unreasonably so. He's the one who insisted on the location. The acre lot is perfect for raising kids and any other living beings we decide to take on. He also said since he returns to town daily to visit his mom, we'll have no problem making the trip to bring Ophelia to daycare and, eventually, school.

I shiver at the thought of her growing up. I'm not even close to ready for those milestones.

Bracing the steering wheel with excitement, I turn down a long paved driveway. Around a lazy bend, the trees give way, and the two-story farmhouse comes into view. The white house with black shutters is magazine picturesque. I can already imagine many summer nights on the wraparound porch with a cool drink in my hand while kids play in the large, grassy yard.

"We're here, Ophelia."

"Dat mine?" She shoves a chubby thumb into her chest.

"That's ours, honey. Want to see your new room?"

"Daddy too?"

Her attachment to Dane settles in my heart. I hope these two never lose their bond. "Daddy lives here now too."

"I see him?"

I've already become uninteresting to my daughter. I thought that wouldn't happen until the teen years. Before I can answer, he materializes outside her door and sets her free.

"I have a surprise for you." He hoists her onto his hip and taps her nose.

"You do?" I ask.

"I suppose the surprise is for you too." He winks. The smile spreading across his face implies he intends to beg for forgiveness later. Much later, when little girls are asleep in their beds and mom and dad can be alone. An anticipatory shiver threatens my calm façade.

"Uh-huh." The heavy sarcasm falls too short to be taken seriously.

"This way."

He waits for me to meet him at the other side of the car. His palm claims mine, and together we trek across the lawn.

The front door to our new home opens, and out steps Evie, Rhett, and Tommy holding a leash. Tommy jogs down the steps. The wind blows his brown hair off his forehead, and his chest puffs out for his very important job. A wiggly brown and white pup with long, floppy ears runs behind him.

"Oh my goodness." I cover my mouth at the sight of cuteness barreling in our direction.

"Puppy!" Ophelia screams, wiggling to be set down. Dane lowers her to her feet just as Tommy and the baby Basset Hound near.

"Is that ours?" I ask the thoughtful man at my side. He's always striving to make us happy, and Ophelia is definitely in puppy heaven. She drops to all fours and lets the little dog lick her right on the mouth as she laughs.

"Sure is. Her name's Luna. Rhett and Evie have her brother, Mars." He nods to our friends. I didn't even noticed the little dog lying comfortably in Evie's arms. "Tommy named him, so I kept with the theme."

"You're definitely her favorite now," I mutter. Dane easily kisses the faux pout away.

"I promise you can be in charge of the next surprise."

Hand still firmly in his, he tows me passed the kids rolling in the grass with the dog, barks and giggles drifting in the air, and up the steps. A waved finger serves to greet our friends because Dane hauls me around to the other side of the porch.

"What about Ophelia?" That little twinge in my gut kicks in, though far weakened from two months ago. The combination of therapy, self-care, and challenging my fears with action has considerably lessened my daily sensations to a manageable degree. Each day with practice, the sensations decrease until my heart rarely picks up without reason anymore.

"They'll watch her. You've worked hard today and deserve a rest."

A glance over my shoulder confirms. Evie winks and shoos me away.

Around the corner, two black Adirondack chairs face the sun sinking behind the pine trees surrounding our perimeter.

"When did you get these?" I sit in the one to his left, and he takes the one on the right, hands still firmly clasped.

"Duke and Ronnie made them in their shop as a housewarming gift." His gaze shifts out to the waning daylight.

"They're beautiful." I run my fingers over the smooth surface.

"I want to spend every night with you just like this, in these chairs, watching that sunset."

I look over to find him watching me with intensity. "I do too."

Dane slips out of his chair, dropping to one knee on the porch. He removes his free hand from his pocket and glides a simple gold band over my left ring finger.

"Then marry me, Caiti. It's my turn to love you. It'd be the greatest honor of my life if you and Ophelia carried my last name. I know this is probably scary for you, and fast, but when something feels this right, I can't pass it up. I promise to be by your side and do my best to cushion you from the bad parts and love you for the rest of our lives."

My heart slams against my ribs. I lurch from my seat,

landing in front of him on my knees, and take his face between my palms. I don't even ponder his request.

"Yes. The answer is yes."

His lips touch mine, sealing our engagement with an intense kiss. Not a moment later, Rhett whoops, and Evie cheers behind us.

"I thought only the dude is supposed to get down on one knee," Rhett jokes, a wide grin splitting his face.

"I'm sending you the video now. I got the entire proposal," Evie says through a watery voice. "I have to send it to the girls."

"We saw the entire thing from the window." Cami rounds the corner with her hands folded against her chest, leading the pack of the rest of our friends. "But send the video anyway."

Dane helps me to my feet, and Rhett moves in for a hug.

"You knew?" I ask over his shoulder, eyeing my sister.

"Of course I did. We all knew. I knew about the puppies too. Do you know how hard it's been keeping secrets from you?"

"I'm surprised, honestly. I thought you might blab," Dane jests.

Evie pulls him in for a tight hug. "Never about something as huge as this, but if you ever do anything behind her back and I find out about it, you better watch the hell out."

"Noted." Dane releases her, and she moves to me.

I tuck my face tight to the side of her neck, hiding my expression from the rest. "I have so many things I could thank you for. Thank you for being the best sister-in-law. Thank you for finding this town and the wonderful people here who've welcomed me with open arms. Most importantly, thank you for not giving up on me and holding space, even when I wasn't around."

"Stop." Evie bursts into a loud sob. "I can't hold it in when you say it like that. I love you too."

I kiss her cheek and move smoothly back into my fiancé's arms. The gold band on my ring finger glints in the fading sun.

I can't predict what the future holds. But even if I had a crystal ball, I'm not sure I'd ask it for answers. After I lost Eric, I stopped living. I'd take each new day as something I needed to get through, only to wake up in the morning to do it all over again. For three years, I repeated the monotonous process.

But in the past two months, I've learned to stop fearing the future, and I no longer wake up wanting to simply get through the day unscathed. I wake up with anticipation and love in my heart, even if it still shares the space with a few quickened beats of discomfort.

I've truly survived the worst a person can experience—nearly twice. Even if I did have to double my therapy appointments to help me process after Dane's accident. The journey, no matter how hard, has given me opportunities of hope that have made the pain of it all worth it.

Tucked in the arms of a man who loves me unconditionally and true, on the porch of the house we plan to spend the rest of our lives in, with our friends present and the family we're starting together, I can finally admit what I've been trying to deny.

I'm ready for our turn to begin.

ALSO BY A. M. WILSON

Where We Meet Again

An unexpected pregnancy by a man wielding sweet words and empty promises forced Cami to flee from home.

At sixteen, she gathered her torn and tattered heart, determined to construct the best life for her daughter.

Years after settling down in Arrow Creek, West Virginia, her life flourishes in all areas but one—love. She's convinced the sacrifice is necessary to keep her daughter happy and a roof over their heads.

Until she stumbles into her childhood best friend Lawrence 'Law' Briggs at the local coffee shop, and a painful confrontation ensues.

Their long-buried feelings for one another quickly resurface and challenge a carefully constructed reality. Her strength wavers as Law's reappearance exposes half-truths, and memories flood through the barrier.

Her daughter is a gift she'd never regret, even if it meant she lost him forever. Dark secrets hold them apart. The deepest betrayal imaginable.

Years of hurt and suffering can't disguise that Law's love remains, and Cami's is equal in measure. But is love enough to find a way forward through their murky past?

When Morning Comes

There are worse things than getting knocked up by your best friend.
Right?

Kiersten won't make excuses for living her very best life. But being the life of the party has its downsides—like waking up naked next to her best friend.

Ever since Nathan's wife died a few years ago, he's avoided commitment. He went from living the family life to a one-and-done mentality. Until Kiersten breaks the news.

She's pregnant with his baby.

She shoves him back in the friend zone. But there's no return to normal when he's already falling in love with her.

Convincing her that his affection runs deeper than their new reality isn't an easy feat. Not when her lips are his addiction, and her touch is a brand. He's determined to become more than friends.

Kiersten wants to play it safe, but Nathan is ready for risks. The problem is relationships can go south fast.

And they might learn the truth about what's worse than getting knocked up by your best friend.

Losing them forever.

What Tears Us Down

Rhett Senova could charm a woman out of her panties and in the next breath, thank her mother for dinner.

Smooth doesn't even begin to cover his moves. But the hottest playboy in Arrow Creek wasn't always this way.

He had dreams of a one-woman future, and the cry of his firstborn brought him to tears.

He never thought his wife would cheat on him with her boss.

Each day is a feud over the dream home he had built for his ex and learning to raise his young son without the jaded lens now coloring his world.

Starting over in his thirties isn't on his agenda. Not now that he's raised impenetrable walls. His ex left the sour taste of infidelity in his mouth, and he's not sure he can trust anyone new.

That is until he meets a vision passing through town and nearly gets mauled by her she-demon dog.

Her sassy wit makes other women seem inadequate, along with those luscious curves and burgundy curls.

The fact she hides beneath her tough exterior that she might be in trouble sends up red flags he'd be smart not to ignore.

Using his charm to win over the pit bull is the easy part. The question is whether he wants to win over the guarded redhead too.

Where Our Turn Begins

Caiti Harris thought her story ended the night her husband died.

She packed their history away like trinkets in an old box and held steadfast to the ache. Life granted her one love, and after he was cruelly ripped away, she knew there wouldn't be anyone else.

When a tempting bartender invites her to stay for a drink after closing, she agrees to one night, not a lifetime commitment. His sinful smile promises to chase away the pain of the past while his chiseled body guarantees to ward off the unrelenting chill.

Her love life ended, but that doesn't mean she's sentenced to an existence of total solitude.

Dane's world is exactly the way he wants. Tidy. He keeps a watchful eye over his bar, and remains a pillar for the people he cares for most. So when the woman he's dreamt about for three years shows up at his door with a toddler in tow, he's ready for the challenge. The two come as a package deal.

Caiti only wants to establish a connection with him in the event something happens to her. A backup plan to keep their daughter safe. She didn't expect to be whisked away in an ambulance before she could explain her sudden return to Arrow Creek.

Dane's vision soars beyond an eighteen year commitment. He sees a lifetime of settling down. And he's not ready to give up his turn without a fight for their daughter.

Or her.

Pitch Dark

One girl disappeared. After fifteen years, her cold lifeless body was found on the damp forest floor. Not an inch of her was unmarked by the horrors she endured. Alone, malnourished, abused in horrific ways; this was how she died.

One girl was found walking the streets, covered in dirt and scars. She had no memory of who she was, where she came from, or what happened to her. Even though the marks on her body attested to years of heinous abuse, her strength shone through at every turn.

Revenge and justice were sworn.

Years of searching brought up nothing but dead ends. Detective Niko James was too late to save his childhood friend, but he vows not to let down another.

The clock is ticking and the trail is pitch dark.

Broad Daylight

Lightning never strikes twice in the same place. Or so they say...The small town of Westbridge isn't so lucky.

When his brother's best friend went missing eighteen years ago, Reece James swore to himself that the pain of loss would never touch him. Walls of concrete fortified his resolve, and as a grown man, he keeps to himself and works hard to earn an honest living. No wife, no kids, not even a dog to rely on him.

His quiet life is upended when strange things start happening to him. As the events escalate, he can't continue to blame the neighborhood kids who roam freely at night. Forced to report a break in, he anticipates a swift investigation and the person responsible to be caught.

What he doesn't expect is the woman he's loved in secret for twenty years to return to town and lead the investigation.

His attempt to protect Dani as kids was pathetic at best, but when his stalker gets wind of a woman in his life, no matter that she's merely investigating a case and nothing more, Reece will do anything to keep her out of harm's way. Including sacrificing himself.

What his captor has in store will rock the very foundation Reece lives upon and will force him to face his past head on for a chance at survival.

Poor Reece has no idea what's coming for him.

Indisputable

Eighteen year old Tatum Krause wants nothing more than to finish her senior year without any more drama. After the near overdose of her drug abusing mother the previous year, she moved out in the hopes of making something better for herself. However, the week before her final year, she ends up needing the help of a sexy stranger who's about to flip her world on its axis.

Jacoby Ryan only wants one thing: to forget his past. The last two years have been filled with empty feelings and women in an attempt to stem the heartache and guilt. He's ghosted blindly through the motions until late one night he finds a car stalled on the side of an empty highway, where he meets a beautiful girl with a haunted look in her eyes.

She has a secret, but so does he. Despite their magnetic pull, the two come to the shocking revelation their relationship isn't so black and white. Is it possible to fight a bone-deep attraction when the entire universe is telling you it's wrong?

Unleashing Sin

My name is Alex 'Sin' Sinclair, and they don't call me Sin for nothin'.

After losing the person who meant everything to me, I lived up to the connotation. Saintly behavior wasn't in my repertoire when I f*cked countless women. I made my home at the bottom of a bottle, and my only acquaintance was heroin.

I existed in my own personal hell while I vowed to end the lives responsible for ending her.

Then I found you.

Feeble, alone, needy. Everything I don't want. A distraction from the task I set my sights on years prior. I tried to resist you, but something about you calls to me. I'm not good for you, but the truth is, I think you're exactly what I need.

I pushed. You pulled. I tried to protect you from my darkness. You fought to pull me into a different light.

We became distracted.

Redesigning Fate (Revive Series Book 1)

When my boyfriend threw me down a flight of stairs, I knew there was only one place left to go—far, far away. I packed up my car and left everything I'd known for the nearly twenty-two years I've been alive. One hundred and fifty miles of highway separated me from the life I grew up with and the one I needed to find.

The same day I was offered a job in my new city, I met Elias. He was an enigma. A mystery. One that I wanted to uncover. One I didn't know if I could trust.

He pulled me in with adventure and the melodies of his guitar, but his secrets held me at a distance. He couldn't tell me about what he did for a living, or why he took phone calls in a different room.

Then my ex returned. Travis wove a sordid tale of danger; that he was only there to keep me safe from Elias.

I never expected truth to be nestled in his lies.

Resurrecting Her (Revive Series Book 2)

When I was kidnapped, half-truths were shared by the monster who took me. Half-truths that tested the bounds of my relationship.

A web of lies obliterated my last shred of security.

The man I love vows to protect me from both our demons, but in doing so, he treats me like glass.

I hold the secrets this time. They're slowly destroying me from the inside; igniting in me a fight for righteousness, even if that means leaving behind the ones I love.

Travis is still out there. Watching me. Waiting. And even though he's dangerous, he's not the only villain in this story.

His Deliverance (A Revive Series Novella)

Five years before *Redesigning Fate* comes Holt and Brandi's story...

My alias is Brixton Holt. Using my real name could get me killed. When the FBI needed a man undercover, I was the perfect candidate. Unattached and an all-around badass.

Two years of infiltrating the largest sex trafficking ring in the country, I feel as dirty as the monsters I work for. That is, until she catches my eye.

I call her Brandi. Her real name is no longer significant. She knows the rules. Nobody leaves unless it's in a box--a shipping crate or a coffin. My first mistake was following orders.

The second? Falling in love.

Revive: The Series

ABOUT THE AUTHOR

A. M. Wilson is a *USA TODAY* Bestselling Author. She loves infusing her stories with real life--the good, the bad, and the steamy parts. There's something special about that pivotal moment when two characters realize their love for each other, but she likes wading through a little angst to get there. When she isn't furiously typing on her computer, she can be found searching for her next all-consuming read. A. M. lives in Minnesota with her husband, two children, and black lab.

Visit her website at http://amwilson.net

Made in the USA
Coppell, TX
02 March 2025